SNOW
IN
JULY

SNOW IN JULY

HEATHER BARBIERI

Published by
Soho Press, Inc.
853 Broadway
New York, NY 10003

Library of Congress Cataloging-in-Publication Data

Barbieri, Heather Doran, 1963-
Snow in July/Heather Barbieri
p. cm.
ISBN 1-56947-384-6 (alk. paper)
1. Sisters—Fiction. 2. Single mothers—Fiction. 3. Women—Montana—
Fiction. 4. Narcotic addicts—Fiction. 5. Butte (Mont.)—Fiction. I. Title.

PS3602.A765866 2004
813'.6—dc22   2004048239

10 9 8 7 6 5 4 3 2 1

For my family

It is only with the heart that one can see rightly;
What is essential is invisible to the eye.

—Antoine de Saint-Exupéry

ACKNOWLEDGMENTS

With love to those who've been there since the beginning, especially Mark, Sian, Connor, and Sera—you inspire me every day; Robbi Anderson and Tessa Effland, little sisters with the biggest hearts; Robert and Michelle Doran—thanks for so many things, including the prayers—I owe one to St. Jude, the Patron Saint of Impossible Causes; Jim Doran, visionary, blood brother—fight on, man; Kyle Lindskog, fellow conspirator and creative mastermind from the early days—your friendship is such a gift; the adventure girls, Jeannie Berwick and Marcellina Tylee, for helping me get out of town—or on the town—when I need it the most; the Dorans, past and present, expecially Papa Tod for valuing family above everything; Ginga Loretta for helping introduce me to the joys of books, and Mun for keeping the stories alive; Tina Albro, Marie Allen, William Andrews, the Barbieri clan, Jennifer S. Davis, Julie Fay, Alison Gilligan, Maura Hayes, John Keegan, Colleen Murphy, J. Kingston Pierce, Monica Prevost,

Dennis and Linny Stovall, Grace Van Zandt; my agents, Anna Cottle and Mary Alice Kier, for enduring faith, enthusiasm, and good humor; Laura Hruska for her passionate belief in this book and willingness to take a chance on me; and the Artist Trust Washington State Arts Commission Fellowship program and its 2003 literary panel for early support of this project.

CHAPTER ONE

The night my sister almost dies for the twelfth time, a foot of snow falls, which makes it harder, though not impossible, to save her. Under normal circumstances—as if they're ever normal when it comes to her—snow doesn't pose much of a problem. As Montanans, we're used to driving the white drifts, crunching down unplowed roads like the trailblazers we pride ourselves on being. But this storm catches us off guard. It's July, after all, a time of beach vacations and ice cream trucks and waterskiing, everyplace but here. We let ourselves get suckered in, stored the chains and boots and parkas in the attic in anticipation of scorching, dry days. I suppose we should have known better. Weather can be unpredictable in Butte.

So can my sister.

As snowflakes tumble from the sky, the telephone wires hum a dirge, black lines tying us into the network, tying us down. The phone hiccups, bring-bring, bring-bring, bearing a message from my sister, who has the habit of disappearing and reappearing like a sequin-clad girl in a magic trick. I know something's wrong the minute Mama picks up the phone. She gets that pained look around her eyes, as if a splinter has lodged deep in the optic nerve.

That doesn't stop her from seeing things clearly. Or, at least, as clearly as you can when you're the mother of a sister like mine.

Mama sits down at the kitchen table, the receiver to her ear, listening. For a fleeting moment, she has a this-isn't-really-happening look on her face, distant, dazed. She gazes past me, past the whole town maybe, to the life she'd never managed to have. Her name is Finola McGann Mulcahy, though everybody calls her "Fi." She was the first in her family to go to a university. Even though she had a beautiful singing voice, she took the practical route and studied nursing. She returned to Butte on weekends to see her friends, to see the guy who would become our father. She couldn't separate herself from this place.

Neither can the rest of us.

Then she got pregnant with my sister, came home, and married my father, a boy she'd known almost her whole life. The same old story. He was a good man, even if he didn't have a good heart. By that, I mean one that worked right. His heart was too big in some ways, too small in others, a hidden defect no one discovered until it was too late. He died at the age of thirty-seven, when I was twelve. Ancient history, since the years have collapsed on themselves, like folds of an accordion.

I'm eighteen now. My mother is forty-two. My sister, twenty-one.

Mama knocks a cigarette out of the pack on the table with the same wrist-snap required to roll dice. She does this with the practiced grace of someone who's gone through the motions for years. She doesn't miss the irony of smoking, though she's a labor and delivery nurse at St. John's. She says you've got to have a vice or two, to keep things interesting. As long as it doesn't hurt anybody. That's the crucial point.

I guess she doesn't count hurting herself.

She only smokes outside, out of consideration for me, even if that means freezing her butt off. She wraps herself up in an old blue chenille robe with a faded bouquet of flowers appliquéd on the back (my father gave it to her years ago, for Mother's Day) and plunks down on the steps of the front porch, the embers of her cigarette like the lights of a small plane unable to land.

She'd be there now if she could. She needs a hit of nicotine bad. She runs her finger along the phone cord—she knows it won't reach as far as the porch—and glances at me. She's thinking about asking for the cordless, but she doesn't dare break away for one second, because she's afraid if she does, Meghan will hang up.

We're waiting, waiting in a silence that causes me to think the worst—that Meghan has dropped the phone, that she's passed out on the floor, spit and vomit dribbling from her mouth. I imagine her with a knife in her chest, because she pissed off the wrong person. Again. "What's going on?" I ask.

Mama shakes her head. "She's there. I can hear her breathing. Honey? Hello?"

I pick up the portable phone. Mama doesn't care if I listen.

3

I'm part of it, too, whether I like it or not. I always have been. The power of blood ties. Or the curse of them.

Sure enough, I hear breathing on the line. My sister does this frequently. When she's coherent enough, she begs us to put her back together again. *And Meghan Mulcahy had a great fall, and all the king's horses and all the king's men couldn't put her together again.* Problem is, the cracks are starting to show. You might mistake her for a statue that belongs in a museum, but you'd be wrong, because she's not that type of high art, not along the lines of the Venus de Milo or the statue of David. Yes, her skin has a marble-like quality to it, an undertone of green—from the toxins she's pumped into her body, the exploded veins. The broken pieces don't fit together quite right, though you won't notice unless you look real close. Unless you know her as well as we do. She's good at fooling people. At fooling herself, most of all.

"What did you take?" Mama asks with the calm delivery of a dispatcher for the emergency service, talking someone out of jumping off a ledge. "Megs, I have to know if I'm going to be able to help you." The radio crackles and pops on the counter, an old song by the Police, "Message in a Bottle." Mama has their tape somewhere.

Meghan doesn't give us anything to go on. Nothing but breathing. At least she still is. Breathing.

"You need to tell me." Mama's face tenses, as though her head is a jar lid that's been screwed on too tight. The pressure's building, but she won't blow. She'll keep it together, because that's what she does, what she's always done.

Then: "I didn't take anything, Grandma. Honest," says a voice

4

so tiny you could tuck it into your pocket and there'd still be plenty of room.

Mama and I look at each other across the kitchen. That glance contains a landscape with a little girl all alone in a garbage- and needle-strewn cesspool, a place where no child should be.

"Teeny, is that you?" Mama spreads her fingers on the table, as if she could reach across the distance and pull her to safety.

"Uh-huh." She hiccups, the sound a dot-dot-dash of Morse code.

"Where's your mom? I need to talk to her." Mama picks up the cigarette with shaky fingers and taps it on the table. The tip crumples, like the bashed-in front of a car that's been totaled.

More adenoidal breathing. "She's sleeping. She won't wake up."

Mama leans forward in her chair, elbows on the table, fingers pressing into her temples. "Where are you?"

"Don't know. We had to climb lots of stairs. My legs got tired." Her voice gets smaller and smaller, as if she's disappearing.

We can't let her do that.

Mama closes her eyes and pinches the bridge of her nose. "Look out the window, honey. Tell me what you see."

There's a clunk as Teeny puts down the phone. We wait for her to pick it back up. "A big night light with a dancing lady on it," she says finally.

"Don't you worry," Mama says. "We'll be right there."

"Shit," Mama mutters as she slams down the phone. She turns to me, her expression grim. "She must be at the Pair-A-Dice Hotel." It's the only place in town with that kind of sign. Doesn't exactly have a four-star rating—unless you're talking about the kind of stars you see when someone punches you in the face, which happens often enough, judging by the brief

5

stories in the sheriff's blotter of the newspaper. To say it's rough would be the understatement of the year.

"The car won't make it. Not without chains." I start toward the basement stairs. The storage room, where we shove everything we don't need routinely, is located down below.

"Never mind. We don't have to drive," Mama says. "At least she's picked a flophouse within walking distance this time."

As we grab whatever coats and sweaters are handy off the hook near the front door—cotton blends that are more convenient than effective—we avert our eyes from the living room mantel, where vestiges of my sister's former glory remain: the honor certificates, a first-place trophy in track, a gold medal in the 100-yard dash.

Meghan does a different type of running now, the kind nobody gives prizes for.

Mama wraps a peach-colored knit scarf around her neck and head. The ends poke straight out, which, coupled with her intense eyes and pinched mouth, gives her a look of alarmed—perhaps even deranged—determination. The scarf is one of many she knitted in the nights she spent waiting for Meghan, nights she never came home. Mama cast on, and on, and on, as if it were another way to bind us together. It didn't work.

I take a scarf too, one that's long enough to hang myself with, if I were so inclined, more suited to a 7-foot-tall basketball player rather than 5′3″ me. Mama must have gotten distracted while she was working on it. We don't know anyone that big. I wind it round and round. A glance in the mirror confirms the embarrassing truth: We look like bag ladies. Me in a pair of gray sweats and windbreaker, Mama in holey jeans, sweater and beat-up barn jacket. Big deal. We're not on a designer's catwalk. We're on a mission of mercy.

We trudge to the narrow street that twists through our part of town, where the roads are still gravel and dirt and the houses cling to the hill for dear life. Houses that seem as though they might slide off in a good hard rain, which we never get, except for the occasional deluge after a thunderstorm, which dries quick as spit and makes you wonder if you imagined the whole thing.

Abandoned mine shafts riddle the landscape with hidden dangers. When we were kids, Meghan and I stared down into the great gaps in the earth and told each other ghost stories about the men who had died there nearly a century before. Skeletons of rusty ironworks still loom over us, like gangly old men loitering outside a tavern with nothing to do since losing their jobs to the open-pit mining scheme that took hold in the '60s. The open-pit concept. More of an open sore. Another twist on strip mining, the peeling away of layers. Too bad you can't put them back on when you're done, the way you can after you've lost a round of strip poker. Because even though it must have seemed a fine idea at the time, now most of the hill is gone, munched away by machines—and once it was lost, there was no getting it back. We're right on the edge of the hole. It stopped less than a mile from us.

Most of Mama's friends viewed the incursion as an opportunity to move to newer houses on the Flats, the kind with updated wiring and foundations that haven't settled. We're the only ones in her circle who stayed. Mama claims to like the eccentricity of the neighborhood. "Those other houses don't have the vintage charm of our place," she says. Our place, with its neat white paint and planters of red geraniums, now recoiling with shock from the cold shower of snow.

I like vintage too. Except when it comes to plumbing. Except when it isn't based on conscious choice, but necessity. The fact is, we don't have the money to move. And we won't any time soon.

Ours are the only footsteps in the snow tonight, Mama's slightly turned out like a ballerina's, mine slightly pigeon-toed. No one's bothered to shovel their walks, operating under the assumption that the snow will start to melt by morning. Maybe it will, maybe it won't. It certainly acts like it's here to stay, squeaking as it packs into the grooves of our soles and sneaks into the tops of our boots. It's deeper than we thought.

"Beautiful night for a stroll!" Yo-ho raises a bottle of beer at us from his front door and swipes a hand across his grizzled chin. He hasn't stopped celebrating his eighty-fifth birthday, which occurred three days ago. Maybe he never will. He'll take any excuse for a party. Any excuse to forget.

His pirate flags snap in the breeze: skull and crossbones, a scimitar. Quite a collection. He started to accumulate it when the mine shut down and he found himself jobless. His real name is Frank. But no one ever called him that except his wife, Maybelle, who died a couple of years ago. That's when he adopted the pirate motif in an extreme way and began to imagine alternate realities. In his mind, the porch morphs into a ship's deck, complete with wheel. His house is a galleon, sailing over a dried-up sea. He has a parrot named Methuselah, who squawks from his perch inside the front window.

Methuselah is his first mate. "My second, if you count my wife."
Yo-ho laughs until he coughs hard enough to bust a rib, tears in
his eyes, not so much from physical pain, but because he misses
Maybelle, which is funny, because they used to fight often
enough. You'd never know it now. You'd think she was a saint.
That's the way he sees her these days, the figurehead on his vessel, the one he navigates by, who he talks to night after night,
as if she's really there, his words never harsh, but soft, soft as
falling snow.

His daughter, Marlene, lives down on the Flats and visits
often. But Mama, the devoted caregiver, the original Ms.
Bleeding Heart—how much can you bleed before the life goes
out of you?—checks on him every couple of days, brings a
casserole or soup to keep the beer bottles company in the
fridge. It's her nature to take care of people. And she knows
how it feels to miss someone that bad.

Yo-ho gets so caught up riding the high seas, he sometimes
forgets to eat—or, rather, he says an old salt like him doesn't
need much, that the ocean blue will sustain him. In his lucid
moments, he knows the maritime scenario isn't real. He isn't
crazy, not totally. He's aware that land surrounds him. He's
probably as land-locked as a person can get. But he chooses to
ignore it, to hold on to the dream of the sea, a survivor, clinging to the edge of a capsized boat.

Mama waves. She uses her whole arm, a semaphore, to make
sure he knows it's us, not some other passersby, because it's
dark and his eyes aren't what they used to be. "Where are you
tonight?" she asks.

"The Falkland Islands and it be snowing. But I'll press on.

North to the Caribbean!" He raises a toast and flashes a tooth-less grin. He must have misplaced his dentures again.

"North to the Caribbean!" We cheer. It sounds pretty good about now. A sugar sand beach on Antigua. Warm turquoise water as far as the eye can see. No snow. No strafed landscape. And no drug-fiend sister.

If only we could join him and make the world our oyster. But there isn't time to sit on the porch and dream. We have another port of call tonight. Another heroine to save from heroin.

"Are you going to call the police this time?" I ask. Mama has threatened to do it, but she always relents at the last minute. It's not easy to have your own daughter thrown in jail. Mama doesn't answer right away. I squint at the statue of the Virgin Mary on the ridge, ninety feet of monumental grace. Always calm, always bright. The biggest nightlight you've ever seen in your life. Once, not too long ago, I had a dream about her coming alive and stomping down Main Street like Godzilla, a beatific expression on her face as she flattened cars and busted water hydrants and said "Bless you, bless you, my child."

"I haven't decided," Mama finally replies. She hunches her shoulders against the cold and whatever might be waiting when we enter the room that contains my sister and her children, five-year-old Teeny and baby Si-si, short for Siena. (Apparently Meghan saw a magazine article about Italy when she was in the waiting room of a doctor's office, probably one of the few times she made—and showed up for—an appointment.)

Mama keeps her thoughts to herself, holding them close as a hand of cards she doesn't want anyone to see. She's trying not to judge, to cast the first stone, though circumstances being what they are, most people would agree she's allowed. She fights the inclination, being no angel herself. She had wild times when she was young, riding shotgun in drag races, running down the street naked on a dare, drinking until she passed out. She still goes to the bar now and then with her friends. She puts on jeans and a pair of biker boots from the days when she and my dad rode Harleys together. She's had the boots so long, they're back in style.

As for the bikes, she sold them years ago when I burned my leg on the exhaust pipe in a major wipe-out. Meghan and I had decided to go for a spin a month after my dad died, half-dare, half-skewed tribute to his memory. Neither of us knew how to ride. He'd promised to teach Meghan but never got around to it. Meghan didn't let that stop her. When I got home from school that afternoon, there she was, straddling the bike. She'd cut her first class that day, a pattern that, over the course of the next few months, would repeat itself. She pruned her academic schedule one subject at a time until she didn't go at all.

"Get on," she said, not a request, not an order. A statement of fact. A foregone conclusion. She wore my dad's leather jacket, which, though too big for her, looked right somehow. Her eyes had a peculiar shine, the deeper color rocks get when they're under water. I felt a twinge in my chest, a mixed drink of certainty, fear, and excitement that tended to accompany my misgiving-laced participation in her schemes. I didn't ask if she knew what she was doing. If she didn't, I assumed we'd wing it the way we always had when we were younger and things didn't seem so complicated and our father was still alive.

We didn't wear helmets, flouting the law and everything else. It was only us and the bike, full-throttle. She roared out of the narrow driveway on instinct, the sound coming from her throat blending with the screaming engine. I began to have serious doubts as to the wisdom of the excursion, but it was too late to get off. She couldn't hear me—or pretended not to hear me—when I yelled at her to slow down. Bugs and grit, nature's shrapnel, peppered us. The wind whipped our hair into flames. I tightened my grip on Meghan's waist and hugged the seat with my thighs. She nearly lost me when she accelerated out of a bump, but I held on. That was something I knew how to do. I followed her lead and leaned into the curves. It was as if we were the same person, hearts beating, breaths coming, with a synchronicity we hadn't had in years.

Pure excitement and adrenaline took over. We were going for it. We were really going for it. I imagined my father laughing and shaking his head. His girls, his girls. I didn't want the journey to end, the sight of the town whizzing by in a surrealistic blur, the place made beautiful by virtue of speed, hard edges softening, melting into a harmonious whole. The land became the people became the buildings became the sky became the sun became the clouds. My sister became me and I became her. I expected the tires to lift off the ground any moment and we'd sail away and wave at my dad as we passed by heaven.

The tires did rise—as we hit a pothole and crashed into a ditch, back to zero in an instant. Everything stopped. Heaven pulled away from us at warp speed. I lay blinking up at the sky through a cloud of dust.

"We're not dead," my sister said, again a statement of fact, tinged with a dash of something darker she'd explore in other ways as time marched on.

I wondered if we were supposed to be. I didn't ask. Maybe I was afraid to learn the answer.

As luck would have it, we'd landed in a large clump of tumbleweeds, though we sustained some minor injuries. We had cuts and bruises and my leg got seared like an overdone pork chop on the exhaust pipe. It hurt like hell, but we were alive. That counted for something. We limped home, pushing the bike—which, though a bit scratched and dinged, wasn't much the worse for wear—up the hill, arriving back at the house just as my mother pulled into the driveway in the copper-colored Volkswagen Bug she'd gotten for her high school graduation. Meghan and I exchanged glances, knowing shit was going to hit the fan, glances that said we wouldn't betray each other, that we'd stick together the way we did when our lives—or allowances—depended on it. Besides, we were too tired to lie or make excuses or argue. The bike was heavy and the hill long. We felt as if we'd returned from a cross-country odyssey, not a two-mile joyride.

Mama's face underwent a series of subtle shifts, resembling one of those time-lapse photographs. She clenched her fists at her sides. The fury inside her radiated like heat. She didn't say anything. She didn't have to. I counted to ten. I figured that was all the time we had before she let us have it.

But she didn't.

I suppose she knew why we'd done it. She'd probably wanted to do it herself, with more dramatic results. Maybe she would have, if she hadn't had us to consider. There were times, in the darkest hours of the night, when I'd catch her sitting at the kitchen table with a knife in front of her. A still life an artist might paint, *Widow Contemplating Death*. She didn't move. The clock on the wall ticked and ticked, and she stared at the blade, as if she were trying to memorize its edge. Sometimes, instead of the knife, she'd consider the possibilities contained in a bottle of pills the doctor had prescribed to help her sleep. With a chill, I thought of the prayer I said before I'd go to bed, *Now I lay me down to sleep, I pray the Lord my soul to keep and if I die before I wake, I pray the Lord my soul to take*. I'd watch her from the doorway. I didn't say anything to interrupt the silence. There was an intimacy between her and the knife and the pills that I didn't dare penetrate until one night her hand moved toward the bottle of medication, crossing a boundary that had never been breached before. I wanted to say "What are you doing?" Or "Don't do that!" Or "No!" Instead, I said "Mama, may I have a glass of water?" Her hand stopped in mid-air, fingers curled into her palm. She turned toward me as if I'd awakened her from a trance. She didn't say "Why didn't you get a drink in the bathroom upstairs?"; she said "Sure, honey. Do you want some ice?"

Maybe that was why, on the day of the motorcycle incident, she held her tongue and guided my sister and me into the house, a trembling hand on each of our backs, knowing how close all of us were to the edge. How we had to walk the line between life and death, to test it, to confirm which side we should be on, to kid ourselves that it was something we could control.

Mama's movements were swift and decisive as she retrieved the first aid kit from the kitchen cabinet. She dressed our wounds in silence, as we experienced the sting of antiseptic, the precise, tight wrapping of bandages. We knew better than to complain. Her expression remained unnaturally still, though, beneath the surface, her emotions were anything but calm, which was why she didn't look at us directly: the thought of what she could have lost that day compounding the loss she'd already had to endure. In the end, she didn't ground us for a week or withhold our allowance. She merely took the keys to the bike and placed an ad in the paper. Both bikes sold within a day. She gave a discount on the damaged one, the one we'd taken, which had belonged to my dad. She gave away the leathers too, folded into a doubled-up Safeway grocery bag.

Now, but for the boots, she doesn't own biker clothes. She mostly wears cotton button-down shirts, open at the neck. She isn't into the tight T-shirt thing, which I'm grateful for. It's embarrassing to have your mother grasping after her fading youth. Her hair hasn't gone gray yet, at least not in an obvious way, thus sparing her the risk of a dye-job-gone-bad. When she's tired or stressed, the lines around her eyes and mouth deepen, but she still looks more than a decade younger and people who don't know us or our situation think she's my older sister, which she appreciates more than I do.

Sometimes she returns late from the bar, not late enough to cause worry, but enough to make me wonder if she's seeing someone. She spends time with Joe Flanagan, though she insists he's just a friend. She met him when his daughter,

April, who was a couple of years behind me in school, had a baby at St. John's. Mama was the nurse on call that night. (April used to run with the cheerleader/jock clique. After her mother died of breast cancer, she started hanging with a rough crowd. She gave the baby up for adoption and left to study acting at Juilliard—as if we don't have enough drama around here already.)

I can't picture Mama getting romantic with Joe. People call him Average Joe Flanagan for a reason. Average height. Average looks. Average everything. Mr. Middle of the Road. Literally. He works in the Department of Transportation, maintaining streets. He specializes in patching potholes, smoothing buckles, making new routes, a skill that comes in handy in a place with extreme weather. I've never met him. But I've heard my friend Alex's dad talk about him, saying he's as quiet as they come. He'll sit with a group of guys at the bar, but he isn't one of the talkers. He hardly ever says a word.

Joe never calls. He never drops by. He picks Mama up directly from work. When I ask her when we're going to get to meet him, she shrugs, saying it's not serious, that it's easier this way, that she's gotten used to being on her own.

What she doesn't say is that she doesn't want to lose anyone else. Not ever again.

Neither do I.

Mama and I have almost reached the Pair-A-Dice Hotel. The neon light flashes over our faces, turning our skin green and yellow and red, as the hula girl on the sign whips her hips back and forth, red dice forming the squared-off cups of her bikini top. Yeah, you go, girl. A running shoe, all the nap worn off the gray suede so it resembles the mangy fur of a stray dog, lies on the sidewalk by the door, pointing east. I guess whoever lost it didn't feel the cold—or sat, fascinated, in a snow bank, watching his skin turn colors and begin to die.

Mama takes a deep breath and pushes open the glass door, which is covered with greasy fingerprints and other less-identifiable bodily imprints. I pull down the sleeve of my coat and shoulder my way in so I don't have to touch it. The red carpet extends before us, a contaminated crimson sea, splotched with rusty islands of brown and sulfur. The Pair-A-Dice is a place where people leave bits of themselves behind, because they can't hold themselves together any more. That shoe outside. The odd stain of pee or vomit in the corner that won't quite come out. No nightly turn-down service or mints, only drops of blood on dingy pillows, weeping from old wounds, needle marks, or singed sinus passages.

At the end of a narrow corridor, another door connects to a casino, where banks of lights blink like a carnival arcade. The sign indicates there's a Thursday night special this evening, though it doesn't say what it is. We don't bother going in that direction. We know we won't find Meghan there. She doesn't gamble—not that way.

I lean on the front desk, the edge of which looks as if a large animal has gnawed it, and ding the bell. A man lumbers out of the back room, slope-shouldered and small-eyed as a bear.

"Yup?" He squints at us, a cheap cigar clamped between his blubbery lips. He stinks of smoke and stale sweat. There's a grease mark on the placket of his short-sleeved shirt, the mustard yellow color of which does nothing to flatter his sallow complexion.

"I'm looking for a girl who came in tonight with two small children," Mama tells him. "The name's Meghan Mulcahy."

He shrugs, regarding us with bored, blood-shot eyes. "People come, people go."

"Forgive me for being blunt." She lowers her chin and glares at him. "But she might have OD'ed again. You want the police coming around? Maybe even shutting this hellhole down? That would be something, wouldn't it?"

"No need to get your panties in a bunch." He waves us away, as if swatting flies. "Room 470."

"Keep your mind off my panties," Mama holds out her hand, "and give me the key." The charms on her bracelet tinkle, silver symbols of luck—a horseshoe, a star, a four-leaf clover—in theory anyway. My father gave her a charm for every birthday, because, he said with a grin, they led such a charmed life. She has thirteen charms (not the luckiest of numbers), which makes the bracelet heavy and noisy. She never buys any charms for herself nor does she take the bracelet off—unless she has to for work—even though it sometimes makes her wrist ache.

The desk dude expels a breath of smoky air. "Now, you know I can't do that." He kneads his doughy cheek with his fist.

Mama raises an eyebrow. She isn't budging.

With the sigh of a balloon deflating, he swipes the key from a hook and drops it into her palm. "Just bring it back, will you?

So we don't have to change the locks." He mutters to himself as we walk away.

"What are we going to do this time?" I ask as we ride the jerky elevator to the fourth floor. It rebounds nauseatingly, as if it's had one too many, before opening to a dim hallway with bald, pool-table-green carpet.

"We'll decide when we get there." Mama doesn't look at me as we step off the elevator and the door crashes shut behind us. Her eyes fasten on the door at the end of the hall. It's made of stuff that splinters when it gets kicked in, the kind that's inexpensive to replace.

I knock. "Teeny, it's us. Erin and Grandma."

No reply.

Mama tries the key. The door won't open. "Bolted." She folds her lips into a thin line. "Teeny, honey, you need to open the door."

"Mom said not to." Canned laughter erupts from a television inside. The volume's turned up loud enough to cause hearing loss—or provide cover for illicit activities. Probably a game show, *The Price Is Right*. Or rather, *The Price Is Too High*. In Meghan's case anyway.

I sigh in frustration. "You know it's us."

There's a pause, then the sound of Teeny fumbling with the bolt. Her small heart-shaped face peers out at us. She came by her name because she was a preemie. She was tiny then, barely four pounds. She's tiny now, all skinny arms and legs and big turquoise-blue eyes that seem to see through everything, because they've already seen too much.

We push inside, and I dab at the strawberry jam smeared on her face and hands. She has the appearance of a snot-nosed little clown.

"I got hungry," she explains. "That's all there was to eat." She points to the sticky jar on the windowsill, on which a fly with iridescent wings perches resembling, for a fleeting second due to a trick of the light, a jeweled brooch rather than the pestilence-carrying insect it is.

The TV roars at us. We can barely hear ourselves over the noise. Mama marches across the room and turns it off with such force the knob breaks. She mutters "cheap piece of garbage," as she jams it back in place. It's hard to know if she's talking about the television or my sister. Her expression darkens as she takes in the condition of the unit—the tangled bedcovers, the length of rubber tubing, the lighter, the burns on the sheets and nightstand, the fist-sized hole in the wall, the dirt-brown shag carpet so worn and grimed it looks like hair that hasn't been washed in weeks. Her knuckles whiten as she grasps a chair back someone has carved with knife-nick x's and o's, but all she says is "Honey, where's your mom?"

"She woke up." Teeny points at an open window near the fire escape. The dingy curtains stir listlessly.

I close the sash, something Meghan should have done to prevent her kids from freezing to death.

"So I see," Mama replies. "Did she tell you why she didn't use the door?"

Teeny scratches a bug bite on her arm. "She said she was taking a short cut." That's one way of putting it.

"She must have heard us coming." I look outside. A few isolated flakes sift down from the sky. The road glistens, paved with sugar.

There's no sign of Meghan. She can still move fast when she wants to. I trace footprints a quarter of a block with my eyes, wondering if they're hers, but lose them in the mash of treads at the corner. She's an expert at covering her tracks.

"She said she'd be right back." Teeny bounces on the bed. The springs jangle, muffled sleigh bells. *Dash away, dash away, all.* "She said she'd get me something to eat."

Mama and I trade glances. We both know what Meghan's really getting. She'll do anything, say anything, to score.

Mama touches Teeny's cheek to get her attention. "Where's Si-si? Where's the baby?"

"Sleeping. Over there." Teeny indicates a satin-edged pink receiving blanket spread on the floor on the other side of the bed. The baby's diaper leaks a muddy rivulet and her face is slack and drooly. "I'm baby-sitting."

Meghan sent us a photo-booth picture of her growing family taped to a postcard a couple of months ago, but this is the first time we've actually seen the baby in person. Mama glances from the bottle of Nyquil on the bureau to Si-si and back. "Jesus." Meghan has apparently doped the baby to make her sleep. As Mama changes her diaper, she shakes her head about the angry red rash on the child's butt—and everything else. Si-si's so out of it, she doesn't even cry. I wonder how often Meghan has resorted to this as she careens all over the state. Missoula. Great Falls. Helena, I think. It's not as if she ever gives us an itinerary. Sometimes she tells us she's in California and Texas when she calls collect.

Mama snuggles Si-si on her shoulder. "That does it. We're taking them with us."

"Shouldn't we wait for Meghan to get back?" That's what we've done before, trying to persuade her to come home with us, with the intention of getting her into treatment.

Not that it worked.

"Treatment? Sure. A facial would be great. Go ahead and make me an appointment," Meghan would joke.

And vanish the next day.

"Who the hell knows when that's going to be?" Mama looks around for things to pack. There isn't much. They travel light. She crams Teeny's holey jeans and stained T-shirts into the Hello Kitty backpack she'd given her two Christmases ago. The cat's white fur has gone gray from living on the streets.

"She'll wonder where they are," I point out.

"Will she?" Mama gives me a long stare. "Well then, why don't we leave her a note?"

I check the drawer for a piece of paper. This isn't the sort of place that has its own stationery or that people sent postcards from: *Hi, having a wonderful trip, great place to shoot up!* There is, however, a traveler's Bible with a broken spine, in case you get high enough to think you can see God and want to talk things over with him. *So, about the parting of the Red Sea . . .* or *was Sodom and Gomorrah everything it was cracked up to be? Sounds like my kind of place—*

"Can Mr. Bear come?" Teeny clutches a mildewed blue teddy to her chest. He's missing an eye and his joints are floppy. She's loved him practically to death.

"Of course, honey. Any friend of yours is welcome," Mama says with a brightness that has a hard edge to it, her words like shards of glass. She pushes Si-si higher on her shoulder.

I hold Teeny's hand as we ride down on the elevator. As we pass through the lobby, Mama sets the key on the front desk.

"Checking out?" the desk dude asks.

"Some of us."

"Going to pay the bill?" He pushes a slip of paper toward her.

"We've paid enough." She turns her back on him. To my surprise, he doesn't yell after her. Then again, she didn't book the room. Meghan did.

As we walk into the night, Teeny casts a glance up and down the street, looking for my sister. She blinks, from the cold or the absence of her mother or both. The roads remain deserted. There's only the four of us and a million swirling flakes of snow. The sadness in Teeny's eyes is so unbearable to me that by the time we reach the end of the block, I throw myself into a snowbank to distract her.

Mama almost smiles. Almost.

"What are you doing?" Teeny flings herself down beside me.

"Hasn't your mom taught you how to make snow angels?" I swish my arms and legs back and forth with a fury that borders on hysteria. I want to scream. I want to tear the night to blackened bits and glue it back into a shape that makes sense to me.

Teeny moves her limbs in tandem with mine and squeals. "I'm flying, I'm flying!"

In her voice I hear my sister when we were children, the two of us standing on top of the corroded metal swing set, willow branches tied to our arms, jumping off and expecting to soar, like red hawks riding thermals over the lake, if you can call it that, the small body of water poisoned with ten types of deadly chemicals at the bottom of the open pit mine.

My sister who, on more than one occasion, has run down the street, flapping her arms, her shirt gaping open in front, laughing wildly, "I'm flying. I'm flying!"

My sister. A snowbird, snorting flakes of God-knows-what. Lost somewhere in the storm.

CHAPTER 2

While Mama fixes Si-si a bottle, I give Teeny a bath in the clawfoot tub upstairs. We peel off our damp clothes—Teeny's Tweety Bird T-shirt and jeans, me the sweats I'd thrown on over a pair of boy shorts and a tank top—and drape them over the radiators. Puffs of steam rise into the air, like smoke from distant fires or a smoldering volcano.

Through the window, a streetlight burns, flakes go-go dancing in the beam it casts on the sidewalk below. Snow piles up on the beater cars parked outside tumbledown houses and forms a thick layer on the sill that reminds me of frosting on a cake. My breath fogs the pane before doing a slow fade.

"Will they dry soon?" Teeny eyes the T-shirt. She doesn't have much to wear. Maybe Meghan left the rest of her wardrobe behind when they last cut and ran. Teeny rubs her nose with the back of her hand, the furtive movement of a small animal, then answers my unspoken question, because she's gotten used to making excuses for her mother. Wherever she goes, that's something she has to do, part of the job description of having an addicted parent. "She said she was going to take us shopping."

I nod. Maybe she did. Meghan says a lot of things. It isn't even as if she's lying or doesn't mean it. Not all the time anyway. What it boils down to is, she's not great with followthrough. Never has been. It's all impulse, spontaneous bursts of energy that radiate blindingly but ultimately go nowhere.

I wrap myself in a kimono, another reject from Funkified, the vintage clothing store where I work part-time. The silk is discolored in places, but I pretend it's part of the design, the faint outline of waterlilies rather than an old wine stain. I like the smoothness of the silk against my skin, the way it makes me feel beautiful and exotic and someplace far away, where the scent of spices is in the air and there are tropical flowers and birds with brilliant plumage.

I roll up my sleeves and dip my finger in the water to test the temperature. Seems a little cold. I add more hot water and another shake of bath flakes from a box of Mr. Bubbles, whose goofy face promises the most fun bath time on the planet.

Teeny strokes my sleeve. Her knuckles are skinned. She's got a lot of scrapes and cuts, as if her skin is too thin, as if it's being rubbed away. Stuff happens when you're a kid. I mean, I know Meghan never hurts her. But sometimes she doesn't pay close enough attention. "That's pretty." Teeny flutters the kimono sleeve, making the printed butterfly fly.

"Thanks. Is this okay?" I hold Teeny as she sticks her toe in. There's no softness between her skin and bones. She's all angles, a tinker-toy girl.

"Uh-huh." She slips down into the bubbles with a sigh. Her skin turns pink from the warmth.

"You sure it's not too hot?" I test it again, this time with my elbow. I don't want to scald her.

"Nope. It's just right. Look, I'm a boat." She slides up and down the length of the tub, making waves. Good thing I didn't fill it too full or it would slop over the side, seep through the cracked tiles, and add to the water damage Meghan and I caused when we were kids. "Ahoy! Ahoy!" Teeny brandishes a make-believe sword. "Hey." She stops, imaginary cutlass poised in mid-air, water sloshing against her waist. "Are there girl pirates?"

"You bet there are. Or were. Grania O'Malley, for instance." I have a book about her in my room. My father gave it to me for my eighth birthday. *To my little mariner, love Daddy.* I don't know why he wrote that particular inscription on the flyleaf. Maybe he thought I loved the water as much as he did. Reading the currents in the river at the family cabin near Divide, trying to land the biggest trout, dreaming of sailing around the world, away from this ghost-filled dustbowl.

"Grania. That's a funny name." Teeny blows bubbles, puffer-fish cheeks inflating.

I rest my arms on the side of the tub. "Grania is an Irish version of Grace," I explain. I'd sit on my dad's lap in the evenings before bed and he'd read me stories. I'd ask for the pirate book over and over again, because I wanted to sail the high seas and have magnificent adventures. I wanted to be someplace where it rained day after day and the land was green and surrounded by water. I wanted to be brave and beautiful. A heroine. Like Grania O'Malley. Clear-eyed. Unafraid.

"Are pirates good?" Water streaks Teeny's face with faux tears.

"I guess it depends on whose side you're on." I dangle my fingers in the water. "Usually they were considered criminals, because they stole things from other ships. But in Grania's case, some would say she had her reasons."

Teeny looks solemn. "Is Mom a pirate?" she asks. "She steals stuff sometimes. I've seen her. Does she have her reasons?"

I shrug. I don't want to go there. Teeny doesn't need me to diss her mom. She probably already gets that from plenty of other people, good, bad, and indifferent. "I think she dressed up as one for Halloween once." I steer the subject to more neutral ground. "What are you going to be this year?"

"A cat. Meow. Meow." She makes whiskers with her fingers. "Is that a good cat sound?"

"It's purr-fect." Corny, I know, but I say it to make her laugh, and she does, right on cue. I grab a sliver of soap, shaped like a small ear, and wash her back. I feel the knobs of her spine, her delicate shoulderblades, the bones of a bird, as the soap dissolves in my hands. Teeny's hair straggles over her shoulders in greasy hanks. I reach for a bottle of children's shampoo left over from their last visit, Johnson's Baby Shampoo, the kind that promises no more tears. "Close your eyes and tilt your head back."

Teeny contorts her whole face as though she's sucked a lemon, while I lather her scalp. "Like this?"

"Uh-huh." It doesn't take much to get it good and sudsy.

Teeny palms a handful of lather and slaps it on her head. "It's whipped cream," she announces, "and I'm a sundae."

"What kind?" I rub behind her ears, a vigorous power wash to dislodge grime.

"The best." She licks her lips. "Chocolate."

"M'mm. My favorite. Maybe I'll have to eat you up!" I bare my teeth and tickle her.

She screeches with glee. She knows I'm someone she doesn't have to be scared of. I keep scrubbing as if I can scour away all the dirt, not only the kind that's skin-deep. I check the back of her neck and let out a sigh of relief. Thank God, no lice like last time. Teeny's hair is thin and fine and the color of weak tea. She doesn't have the McGann curls from my mother's side the rest of us do. Her straight locks could be due to a recessive gene from the Mulcahy branch. Or from The Unknown Father. We'll probably never be sure, since neither Teeny's nor Si-si's dads are involved in their lives (which might be a good thing). We don't even know who they are. Teeny's features are pure Meghan, the sharp, elfin chin, the high cheekbones, no baby fat to soften her edges, though her voice is sweet as a bell.

And I wonder, how much of who we are is inherited? How much is learned? Do we have a choice in shaping who we become? Our weight? Our temperament? Our desires, for love, for drink, for drugs? Living hard was part of the package back in the early days of our town. We're the only Mulcahys left here now. The end of the line. Dad's parents, Nana and Grand-da, a retired Montana Power Executive, live down in Arizona full-time, drinking cocktails, playing golf, and soaking up the sun in a place where snow never falls. Mama's parents are dead, victims of a plane crash years ago. I was too young to remember.

My maternal great-grandmother, Ginga, died a few years ago. She'd been known as Tana to her friends, which was short for Montana. A big name for such a little woman, Mama used to say, since she stood 4'11" and weighed 90 pounds. But what she lacked in physical size, she made up for with an out-sized personality. Teeny met her once. She doesn't remember her.

I pull sections of Teeny's hair away from her head so that they stick straight up. "You're a sea monster." Little Miss Loch Ness. All she needs is a banner across her chest.

"Ooo. Let me see!" She claps her hands. Bits of foam fly, spattering the tile with bubble buckshot.

I hold up a hand mirror with a faded rose on the back that used to belong to Ginga. Relics are everywhere in this house. The mirror's fogged and veined black around the edges, but the center remains clear, reflecting Teeny's face.

Teeny giggles with delight. "Do another one."

"Okay." When we were little, my sister and I took baths together. We washed each other's hair and backs, slippery and playful as young seals. We had contests to see who could fart the biggest bubbles, yelling "torpedo!," and hold her breath the longest (usually me). I'd make my eyes bug out and lie so still Meghan thought I was dead and would haul me to the surface and yell at me not to die and then I'd spit water in her face and laugh and we'd get into a big splashing fight and Mama would get mad because we'd trashed the bathroom for the billionth time. On other occasions, we lay side by side and pretended to be scuba divers on a mission for Jacques Cousteau exploring the Great Barrier Reef or the Blue Hole—*look out, there's a hammerhead shark, a blue-ringed octopus, an olive sea snake.* Or we were mermaids with long flowing hair, living in a giant pink shell, not needing air to breathe, not needing anything except each other.

"Auntie Erin, you're not paying attention!" Teeny splashes me the way Meghan used to. "Do another one!"

"Sorry. I was spacing out." I wipe drops of soapy water off my cheek and return to the present. "Here goes." I twist her hair into a bun on top of her head. "There. You're Cinderella going to the ball."

"But I don't have any clothes on!" She crosses her arms over her bare chest. Her bony knees jut from the water like miniature mountain peaks.

"Then the mice will have to sew you some," I squeak, and make her a gown of bubbles, an off-the-shoulder style whose skirt slowly breaks apart and floats away. "See?"

Teeny looks in the mirror again, nodding at her reflection in approval. "Pretty." She tilts her chin regally and moves her arms as if she's dancing with an invisible partner, waltzing this way and that. I can almost hear the string section of an orchestra providing the music.

I point to the dial on my watch. "Oh, no—it's after midnight!"

She stares at me, wide-eyed. "After midnight—I have to go!," then ducks underwater and rinses off. Bye-bye, bubble couture. When she surfaces again, she's no longer Cinderella. She's just Teeny, and she's ready to give me what little kids prize most, The Complete Owie Tour. I feel like a real insider now. "This one happened when I fell down on the sidewalk." She points to a postage-stamp-sized scab on her elbow. "I got this one from falling off a bike." She indicates a scar on her knee.

31

I run my finger over the raised white line, where her skin pulled together to heal itself. It's curved into a tiny smile or a frown, depending upon which way you look at it. "I didn't know you had a bike."

"It wasn't mine. It was at a place where we were." She squeezes the bath sponge and makes a foamy waterfall. "A kid said I could ride it."

I let the water dribble from my fingertips and drip into the bath, my own little rainstorm. "And your mom said it was okay?"

"She wasn't around." Teeny shrugs.

That figures. I imagine Meghan sprawling on a mildewed mattress, slack-jawed, spit-slimed, needles scattered on the dirt-encrusted, warped wooden floor. A ragged curtain flaps in the breeze that comes in through the busted window, a breath of fresh air that manages to stir the smell of barf and shit—give a hint that something better awaits someplace else—but can't totally displace it. The walls are a collage of sprayed urine, illegible screeds, grimy handprints, peeled paint, and yellowed, torn advertisements from old Frederick's of Hollywood ads. From the bed, if you're lucid enough to see beyond the windowframe, you can glimpse the shiny dome of a church or an observatory and dream about going there some day and seeing the stars. Real ones, not just the ones in your head.

And I see Teeny in that scene, ducking around bodies slumped in hallways, making her way downstairs to the sidewalk where weeds sprout from cracks in the pavement, grateful for something to hold on to even if they risk getting stepped on or dying of thirst. She steals a glance at the window above, where, in the shadowy region beyond the paint-peeled sill, her mother is tripping. Then Teeny turns to the boy sitting on the bottom step, a boy with a bruise on his cheek where somebody hit him and clothes as dirty and torn as her own, and a rusty bike with tires that are almost flat.

"You want to ride?" He hits the corroded railing with a piece of wood that he has broken off from the frame of the front door. It's that brittle—and he's that bored.

And she says "Sure."

"It'll cost you." He squints at her.

"I can pay." She digs in her pocket for the tarnished dime she's found on the floor, the one she's been saving to buy a piece of hard candy, her favorite, a green apple Jolly Rancher, the next time they go to the store—when will they go? she's so hungry—but she places the coin in his outstretched hand, with its cuts and chewed nails and cigarette burns. Because maybe she can fly away on that bike, out of that neighborhood to a place where there are green lawns and mothers who bake cookies and kids who think going on a trip means taking a family vacation.

The first few times Teeny gets on the bike, she can't keep her balance. She gets some minor scrapes. She doesn't cry. She almost never cries. The boy snickers to himself, which only makes her more determined. She'll show him. She pushes off again. It feels as if she's on a tight-rope. She jerks right, then left, sensing the limits, poised on the blade of a knife. You can do it, she tells herself, you can do it. But as she wobbles toward the end of the block, past the burned-out cars and shifty-eyed dealers huddling at the corner, the front tire dips into a pothole, and she falls and cuts her knee, a deep gouge that bleeds freely and will eventually become a scar to add to her collection.

The scar I'm looking at now as she frolics in the bath.

Teeny's been so many places, done so many things, that we don't have a clue about. There's a map inside her no one can read, a map leading from one hellhole to the next. Because none of the places they shack up are any good. Not for kids. Not for anybody.

"Where were you?" I ask.

Teeny flicks a drop of water from the tip of her nose. "When?"

"When you rode the bike." I sponge her back and arms, careful not to put too much pressure on the scabs.

"Someplace where it's sunny all the time and there are palm trees and swimming pools and sand to build sand castles not in sandboxes, but at beaches, real beaches." She spits water from her mouth like a fountain. "It's called Califorkia."

I stifle a laugh. "You mean California?"

"Yeah." She sprays droplets of water, as though she's a dog shaking itself dry after a dip in a lake. "You know, the place Mickey Mouse lives."

Southern California. "You went to Disneyland?" I ask.

"Uh-huh. Look, I'm a dolly-phin." Teeny submerges again and wiggles her elbows, pretending she has fins. She has a good vocabulary, though she sometimes messes up on pronunciation. But then she's only five.

L.A. Interesting. Meghan must have found herself a guy with money this time. "Why did you leave?"

Teeny shrugs. "Mom said it was time to go home."

H'mm. Meghan doesn't come back here unless something's wrong. Seriously wrong.

"But everything was okay, right?"

Teeny gives me a quizzical look. "Sure. Mom was tired of get-ting sunburned. You should've seen how red she got. She has a gazillion more freckles. She said Califorkia isn't for fair-skinned girls like us. It never snows. It's hot all the time."

It was probably a different type of heat that made my sister run. She can take extremes in climate; she's a Butte girl. But the type of heat that comes from cheating a dealer or pissing off a boyfriend? That, she can't take.

"How did you get back?"

"People gave us rides and money. We got to go on trucks and buses and cars." Teeny stretches out on the bottom of the bath. She's small enough to flutter-kick without her feet brushing the other end. "Do you have any little kids' bikes around here?" She picks up an old thread in our conversation, the one that inter-ests her most.

I think of how Meghan and I used to take our bikes—retro, banana-seat numbers Mama had gotten at a garage sale—out onto the hill, how we careened down unused gravel-mine roads and made jumps from pieces of board and rock, in search of the biggest thrill. We drove Mama crazy with the stunts we pulled. In some ways, I guess we still do.

"Yeah. I think our old ones are down in the basement," I say. "You want me to teach you to ride?"

"I already know how. I taught myself," she says importantly. "Look. I'm a submarine." Teeny periscopes her head, adding: "Does Mom have one too?"

"A bike? Sure." Mama never gave Meghan's stuff away. I sit back on my heels. My legs are falling asleep, pins and needles from ankle to thigh. "We used to ride them everywhere."

"I'm a blue whale. The biggest fish in the sea." Teeny spews a stream of water. "Maybe now that we're here, she'll ride with me."

"She hasn't before?" I reach for a towel.

"We aren't usually at places with bikes her size. Everybody drives boom-boom cars." Teeny shakes her head. "One time there was a bike for her. But she said she didn't have on the right shoes."

I smile, thinking of Meghan pedaling down the street, wearing cowboy boots and a mini-skirt.

Teeny submerges and surfaces again.

"Who are you now?" I push up the sleeves of my kimono again so they don't get wet.

Teeny thinks for a moment. "Just me." Goosebumps cover her arms. The water's getting cold. She is too. "Grrr. Did I scare you?" She waves her fingers at me. They've gone all raisiny.

"Yeah." I pretend to shudder as I reach for a towel. "Do you want to get out?"

"Okay." She swings her leg over the side of the bath, but the lip's too high for her. I lift her up.

"You're strong, Auntie Erin, stronger than Mom." Teeny steadies herself by leaning against my shoulder. "Sometimes she's so tired, she can't lift anything."

I flex my arm. "Look at these muscles." Inside, I'm thinking, I don't want to be the strong one. I don't want to carry the load. But I don't say the words aloud. Teeny doesn't need to hear them. She wouldn't understand. Or maybe she would. And that would be worse.

I wrap Teeny's hair in the towel, turban-style. "There. You're a swami."

"What's a swami?" she asks suspiciously.

"It's a good thing. Kind of like a magician," I assure her.

"Cool. I'll turn everything into candy. I'll make no one fight ever again. I'll make Mom come home." She waves an imaginary wand. Abracadabra. Alacazam. "Can I wear my hair like this tomorrow? Even after it's dry?"

"Sure. If you want to." I tuck a damp strand of hair behind her ear.

She has the appearance of a small Hindu deity. All we need is some sitar music and incense and we could build a shrine for her, gild it with fake gold, and people would come and ask her for words of wisdom.

In a way, I wish she really were. Then she could give me some guidance.

I lead her to the bedroom, the one that used to be Meghan's, a shrine to different times, a different girl. It's hard to reconcile the Meghan of Then with the Meghan of Now. Meghan's last school picture (freshman year) is on the bureau. She has that well-scrubbed Catholic girl look and wears a Peter Pan collar blouse and navy crewneck sweater, something she wouldn't be caught dead in two years later when getting smashed at high school parties wasn't enough and she started frequenting biker bars. (She has a thing for guys with motorcycles.) She'd drink until she passed out. But it still wasn't enough. She kept seeking the perfect high, taking one drug after another, trying to fill the empty space inside her, chasing that elusive feeling with all those elusive men, chasing it—and then she had Teeny and Si-si, chasing it—and then it almost killed her. Chasing it. Over and over and over again. Over. Dose.

"Who's that?" Teeny points at Meghan's photo on the vanity, next to a Lucite cube filled with tubes of lip gloss and eyeshadow, the makeup my sister was experimenting with when she ran away for the first time. In the drawers are her clothes and her journal, which Mama broke down and read, trying to reach her. But after a couple of entries, the pages were torn out or blank. There were things Meghan didn't want us to know, places we couldn't go. She wouldn't let us follow her. She was good at disappearing, then popping back into our lives when we least expected it, a Jack-in-the-Box in drag.

I put a finger to my lips, because Si-si's sleeping in the cradle on the floor near the closet. We were going to set her in the guest room, but Teeny insisted on having her close by.

Too late. The baby opens her eyes. But she doesn't cry.

"That's your mom." I touch the silver frame. The stand almost topples over. I steady it, then carefully let go.

Teeny frowns. "Doesn't look like her."

"It was taken a few years ago. A school picture." A few lifetimes ago. When Meghan had a sweet innocence to her smile, a childlike roundness to her face. When she thought anything was possible. *I'm going to be valedictorian. I'm going to be the best rock 'n' roll singer in the world. I'm going to be—*

An addict.

"I'm going to kindergarten this year. Mom says so," Teeny informs me. "I'll get pictures taken too, huh?"

"Yeah, you will." I wonder if they'll stay in one place long enough to enroll her. Will she still be with Mama and me in the fall? Will I still be here? Or will I fly away and put some distance between myself and this messed-up situation?

Teeny studies the photograph and steals glances at herself in the mirror behind it, comparing the two images. "Do I look like her?"

"What do you think?" I sit on the bed. I don't want her to resemble Meghan too much. Who knows who she'll become as she gets older, what genetic glitches will rise to the surface.

Teeny burrows under the covers. The pink satin of the quilt matches the flush in her cheeks. "Sometimes," she says, her voice small. "On one of her good days."

I lay my head on the other pillow, the cotton case soft, rose-bud print faded from years of washing. I remember how Meghan and I used to fall asleep this way, when I'd come into her room in the middle of the night, frightened from a bad dream. After she'd gone for good, I'd still stand on the threshold, waiting for her sleepy voice to tell me to come in. "What are good days?" I ask.

"When she comes back." Teeny makes her favorite—and only—stuffed animal, Mr. Bear, dance on her chest. "When she doesn't sleep all day. Her sleep is different from other people's. It's like Sleeping Beauty's."

"It is?" I turn and look at her.

Her eyes are round and serious. "Yeah. Because it takes forever for her to wake up." She hugs the bear and stares at the ceiling. The false stars of glitter in the plaster wink at us.

I sigh. Teeny's this funny combination of old soul and little girl. Sometimes she blows my mind, the way she sees things. I asked her once how she got to be so smart and she said it's because she watches a lot of TV. Because there's almost always TV where they are, no matter how crappy the accommodations, how tripped-out and broke their hosts are. TV is there. A fact of life. An essential element. *News at eleven. And now a word from our sponsors. Back to you, Jean. This just in. This is a test, only a test.*

"How about a bedtime story?" I go over to the bookcase and pull out a copy of *The Lonely Doll*, jammed into the far side behind stacks of paperbacks that Meghan read by flashlight when she was in elementary school. She'd stay up the entire night reading, go to class, then tear around the neighborhood, looking for trouble. She never got tired, never let herself slow down.

"Wait. Si-si wants to listen too." Teeny slides out of bed and picks up the baby, lumbering toward me as if she's carrying a large sack of potatoes.

"Here. I'll help you." I hold out my arms to take Si-si.

Teeny shakes her head. "It's okay. I do this all the time." I hover nervously as she sets Si-si on the bed, away from the edge, climbs up, and cradles the baby in her lap. Si-si doesn't protest. She stares into Teeny's face, serene.

The cover of the book crackles when I curl up next to the girls and open it. No one's read it for a long time. The book used to be Mama's when she was a girl. It's about a doll named Edith who becomes friends with two teddy bears. The author tells the story using a series of black-and-white photos.

"Look, Si-si," Teeny says, "there's another Mr. Bear, just like mine!" Si-si doesn't reply. She's sleeping soundly in Teeny's arms. Teeny listens raptly, forgetting about her mother and her habits, sleeping and otherwise. She loses herself in a simple story of friendship, where people get mad but forgive each other, run away but come back and live happily ever after.

As I turn the last page, Teeny's nodding off. After I tuck Si-si in the cradle, I pull the covers up to Teeny's chin and smooth the hair out of her face. She looks warm and happy and I want to take a picture of her, to capture that contentment, as if that will make it last, and put it next to the photograph of my sister, to create a tableau of not only what had been, but what might be.

I wipe the dust from Meghan's picture with the sash of my robe. I can't touch my sister's face. The glass comes between us. Something always comes between us. I grasp the handle of the drawer, consider tucking her away out of view. But in the end, I leave her framed image on top of the vanity to watch over us the only way she knows how.

CHAPTER 3

Once the kids are in bed, once our anger cools by a degree or two, Mama and I stare at each other across the kitchen table. She sips a cup of coffee. I have peppermint tea, like an old lady. What can I say? I like the smell of it. I close my eyes and I'm lying in the sun along the Mediterranean coast. A Greek island with a Greek god. The scent of mint in the air.

Well, maybe not. The truth is, the closest I can get to Greece right now is the Athens Restaurant on Pyrite Street, and my only hero is a gyro. I spin my cup. My leg jigs a dance of restlessness. Sometimes I feel as though I'm tethered here, a hound at the end of a chain, and I'd have to chew off my own foot to escape, because it's about family, because I'd have to lose a part of myself in order to leave. And I want to. And I don't.

Patches of black, star-flecked sky slide out from behind the clouds like broken slabs of granite. Somewhere up the hill a dog howls, long and mournful as an oboe, until it emits a strangled yelp and stops. The windows reflect our pensive images, wavering against the background of the vast night. Our profiles and gestures are nearly identical, which is kind of disconcerting. The curly black hair, the green eyes, the freckled skin. McGann women all have them. My sister too. Still the beauty of the family, in spite of everything.

Beyond the windows, the hills loom over us, where scores of people dug deep and a chosen few struck gold.

Funny. When *we* dig deep, all we find is more dirt.

I don't know exactly how long we sit there. Can't be much more than a few minutes, though it feels like forever. Our world almost constantly revolves around Meghan, whether she's here or not. Always has, one way or another. At first she was the golden girl, skipped ahead a grade in elementary school because she tested gifted. Mama couldn't help bragging about her. It wasn't that she loved me less. I just didn't draw as much attention to myself, not possessing talents that lent themselves to acclaim. Nowadays, I still don't have her complete attention, but she relies on me. Part of me craves that reliance, the other feels it's a consolation prize. *And the first runner-up is Erin Mulcahy. . . .*

We can't remember whose turn it is to go after Meghan. Mama pulls a loose thread on the sleeve of her sweater, mohair, the texture of angel hair. She watches it unravel, as if it belongs to someone else, then remembers it's something she'll have to fix and ties a knot to contain the damage, though it's already been done. I pick at a chip in the table with my fingernail.

"We should let her lie in whatever hole she's dug for herself," Mama says finally. She presses her lips together, an attempt at maintaining resolve, though they tremble at the corners, giving her away. She might appear hard on the outside, but she's soft in the center, especially when it comes to my sister—who, of course, uses that to her advantage. Then again, I'm no better. I'm always giving her another chance. My sister's the queen of second chances.

I sigh. All I want to do is crawl in bed and close my eyes and dream about being somewhere else. Too bad that isn't an option. "Let's flip for it." I toss a dime in the air, slap it down on my wrist. "Call it."

Mama puts her elbows on the table, charm bracelet tinkling. "Heads."

I lift my hand. Sure enough, the coin lies face up. I slump in the chair, unable to summon much enthusiasm for the task ahead. I never win at games of chance.

"I'll go," Mama offers. Her eyes are shadowed, face haggard. For once, she looks her age or even older. No. I'll have to be the designated martyr tonight. "You have to leave for work earlier than I do." I rise from my seat and stretch. "Besides, like Yo-ho said, it's a beautiful night for a stroll."

I put on Mama's old pea coat this time, which, while not exactly making a fashion statement, will keep me warmer than the windbreaker. I settle for the same boots, because I only have one pair. My feet are bigger than Mama's, so I can't borrow hers, nor can I wear her clothes, except for oversized items such as the coat, because she's the smallest person in the family. It's weird giving your mother hand-me-downs, rather than the other way around.

Mama frowns. "Maybe we should call the police. Let her be someone else's problem for once."

I shake my head. We can't throw Meghan to the wolves. Not yet. "I'll find her."

"I'm not sure I want you going out there."

Mama looks tinier than usual, her mouth pinched. Most of the time she thinks nothing of my tearing around town. Tonight's different, though. Something has reminded her of my father. She sees him in me now and then. I know when it happens from the sudden stillness in her face, the fleeting anguish in her eyes.

"Nothing's going to happen." I assure her. "I'll take your cell phone, okay?"

She folds her lips together and nods as I head into the night, where I become a figure inside a snow globe, small and insignificant and bounded by the finite world of the town and the search for a sister who might not want to be found.

I don't want you to get the impression that my sister and I have some sort of good girl–bad girl thing going. What would the female equivalent of Cain and Abel be? Caina and Abelette? The point is, that isn't an issue for us. Or it didn't used to be until lately. I mean, I'm no prize myself. I've had my own moments of craziness, partying with my friends. Not that long ago, somebody in my motley crew decided we had to climb the giant statue of the Virgin Mary on the ridge, Our Lady of the Rockies, that we had to sit in her prayerful hands at the top of the world (our world, anyway). Never mind that she's made of steel and there's no way to get a mountaineering pin into her, or that we didn't get farther than my friend Alex's

45

house because we were too drunk to assemble the gear in the first place. I think that was the night I had the nightmare about the statue coming to life and leveling Butte.

Mama doesn't know about my escapades. Maybe because, for the most part, I know when to stop. Or can stop. Maybe I have a greater sense of self-preservation. Or am just a chickenshit. Whatever.

Not my sister. She has her foot stuck on the accelerator. She has a tendency to floor everything.

As I trudge down the street, the "M" glows on the hill, a giant, lit-up letter branded on the night. It stands for the Montana School of Mines. I like to think it stands for other things too. When I was a child, I'd look "m" words up in the dictionary, making a list. I suppose I still have it in a drawer somewhere.

Miasma. Monster. Multitude. Mercy.

Meghan.

A couple of nights ago before the weather turned on us, my buds and I sat in the light of the "M," along with the moths hurling themselves at the hot bulbs, singed wings accumulating like fragile shells, the kind that turn to dust if you step on them, on the beach of a dead sea. We talked in an aimless way about what we were going to do now that we'd graduated from high school. The biggest news is that our friends Lisa and Dillon are getting married soon. They've been dating for about a year. A lot of people around here get hitched right after graduation. Lisa and Dillon have additional motivation, since she got pregnant. Alex and I are bridesmaids. Because the whole thing is happening at warp speed, we bought dresses at a tacky bridal store in town, pale pink puffy numbers that make me feel more like a soda fountain drink than a member of a wedding party.

A couple of us are heading to college in the fall. I've been accepted to art school back east, though I haven't told anyone except Alex. When Mama asks, I tell her I haven't heard yet. Maybe I'll say I'm on the waiting list, because I *am* waiting—to decide if I can afford to go, both financially and emotionally. Even before this latest episode of Meghan's ongoing soap opera, I wasn't sure I wanted to leave. I've never been that far away before—or for so long. I'm holding on to my job at Funkified, just in case. It's a vintage/costume store run by a couple of guys named David and Daniel, who call themselves the Double Ds. I got the position because I'm good with a needle, though not in the same way my sister is.

"Hey, Erin!" Alex and the rest of our friends are out in the snow, hauling sleds up the slag-heaps for what will undoubtedly be a bumpy ride down. She has a total Nordic thing going, blond braids, snowflake-patterned sweater, and pom-pom hat. "Come on!"

I shake my head. "Can't." I cup my hands around my mouth. "Have to run an errand."

"What?" She puts a hand to her ear.

"Errand!"

She doesn't get it. It probably sounds like I'm saying my own name over and over again. Erin. Erin. I shake my head from side to side in an exaggerated way. Now she has the idea. I'm glad she doesn't come over and try to talk me into it. When I have to make excuses for Meghan, I end up feeling like a loser by association.

"Okay. Later!" Alex shoulders the rope and makes for the

crest. She's what I call a three-exclamation-point person. She brims with enthusiasm in an almost indiscriminate way. She's the exact opposite of me. That's probably one of the reasons she's my best friend.

I turn away from their boisterous expedition and back to the snowy silence, feeling increasingly resentful that I can't accompany them because I'm stuck with Meghan-duty. Hopefully it won't take long. I've climbed over too many semiconscious addicts in too many squats looking for her. I'm tired of getting puke and crap all over my shoes. I'd rather endure the freezing cold than deal with that again.

The town has on its poker face tonight, oh-so-familiar yet giving nothing away. There's my place of employment on the corner. Since the lights are out, only the items in the front of the store are visible: a doll with bruised eyes and frizzled hair who reminds me, in a creepy way, of my sister at her most strung-out; a beaded black flapper dress on a headless mannequin; and a wide-brimmed wool felt hat with an ostrich feather, something my great-grandmother, Ginga, might have worn. Mostly things people left behind after they died, or sold because they needed the money. The window display definitely could use work. I'll deal with it tomorrow. I can't stop trying to bring dying things back to life.

At the moment, I have a different type of reclamation project to handle. "Meghan? Meghan?" The snow muffles my voice. I'm the one who sounds lost, not her. I'm a child again, looking for her big sister. The tag-along. The baby.

"Hey," a male voice says behind me. "Girlie. What're you doing out tonight?"

It's Marlon Jennings, one of my sister's old boyfriends. He's so gaunt, everyone calls him Bone. We're as close as he's got to family—and that isn't much. His mother died young in a car wreck when a drunk driver crossed the centerline on the highway. The irony of her cause-of-death, given Bone's current condition, isn't lost on him. His dad died of kidney failure, the last of long line of failures in his life, business, health, and otherwise. Bone's brother, Leroy, left town ten years ago and never looked back. Word has it he's selling cabin cruisers in central Florida.

Bone's dirty pants have the texture of tanned hide. One of his shoulders isn't quite even with the other. He broke his collarbone and never had it set right. He's broken a lot of things—and been broken himself. He takes a perverse pride in having a mutually destructive relationship with life.

"Guess." I ask.

"Gone again, huh?" He exhales a long plume of smoke. The tip of his cigarette glows, then fades to ashes. He's hunched over in his usual doorway, an abandoned building that's been for sale for years, no one fool enough to buy it.

"You know where she is?" I stamp my numb feet.

"I try not to, 'cause it'll just mean she'll leave all over again." He squints at me.

Marlon can't be more than thirty-five, though he looks fifty. He'd been one of the town's bright lights, a star basketball player and honor student. Everyone thought he'd play college ball, but he wasn't big enough. He was used to working hard and fighting his way through anything. To his great frustration and disappointment, his height wasn't something he could change. So he moved to Seattle with his high school sweetheart, put her through college washing dishes in a Mexican restaurant. He figured he'd have his turn when she was done. It turned out she was done with him first, and the education he received wasn't the type you get a degree for. He roared home in a fury, leaving everything behind, including half his face when he crashed his motorcycle just shy of the Continental Divide. His mouth still crumples at the edges, even when he isn't sad, which is most of the time.

"Anybody in your life now?" He stubs the butt in the crumbling mortar between the bricks.

I cross my arms over my chest. "Too many people."

"You know what I mean." He looks down the empty road.

I shake my head. "I'm not like her."

"You don't have to be." He tips snow from the brim of his hat. His style isn't usually so Gunsmoke. He must have found the soggy ten-gallon in the ditch. "Last time I checked, it wasn't a crime to let yourself care about someone."

I roll my eyes. "I don't need a matchmaker, Bone."

"That's right. Just a bunch of hicks and drunks and cowboys in this town. You're destined for bigger things." He grins at me with a mouthful of chipped teeth he's never bothered to get fixed.

I bite my lip. I didn't intend to make him feel bad. Marlon has a good heart. He doesn't get mean the way some of Meghan's men do. "She liked you."

"Yeah. But not enough." He stares at his blackened fingers. He looks as if he's been burned.

I lean against the wall. "She has a way of using people up."

"She has a way of using a lot of things up." He nods. "She's probably the hungriest person I've ever known."

I draw a line in the snow with my toe, watch the flakes rub it out. "I have to find her."

He sucks in his cheeks. "Maybe it's best not to."

"For her kids." I add.

"Like I said." He has an edge in his voice now. "Maybe it's best not to."

I sigh. "I have to try. I can't not try."

"That's the curse of blood, isn't it?" He turns up his collar against the cold. "Give her my best. Or what's left of it."

I sigh a puff of exasperated fog and straighten my shoulders. I have to be tough tonight. Maybe if I am, Meghan will finally start taking responsibility. Ha. I laugh out loud. Nobody's around to hear, only the old brick buildings that look down on me with black eyes. I'm keyed up. I don't know which way to turn or whether I'll find her dead or alive. Everything's surreal, partly because this section of town resembles the set of a Capra film, except it isn't exactly a wonderful life and there aren't any guardian angels to help us so they can earn their wings.

Moldering facades flank Main, faded Painted Ladies of another era. The ghosts of those who'd once jammed the avenues a century ago—miners, whores, drummers, boss-men—are everywhere. Our ancestors were among the lower orders, the thousands of Irish who'd sought their fortunes and ended up with next to nothing. With each subsequent generation, more mines closed, more people died and moved away, and no one spoke the mother-tongue in the place that once had the largest Gaelic-speaking population outside of Ireland, though some people still have a slight lilt in their speech, if you listen close enough to hear it. Ginga did.

Signs along the freeway court tourism, touting the mining museum, the speed-skating oval where Bonnie Blair trained for Olympic glory, even a museum dedicated to Venus Alley, where prostitutes worked in rooms no bigger than closets to feed opium habits. I suppose some of our ancestors were there too. Smoking pipes seems slightly more elegant than shooting up, though the result's the same.

Meghan's done it all. Now, to get high, she has to get the hardest stuff on the market—or go for a vein. She doesn't have many good ones left.

I remember the first time I realized Meghan was using. It was right before she dropped out of school. I needed to go to the bathroom; we shared one on the second floor. Something blocked the door from the inside. I thought she'd shut me out, so she could continue to primp, uninterrupted, in front of the mirror, a process that could take an hour or more.

I banged on the door. "Open up. It's my turn."

I heard a groan and a thump. When I pushed again, the door opened enough for me to squeeze in. Meghan had collapsed on the tile floor next to the vomit-filled toilet. Her skin had a green cast to it, as if she had chlorophyll in her veins instead of blood.

I was scared. She looked like something from a horror film. "What's the matter? Are you sick? Should I call Mama?"

"No." Her chest heaved. "It's just the flu."

It wasn't any flu I'd ever seen. "You'd better not give it to me." I almost left right then.

"Shut up," she croaked. Usually, she could at least muster a good yell or shove. I tried to help her. She shrugged me off.

"Leave me alone." She slurred her words.

I hesitated.

"Get. Out." She glared at me with vampire eyes.

"Okay, okay."

I retreated to my room and opened my science book, but I couldn't concentrate. We were studying botany: namely, the process of photosynthesis. I traced the pictures of leaves with my finger, thinking of my green-tinged sister, who'd wrapped herself around the toilet in the next room. A seething being so different from the girl I'd always known. It was like she was possessed. I wanted to ask *Who are you, and what have you done with Meghan?*

By the time my mother returned from her shift at the hospital, my sister had gotten herself back to a semblance of normal. But I knew something was taking root in her, something she couldn't control.

I blow on my fingers and jam them in my pockets. I had forgotten to put on gloves. Dumb move. I shiver and turn south, up one street, down another. Each one named after a mineral. Galena. Quartz. Granite. I'm on Mercury when I think *Screw it. I'll catch pneumonia. I'm going home.* And yet I can't stop searching, any more than she can stop using.

One more block.

I see a dark shape near a lamppost at the end of the road. It's moving toward me, not exactly in a straight line, and while there are a number of people in town who may get discombobulated like that, I have a strong suspicion it's her. It would make a certain amount of sense to find my sister on this street, named for a substance that measures temperatures, moves fast—and poisons anyone stupid enough to touch it.

Meghan doesn't try to run this time, which probably means she's in post-score bliss. Something involving uppers is my guess, judging by the way she's weaving along the sidewalk. Icicles fall from the eaves of a building behind me and shatter on the pavement like glass.

"Hey, Sis." Meghan gives me a sloppy grin. Her body lists to one side, as if she's a sinking ship. "What are you doing here?"

"What do you think? Looking for you."

A guy slows and honks his horn as he drives by on his way home from one of the bars. I can't see much of him in the darkened cab of the dirty white pickup, but I smell snuff and beer, lots of it. "You ladies need a ride?" he calls, his voice juicy.

"No, thanks," I reply, my voice strong and clipped, before my sister can accept, which I'm sure she would, unable to resist the interaction, the promise of more booze or drugs or danger.

I feel a shiver of adrenaline, thinking he's going to get out of the truck and confront us. But to my relief, the moment passes and he pulls away, spinning slush from his wheels, taillights glowing like demon eyes.

Maybe we look like too much work. High-maintenance, that's us.

Or at least her.

"Why'd you blow him off?" My sister waves after him in delayed-reaction mode. "You're jealous that everybody wants me, aren't you?"

I tap my foot in the slush. It would have been a more effective gesture on hard pavement. "Yeah, everybody wants you. Especially your kids."

This brings her up short—for a split second. "You don't need to talk to me that way. For your information, they're in good hands. Greg's watching them." She slips and grabs my arm, almost knocking us over in the process. "Oops." She giggles, adding, "He's real good with kids."

I shrug her off. "Who's Greg?" I watch her closely. A muscle in her cheek twitches as if a parasite has burrowed under the skin.

She doesn't meet my gaze. She touches a light pole, a not-very-subtle diversionary tactic. "Remember that big storm when we were kids? Bigger than this one by far. You licked a pole and your tongue got stuck to it?"

"Thanks to you." How could I forget? I was four years old and trusted her in everything, even though she'd given me many reasons not to. It was twenty below, relatively mild, compared to the thirty or forty sub-zero temperatures we'd endured for days. Boredom set in while we waited for Mama to emerge from the butcher shop. We'd made the usual snow angels and snowballs. Meghan wanted more. In search of entertainment, she chose to amuse herself, as usual, at my expense. She told me the city had painted the poles with peppermint candy coating. "Go on. Lick them and see!"

It was more like they'd been coated with icy glue. I nearly

ripped my tastebuds off trying to free myself. I thought my whole tongue was going to tear away—or that it would be stuck to the pole forever, a little pink flag.

Meghan teased me for days, *Aren't we having tongue for dinner?* or *Pole got your tongue, Erin?*

"I was more of a sucker back then," I say.

"More of a licker, you mean. Or maybe you just got licked," she snorts, almost losing her balance again, she laughs so hard. "Get it?"

"Yeah. I get it." I'm not letting her distract me this time. We come from a long line of accomplished storytellers. If she gets started in this condition, she'll never shut up. "I get the fact you're trying to change the subject. Who's Greg?"

"Ooh, Ms. Third Degree." She holds up her hands and pretends to tremble with fear. "A guy I know."

"Well, he wasn't watching them." I hate to hear Mama in my voice, but I can't help myself. I'm cold and tired and sick of this shit.

"How do you know?" Meghan tugs at the uneven hem of her dress, a baby-doll style made of see-through fabric. Her legs are bare, feet jammed into cowboy boots. The soles pull away from the toes, like the pointy beaks of scavenging birds. A short, matted, fake-fur coat completes the ensemble. All she needs is a long cigarette holder and she'd look as goth as Cruella de Ville.

"Because I was there." My patience is wearing thin.

"Really?" She picks at a scab on her arm. "You turning into a Pair-A-Dice regular? Maybe I'll see your name in the newspaper, huh?"

"Are you listening to me?" I slap at her hand. "Teeny called us because you were passed out. She was scared."

"That little silly. I was taking a nap. I can't believe Greg wasn't around when you got there. Bastard. Good thing I wasn't gone long. See? I bought the kids dinner." She talks too fast, a freight train of words, piling up on each other, derailing. She shows me a can of formula and a prepackaged meal with marginal nutritional value she purchased at a gas station mini-mart. "Teeny loves Lunchables. She'd eat them all the time if I let her."

Oh, yum, I think sarcastically, but I don't start in on her. She thinks I'm too much of a health nut—emphasis on the second word—anyway. Besides, we need to stay focused—and, in her case, get straight. "Kind of late for dinner. It's after midnight, Megs."

She laughs again, sharp and dry. "How time flies." She looks at her bare wrist. "Guess I'd know that if I could find my watch." She slips every which way as she strikes off in the direction of the Pair-A-Dice.

I put a hand on her arm. The thin muscle tenses under my fingers, tendon and bone and not much else. "The kids aren't there."

"What?" She pulls away, eyes rimmed with smeary black liner and mascara, cheeks hollow.

Now for the tricky part. "We took them home. You didn't leave us much of a choice—"

It takes her a few seconds to register the information, and when she does, she explodes. "You did what?"

"Keep your voice down." I hiss. "We couldn't leave them alone. The place is a total dive. Mama's really pissed."

"Do you think I give a flying fuck about that? I want my kids back." Her breath comes in quick, ragged gasps. "They're my kids. Not Mama's. Not yours. Mine!"

"Then maybe you should take better care of them." My heart thumps as I wait for the time bomb to detonate.

Her jaw works for a moment. She goes for the personal jab. "I'm not the only one who's been screwed up, skeleton girl."

The allusion's impossible to miss. I'd been anorexic when I was thirteen, the year after my father died. I exercised constantly, taking in few calories, eating away at myself by not eating, the human equivalent of an open pit mine with its widening hole of despair. Until, just short of being sent to the hospital, I looked at my reflection in a dressing room mirror while trying on bathing suits—and the image of a starving refugee, all stick legs and arms, confronted me. In shock, I studied this person, ran my hands over her hollow cheeks and knobby hip bones, the jutting cage of her ribs. She was me. *Me*. I don't know how, but I finally saw myself as others did. Some people take years to come to that realization. Others never do. It took me twelve months to add the layers that had been taken away, another year to build a healthy relationship with food.

Now if only I could build a better relationship with my sister. Getting over anorexia was probably easier. "That was a long time ago." I glare at her. "Let it go."

"Easy when it's about you, not me, isn't it?" she taunts.

I half-expect her to bob and weave. Meghan Ali. I take a step back. She has a wicked right. Though I'd be lying if I said I didn't want an excuse to smash my fist into her face.

But I keep my hands at my sides. One of us has to remain in

control. "Look." I take a deep breath. She is their mother, after all. "I'm sorry. We're trying to help. Them. And you."

She stares at me. Her body shakes. She's a puppet, drugs are her master. They pull the strings. "You don't know what it's like." Her voice quavers.

Cue the violins.

"You're right." I can't look at her any more. "And I don't want to."

A tear runs down her cheek, blackish-gray as dish water. "I'm trying, God damn it." She stifles a sob. "I'm getting better."

"I hope so." I don't know what I want to do more, cry with her, or give her a good hard smack. In the distance, I hear my friends whooping and hollering and having a good ol' time. That's where I should be. Not here. Not dealing with this. With her. I press my fingers to my temples, giving myself cat-eyes. I feel as if my head's bursting. "It's late and I have to work tomorrow. I'm going home."

I've done my job. I've determined that she isn't hurt or dead. She's coming down off a high, but she's functional enough to get herself to the empty hotel room where her children used to be.

As I turn away, she touches my shoulder, her hand light and papery as an autumn leaf. "Wait. I'm coming with you."

We trudge along, side by side, the way we used to walk to and from school together, perfectly in step, except the baggage we carry isn't books any more: it has more weight than the sum of all the tomes we ever studied combined. Our breath forms foggy spheres that float in front of us, thought-bubbles in a cartoon. I mentally fill them in. If we're in bitch mode, the conversation would go like this:

Me: When will you stop being such a fucking cliché?

Her: When will you stop riding my ass?

If we're veering toward a *Terms of Endearment* boo-hoo fest, which is Mama's favorite movie, by the way, it would be more like:

Me: I want to help you, but I don't know how.

Her: Don't give up on me, okay?

As it is, we don't trust ourselves to say anything, which is probably just as well. If we start fighting, we might never get home. We take the back way because I don't want to pass the hill where my friends are. I'm not up to introductions or reintroductions or awkward silences. *Hey, guys, you remember my sister, Meghan.* I'm afraid of what they would remember.

My feet are soaked and my teeth chatter. When I finally try to talk, I sound as though someone's shaking me. I state the obvious, because I don't what else to say. "We're almost there."

She knows that, of course. It's her childhood home too. She remembers the way, even when she's fucked up. But for once she doesn't give me a hard time. Her skin has a bluish cast to it, otherworldly and eerily beautiful. The sharp curve of her cheek is high and smooth; an artist might yearn to sculpt her, though she'd never hold still long enough unless she were unconscious.

"What?" She catches me looking at her.

"Nothing." Snowflakes keep falling on us, melting on our skin, piling up beneath our feet in a great expanse of white. I imagine my sister trying to snort lines of snow, crying when it melts. She'd actually done that one winter, so wasted she thought the snow was a blizzard of coke.

She reaches down and pretends she has something in her boot, then quickly packs a snowball and throws it at me, shrieking and slip-sliding up the street as she makes a quick getaway after hitting me in the neck. She's always had good aim. I paw at the snow on my collar, but it's too late. Cold rivulets run down my neck and spine.

"I'm gonna get you for that!" I pack one of my own, smoothing the edges into a globe worthy of a snow cone as I run after her. She can still move fast, muscle memory semi-intact. She isn't tall. None of us are. But her legs are long for her size and her stride a thing to behold, the natural gift of coaches' dreams. Endurance, though, she no longer has. I gain on her, intending to strike as she mounts the steps to the safety of the front door.

She ducks just in time. The snowball nicks the top of her head and smacks into the post, leaving a white skid mark on the wood. She looks over her shoulder and grins at me, the same devilish smile from our youth. *Bet you can't catch me.*

As the moment fades—God, I don't want it to fade, but it does, it has to, you can't hold on to stuff like that—I stare back at her, lungs ice-burned.

Our hands hang empty at our sides, ammunition gone. She on the steps, me on the sidewalk, no path shoveled between us, the way back to our childhood more complicated than we thought, not the sort of thing that can be recaptured by a snowball fight in an ephemeral storm.

• • •

Mama left on two lights on the first floor, one in the kitchen, the other the desk lamp in the den. The door is partly closed, light shining around the edges. For a moment, I almost think it's a visitation by my father's ghost, returned to give us the advice we need so badly.

But no, the lights are on purely for practical reasons. The rest of the house is in the dark, like us. We can see the shape of larger things in the living room and the hallway, not the details, the small things waiting to trip us.

Meghan wails, her voice soft and spooky, the way she did when we were kids. She'd loved to scare me. She'd hide under my bed and grab my ankles. She'd do anything for the big boo.

She still scares me sometimes, though not in the same way. Now she does it without even trying.

"Boo yourself." I smirk.

Snow falls from our shoes and coats in little avalanches, making miniature icebergs on the floor that dissolve into dirty puddles.

"It's weird." Meghan blows on her hands, fingers skinny, nails broken, polish chipped. "I wasn't cold out there, but I am now, where it's warm."

"It's the contrast between the inside and the outside," I tell her, though I figure it also has something to do with nerves—of having to face our mother, her kids, and her own failings.

No amount of intervention has ever worked before. But maybe tonight will be different. She's long overdue for an epiphany.

I leave the sopping boots and socks by the door and enter the kitchen. "Want some hot chocolate?" I eye the ceiling. The dome-shaped fixture is in need of a good wash. It's become a bug cemetery, carapaces accumulating at the bottom, brittle in body and wing. A wolf spider slides down inside, a paratrooper in a war movie. I wonder if it'll get stuck there in the land of the dead, missing in action.

"Maybe after I take a hot bath." Her eyes dart toward the stairs. "Where is she?"

She means Mama.

I shrug. Mama wouldn't have gone to bed. She's probably reading in the den, though you'd think she would have come out when she heard our voices. I peer into the study, my father's favorite room, where he once perused the newspaper, smoked a cigar, had a beer. There she is in the brown leather chair, the one we used to spin on when we were kids. She's slumped forward onto the desk, head resting on her arms, sleeping. The metal lamp makes a halo over her head. Her watch is beside her, red light blinking. She must have set the alarm to wake her in time for her shift. The door creaks as I brush against it, and I hesitate, fearing the noise will wake her. But she doesn't stir, deep in the land of dreams. Her breath continues in exhausted sighs. I tiptoe across the room, turn off the desk lamp, and put an afghan over her shoulders, another project she knit during the long nights without my father, without Meghan.

I return to the kitchen and report to my sister. "Lucky you. She's asleep." I nod toward the den. "In there." I put water on to boil. I'll catch the kettle before it whistles. The pot hisses from a spill on the burner where something boiled over recently. A thin coil of smoke rises as it burns away, leaving an acrid smell in the air that I swat with a wave of my hand. "She has the early shift tomorrow."

Mama thrives on helping bring lives into the world, as if to compensate for those we've lost. She has a special way of holding a patient's hand and speaking to her quietly that makes fear subside. Perhaps it's a gift that works better in a clinical setting—with people who aren't related to you.

The phone rings, then stops abruptly. "Who could that be?" I ask. The only person who ever calls this late is Meghan, and she's already here.

"Must have been a wrong number." Meghan puts the junk food in the fridge. Her foot taps in time with the internal square dance of coming down—and facing the music. "Are the kids in my old room?"

"Yeah. You want the guest quarters?" Aside from logistics, it *is* the most appropriate accommodation for her these days.

"Sure." She pads upstairs, pauses, creeps back down and whispers over the banister. "Where are the towels?" It's been at least two years—maybe more—since she's been in the house. She's not around often enough to register the small changes in how Mama organizes things.

"I'll get you one." As Meghan heads upstairs, I pull a velvety towel—black, that doesn't show the dirt—from the dryer. Mama must have thrown in a final load that evening, because it's deliciously warm.

I hear the bath water run and the fan hum, and I tense, anticipating Mama's footsteps, her sleepy voice calling my name. But Mama tends to sleep hard—like the dead, my father used to say, before he went and died himself.

When I go to give Meghan the towel, the door is open a crack. I remember days when we'd put Meghan in the shower,

trying to sober her up, her body thrashing, then limp, bile dribbling down her chin. I don't have to do that tonight. She's not
that far gone. Or maybe she's too far gone down that yellow
brick road, lost in the field of poppies, and I'm the tin man, in
need of a heart or the lion in need of courage. Or maybe the
wicked witch, envious of her red, red shoes.

A wisp of steam snakes into the hall. I glimpse Meghan's thin
form, the tracks and bruises on her arms. Before she started
using, I would have burst in. But now I knock first, because I
know she's embarrassed for me to see her this way. The only
time she doesn't care is when she's high. Then the bruises are
purple flowers in the garden of her addiction. "See how they
bloom? See how my garden grows?" she cackles.

"Megs?" My voice is quiet, so quiet she doesn't hear me at
first. I don't want to startle her.

She stares at her reflection in the mirror. She touches her face
tentatively, as if the slightest pressure from her fingertips might
cause the skin to tear. She has a look of terrified wonder, not
wanting to believe the image belongs to her. I wonder how bad
it's going to be when she starts coming down. Depends on what
she's been on, I guess. Once, when she first began her long slow
skid to where she is now, we tried to stop her before she went
out of control. We were too late. She screamed and clawed at
us. We stood between her and what she wanted: freedom,
drugs, men. She was sixteen. And then she was gone.

"Meghan?" I try again, more loudly this time.

She freezes, an animal seeking camouflage, though none
exists in the stark white room. She snatches the towel from me
with a quick darting movement, then folds her arms across her

chest, not to conceal her breasts but the needle marks. Even though I've seen them before, her shame remains fresh.

Teeny's voice carries down the hall; she's talking in her sleep, dreaming that Meghan's tripping: *Mommy, wake up. Wake up.* Meghan flinches as if she's been slapped. I take a step toward Teeny's room, thinking she might need me. But she falls quiet again. So do Meghan and I. The words are stopped up inside of us, as if we need some sort of Drano to release them.

The noises of the house fill the silence. The walls and floors creak their complaints, settling, always settling. *Woe is me. Woe is me.* The crybaby tap leaks from the broken gasket we keep forgetting to fix. The radiator moans with the effort to warm the room, as if waking from a long sleep—no, it won't get the summer off—none of us will. It makes the sound Meghan does when she's struggling toward consciousness. Uhhhhhhh.

Our eyes meet briefly before my sister looks away. In that moment, I see how deep she's fallen. Her eyes reflect the distance she's gone, sad and faraway and desperate.

Then she blinks, and it's gone.

"Thanks," she says and closes the door.

CHAPTER 4

Sometime between two and seven A.M., Meghan must have had a change of heart, because this morning she has vanished. No sign of her anywhere. I touch the pillow, which retains the impression of her skull, the case stained with flecks of ashy mascara, and I wonder how I'm going to explain everything to Teeny. What I'll say to Mama when she gets home. Maybe I should pretend I didn't find Meghan. That she's never been here at all.

I feel like shit, because I didn't get much sleep last night. I kept hearing a phone ring. That happens a lot in my dreams— the hospital calling with word that my father has died. My subconscious won't let it go. It's a recurring motif. And yet there's something about the phone that sounds more shrill now that Meghan's here, so that I swear it's real. I don't wake up in time to find out for sure. I remain in the dark with the sense that I'm a second too late.

I smooth Meghan's sheets and fluff the pillow, giving it a

good, hard punch. Everything appears to be in order, even though it's not.

Mama will be home before noon, in time for me to head to the shop. I wonder if she checked the guest room in the middle of the night. I didn't wake her to share the news of Meghan's return. I let her take refuge in the blissful ignorance of sleep. Maybe I had a feeling, even then, that my sister wouldn't stay. Maybe I wanted to avoid another argument.

The one thing I know is I can barely see straight, not only because of my restless night, but because I've been up since six with the baby. She's happy enough as long as you hold her. My arm's killing me. I'm not used to keeping it in that position for so long. Sometimes Si-si gets fussy and baps her head against me, as if she's banging it against a wall. When I sing to her, she quiets down again. I'm not much for lullabies, having a repertoire of two. So I switch to Avril Lavigne's hit, "Complicated," modifying the words to suit the present circumstances.

Si-si doesn't seem to mind—though *I'm* starting to mind the big wet patch on my shoulder. Even with the tea towel draped over it, I have a drool spot on the T-shirt I got at a No Doubt show, one I traveled all the way to Seattle, driving ten hours straight, to see.

I wonder if I'll ever go to a rock concert again. My life is closing in on me, one of those rooms in a spy movie, whose walls move closer and closer together, crushing whatever's inside. The voice in my head that says the kids will only be staying with us for a little while gets smaller and smaller. I'm disappearing. I'm becoming the person my sister should have been.

Si-si and I follow Teeny as she shuffles downstairs in her

undies and T-shirt. Tweety Bird still has a strawberry jam stain on his chest from last night. It looks as if he's been shot. Or Teeny has. I get a sick feeling in my stomach thinking about the likelihood of that scenario. We'll definitely have to get Teeny new clothes. Too bad there are some things you can't buy.

Teeny presses her face against the window. She leaves an imprint of her mouth on the pane, an "o" or a zero. Take your pick.

"Where's the snow?" she asks. There's not much left but dirty slush.

"Most of it's gone." Apparently the mercury surged after Meghan came back last night. Things tend to heat up when she's around, though it would be a stretch to say she influences the weather. I balance Si-si on my hip and set a bowl of cereal and toast in front of Teeny. I'm so good at this, it's scary. "The temperature changed overnight."

"Where's Mommy?"

"She'll turn up." Si-si snores lightly, her face buried in the crook of my arm. Maybe I'll be able to put her down for a nap. "She always does."

Eventually.

The question is, what kind of shape will she be in?

Teeny shreds the edge of a paper napkin into fringe. "Sometimes I wish she wouldn't."

"Why?" I ask cautiously.

" 'Cause I want to live in one place."

I set a cup of juice in front of her, the movement solid, deliberate, keeping things nailed down. "You will."

She looks up at me. She has the most beautiful eyes I've ever seen. We don't have eyes like that in our family. They must have come from her father, whoever and wherever he is. She calls them turquleez—turquoise. The way she says it makes it sound more like a superhero than a color.

"Can't I stay here with you, Auntie Erin," she asks, "for always?"

I have to look away from her pleading face, out the window at the endless mounds of slag and earth, because I'm breaking into tiny pieces and I don't want her to see.

When my sister and I were kids, that torn-up ground outside the house was our playground. We knew how to have fun back then. A time when, if we said "I hate you," it was a passing thing. Now we don't say the words, because they're more loaded than they used to be, dump trucks full of blame. Recriminations lurk underneath the surface, mixed with love. Sometimes it's hard to tell one sentiment from the other.

The hills didn't look so dredged and hopeless in those early years; they were full of possibilities. We scrambled over the hillside in shorts and tank tops and dopey, blunt-toed Keds, garden trowels and penlights in hand. The world's least-likely prospectors, sure we could do anything if we tried hard enough. Our main project was finding gold, preferably enough to buy the entire inventory at Candy Cane Lane down on Main Street. I was five. Meghan was eight.

We idolized our ancestors who'd once worked the mine shafts as warriors on a heroic quest, not simple men trying to get by, who drank too much, whose children went hungry. There are no pictures of them on the mantel. All that had been lost or never recorded in the first place. We only have photos of my great-grandparents, the first generation to break away from the mines and become teachers and office workers, spiffed up for the camera in sailor suits and bloomers and baseball outfits, freshly scrubbed and neatly dressed against the dusty landscape—which essentially hasn't changed much over the years, as far as I can tell.

Third grade had been difficult for my sister. For one thing, she'd been skipped ahead, which made her younger, as well as smarter, than everyone else. Not the best combination when it came to fitting in and making friends. After school, lacking companions her own age, she played with me. Because I idolized her back then, I was only too happy to oblige. In the spring, as soon as the snow melted and the dirt had softened, we scoured the slag-heaps for hidden treasures. During the summer, unencumbered by school schedules, we'd be gone the entire day, until Mama yelled that dinner was ready.

One afternoon, I kicked a dirt clod and dislodged the most beautiful stone I'd ever seen. I danced with glee, nearly tumbling headfirst into the gravel. "I found a diamond!"

"Let's see." Meghan squinted at the clear jewel clutched in my palm. "It's not a diamond, stupid. It's quartz."

I stared in disbelief. "Looks like a diamond to me."

"You gotta go deep for diamonds. 'Sides, there aren't any around here." Meghan chipped at a boulder with a screwdriver she'd filched from the kitchen junk drawer.

"That's what *you* think," I grumbled to myself. There were plenty of holes in the hillside, mines that had been boarded up with now-brittle wood or ringed with corroded wire fencing.

Faded DANGER and KEEP OUT signs only added to their allure. That's where I'd find diamonds. I was sure of it. There was even a gap just my size in one of the fences, which I took to be a good omen.

In Mine 16, I discovered a ruin of a hoist house, the chains rusted and the girders broken. I clambered over toppled spools, like one of the mice in Cinderella. The shaft itself was only half-covered. I could easily slip inside and descend the corroded metal service ladder. I pulled a flashlight from my pocket, a keychain variety that gave no more light than a firefly, and put my foot on the top rung. I had no concept of the mine's depth. I suppose I thought of it as a manhole, a drop of no more than a few feet.

I hadn't gone far when I heard a popping sound. I soon discovered, to my great dismay, that the screws had just pulled away from the wall. The ladder swung backwards. I dropped the flashlight, its inadequate glow extinguished by the black hole, and wrapped my arms around the rungs, feet scissoring wildly. I must have screamed.

"What are you doing?" Meghan's face appeared above me, floating against the blue sky. Her freckles, spots on a connect-the-dots puzzle, stood out more than usual on her pale face.

"The diamonds are down there." I told her. I wasn't as scared now. The ladder held. I was in the center ring of a circus act. Not even Meghan could perform such a trick.

"Diamonds are in places like Africa, dummy," Meghan informed me. She was such a know-it-all. Sometimes I hated her.

"Then I'll keep going until I get there." I'd show her. I'd be rich and famous. If she were lucky, I'd let her be my maid.

The ladder groaned, one of the rungs snapped beneath my

feet. I shrieked and twined my body around the pole. Maybe this wasn't such a good idea after all. Africa could wait. I'd go there by plane instead—when I was bigger.

"You've gotta get out of there. Climb up." Meghan stretched her fingers toward me.

"I can't." I shook my head and clung more tightly to the pole. I couldn't let go. If I did, I'd fall.

"Yes, you can. Just like the rope in P.E. class." Meghan's lips trembled. I realized that she wasn't only mad at me; she was afraid.

And if my sister was afraid, I knew I should be too. My heart beat as wildly as a bongo drum. The louder it thumped, the more I thought about it stopping completely. I didn't want to die. *God, please don't let me die.* I pulled myself up about a foot, but then my hands got too sweaty. I was losing my grip, in more ways than one. "Help me! I'm slipping!"

Meghan hooked her feet on an old pipe above ground, leaned down, and grabbed me.

"Ow. You're pulling my hair." My scalp burned.

"That's not all I'm going to pull when you're out of there. Keep climbing." She gritted her teeth.

She nearly strangled me with my shirt, but she got me up. We sat in the dirt, scowling at each other, breathing hard. "You've got to be the dumbest sister in the world," she wheezed.

I looked down into the hole. "I know diamonds are down there," I insisted. "I would have found them if you hadn't pulled me out."

She took me by the arms and gave me a hard shake. "Promise me you'll never do that again. Promise!"

"Let go!" I scrambled down the hillside.

Mama was calling us. It was time to go home.

Later, when I dared steal a sideways glance at my sister as she passed me the mashed potatoes, she narrowed her eyes like a feral cat. Every time she opened her mouth to say something, I was afraid she'd tell Mama and Dad what happened. But she never did. She seemed to enjoy the novelty of controlling my fate.

That night before I fell asleep, I thought about how my sister had rescued me and I vowed to be as strong and brave as she was, to save her some day too, to be the master of *her* destiny.

Now, years later, she's gone down the deepest shaft of all, the mine of addiction, a place of complete darkness, where the only thing you can hear is the beat of your own heart, the exhalation of your own breath. That is, if you're still breathing. A place with no ladder up to the sky. A place where you're utterly alone.

And I don't know how to bring her back.

I put Si-si down for a nap. Scarcely bigger than a shoebox, the cradle is one my father made for my sister and me when we were babies. The finish on the white paint has crackled, a confusion of dried-up tributaries in a milky river delta. Mama applied another coat of non-toxic sealant to it so it won't peel away and poison somebody. My father carved a heart on each end of the cradle, which gives it an Amish look. They aren't perfect, those hearts. Neither, as it turned out, was his.

Our dolls used to call the cradle home, but now that we have a real baby to put in it, we had to relocate them to the top shelf of the closet. They look as if they've been through terrible experiments. One has her hair half burned off, because Meghan styled it with a curling iron—with disastrous results. Another is missing an arm, severed while we were playing hospital, not realizing our surgical skills weren't advanced enough to reattach it. The doll looks at me reproachfully. I'm sure she'd sue us for malpractice if she could. Even though we stopped playing with them a long time ago, Mama didn't give the dolls away. She has a hard time giving up on anything, possessions or people.

Si-si snores, her mouth a rosebud, a chubby hand under her chin. She stirs when I touch a wisp of black hair clinging damply to her scalp. I make sure she lies on her side and pull the trunk of the musical elephant Mama bought for her. She sighs and snuggles into the angel-patterned blanket. I feel the knot in my chest loosen. One down. One to go. The problem is, Teeny's too old for naps: she told me so, quite adamantly.

If I weren't playing nanny, I'd call my friends or meet them for breakfast at the Fillmore Cafe. I mean, I have a life. Sort of.

I tiptoe down the hall. The floor creaks with every step, moaning like someone getting sucker-punched. Uh. Uh. Uh. My room is two doors down. It has the same '30s-era furniture as the others, but I've hung Chinese parasols from the ceiling and stacked lacquered boxes on the vanity, the idea being to create a room that would transport me to another time and place.

It used to work.

I push pairs of trainers aside and take my jewelry box out of the closet. I figure I'll work downstairs at the kitchen table and keep an eye on Teeny at the same time. When I say jewelry box,

I mean my tools for making jewelry. That's what I really want to do some day.

"Can I help?" Teeny hops up on a chair when I enter the kitchen.

"Sure." I give her a length of string, knotted at one end. "You can make yourself a bracelet. What color beads do you want?"

"Blue, the color of the ocean where the fishes live." She points to some lapis lazuli. Her fingernails are too long, too dirty, despite last night's bath. I make a mental note to trim and scrub them later.

I bend wire with a pair of pliers into an intricate filigree, a series of interconnected question marks accented with antique coral beads. The chandelier earrings look vaguely East Indian. I hold them up to my lobes and study the effect in a hand mirror. Some of the beads aren't hanging quite right. They should be swinging gracefully. I'll have to try again.

I don't realize until it's too late, that as Teeny has leaned forward to get each bead, she's been drawing the hem of the table cloth toward her incrementally, the tide of fabric steadily advancing, until it slips off the table altogether and sends my entire stock of beads shooting into every corner of the room.

What a mess. "God damn it," I mutter before I can stop myself.

Teeny tucks her chin to her chest, as if she's afraid someone's going to hit her. "I'm sorry, I didn't mean to. I'm sorry." She says the words over and over, taking sharp breaths, a little steam engine, ready to blow.

"It's okay. Let's pick them up, huh?" I get down on my hands and knees. My smile feels pasted-on, my movements jerky with barely suppressed impatience. I guess I'm not cut out for this mother-thing after all. Not that I have to be. I mean, it's not as though I'm really her parent. I'm only filling in. A pseudo mom.

Teeny steals glances at me when she thinks I'm not looking, her lashes dewed with tears. "Are you mad?"

"No." I'm tired—and it's not even noon. "It was an accident."

Upstairs, the baby wails. I pause, glancing up at the ceiling, not feeling the least bit maternal. It's as if someone has wrapped a tight metal band around my head. All I can think is *What now?*

The baby falls silent, as if someone put a hand over her mouth. I hold my breath, anticipating the next wail. It doesn't come.

"Sometimes she has bad dreams," Teeny says. "She can't tell me about them yet, not with words. But I know."

I nod and give her the chance to say more.

She doesn't. She needs time. Although she seems to be a fairly open kid, she has a child-proof lid on, as far as some things go.

I try to lighten the mood and make us feel better. "Let's see who can get the most beads the fastest. On your mark, get set, go!" I slide across the linoleum in my socks.

At first Teeny hesitates, but soon she gets into the game. We skid into the corners, scooping up beads, some fractured, some whole, little worlds that we can, for the moment, hold in the palms of our hands.

The side door bangs open. "Hey," my sister exclaims. She has on a pair of jeans and a pale blue long-sleeved T-shirt with rhinestones around the neckline, which coincidentally—or not so coincidentally—looks exactly like one of mine. She's pulled her hair into a ponytail. She's doing everything she can to appear clean and clear. Just like a cell-phone commercial.

A shadow moves across Teeny's face, the sun emerging from behind a bank of clouds, before she smiles brilliantly. "Mommy!" She hurls herself into Meghan's arms. "Where were you?"

"Getting treats." She shakes a paper bag at us, her fingers clutching it so tight they've gone white at the knuckles. It's tricky for her to hold on to even the simplest things.

I stifle the urge to say something pointed, and, from the look on her face, she knows it.

Teeny jumps up and down as she tries to grab the bag from Meghan's hands. "What is it?"

"Donuts!" Meghan winks at Teeny.

Now that Meghan is here in person again, I feel myself softening. She hadn't skipped on us after all. Whatever she'd been doing—I hated to guess—she had come back.

"Si-si sleeping?" Meghan slides into a chair and props her feet on the opposite seat. She has a way of making herself comfortable wherever she is—of making it seem as if she never left. But the truth is, she's always leaving, always moving, even when she appears to be sitting still.

I gesture upstairs with the wave of my hand. "She went down about twenty minutes ago."

"Didn't think I was coming back, did you?" Meghan eyes me over the rim of the glass as she takes a sip of Teeny's juice. She doesn't wait for a reply. "I had to get an early start."

"Yeah?" I close one eye as I thread a strand of silk through the eye of a needle. "Since when have you ever gotten one of those?"

"I signed up for a program at the treatment center and had a couple of job interviews this morning." She leans forward eagerly. "The first was at Joe's Pastry shop."

She'd once worked strip clubs, involving a different type of pasties altogether. She'd given me a line about people not understanding how empowering stripping was for women. Typical Meghan bullshit. I mean, she was doing it to support her habit, not make a feminist statement. "I didn't think they opened until ten."

She shrugs. "I went around the back. The guy would have given me the job, but he said there was a better one at Carl's bakery. So I went over there and they hired me on the spot. They need someone to work the counter, 'cause a girl just quit. They'll train me to decorate."

Perfect. She's good at embellishing things. "What a coincidence. When do you start?" I keep my voice light. I don't want her to think I'm grilling her, even though I'm tempted to, like a thick barbecued steak. Sizzle. Sizzle. To sear the truth out of her.

"Tomorrow." Her tone's light too.

It's a dance we do, careful not to step on each other's toes. We know the moves so well we could teach a class, open our own studio, start a franchise. Two Left Feet. Smart-Assed Salsa. The Bimbo Ballroom. One Step Ahead.

Tomorrow. Saturday.

"That's fast." I want to believe her. She has an ease with people I've never had, an irresistible charm that allows her to collect jobs and boyfriends. Trouble is, she's never been able to keep them for long. Promises are broken. Disenchantment settles in. The other shoe drops.

She has an inventory of excuses for why it doesn't work out. One thing stays the same: it's never because of her. It's always someone else's fault, or a cruel twist of fate, or plain bad luck.

"I've signed up for AA. I'll take methadone or whatever else I need to stay straight. It's gonna be different this time." She reads my mind. At least, that's how it seems.

If I had a dime for every time she's said those words, I'd be rich by now. But I smile and nod. After all, maybe it will be. Who am I to say?

Cha. Cha. Cha.

To be on the safe side, I don't leave for work until after Mama returns. I'm not sure what to expect when she walks in. We look up expectantly when we hear her footsteps on the stairs. The sound is muffled, because she's wearing rubber-soled nursing shoes. She pauses on the doorstep, gathering her thoughts, not realizing she has an audience. That pause contains the distance it takes to move away from the stresses of her job and arrive at a place that allows her to be Ms. Happy Face, even if it's a lie.

She blinks in surprise as she takes in the scene: me and Teeny and Meghan at the table.

Meghan at the table. Where she hasn't been for a long, long time.

For a split second, there's a weariness in Mama's eyes, a sadness that she pushes away with a smile and open arms.

Her daughter is home again.

I watch them exclaim and hug and kiss, the tears brimming.

In spite of everything, they have a closeness no one can penetrate, certainly not me. It's a bond born of the pain and suffering they've inflicted on each other. I can't compete with that. I'm not like them, even though at times I wish I were. I wanted to be Homecoming Queen. I want to be the object of men's desires. I want that gloss and shine without the big hair and the histrionic scenes and the inevitable train wreck.

Maybe that's not possible. I sit with my hands folded loosely in my lap, cupping air, waiting for my cue.

It doesn't come.

"Well, I gotta get going." I glance at my watch and grab my bag.

"Okay, honey. Have fun at work." Mama touches my arm. Her other hand remains on Meghan's wrist, as if she's afraid my sister will get away if she lets go for one minute. Then she does let go. Of me. And I leave with a slam of the door, because that's what screen doors do unless you keep a hand on them to keep them quiet.

Mama's best in a crisis. She thrives on them—and Meghan gives her plenty. They'll be talking about the grand plan, the necessary treatment, the tender care and feeding of a recovering addict. Mama and my father had a similar dynamic. Scares me to think about it.

On the sidewalk I pause, turning to look at the house the way a stranger would. I have a weird sensation of being both a spectator and a character in the movie that is our lives. A loner. An outsider. Sometimes I hold on to that position stubbornly, other times I want to cast it aside and belong. I can't figure out the distance I need from them so I don't have to be angry or sad.

Teeny waves from the window, my sister and mother behind

her, features slightly blurry, glowing, like figures in a impressionist painting. I have the sneaking suspicion van Gogh waits in the wings, ready to let loose writhing cypresses or snake-headed irises, but I try not to think about it, because I want things to work out this time. I really do.

CHAPTER 5

By the time I get to work, I'm totally fried. I exchanged my baby-drool shirt for a peasant top before I left the house, but I still look like hell. The long, hot walk to the shop didn't help either. The snow is beating a fast retreat and the heat has returned with a vengeance.

"Whoa." One of my bosses, Daniel, pushes his Mr. Science glasses, which are so nerdy they're cool, up on the bridge of his nose. He has spiked his short, black hair today, very '80s. "What happened to you?"

"Parenthood." I toss my bag behind the counter. It's a tote made from an old pair of jeans, on which I printed "Fashion Victim" in red block letters. The marker bled into the fabric. Unintentional, but I like the effect. Even though I'm not a big talker, I enjoy making a statement in other ways.

David pokes his shaved head out from behind the linen shelves, which had been recently ransacked by a determined—and rather rotund—customer, whom he dubbed the

Pumpkin Lady. She'd been seeking the perfect orange chenille bedspread. "Is there something we should know?" His eyebrows are raised.

It takes me a minute to realize what he's getting at. "Oh, God no. It's not like that." I assure him. "My sister's kids are staying with us, that's all."

"And here I thought congratulations were in order," David sighs. "I really wanted to be a godparent."

"No way." I sip the latte I had grabbed at the Perkatory Coffeehouse where Alex works. It's a double-tall. The caffeine hasn't kicked in yet.

Daniel rests his elbows on the counter, long-limbed and flexible, face expressive as a mime. "But you're so good at reproduction work."

"Not that kind," I snort.

"Have we met her?" David refolds a rodeo-patterned tablecloth, perfect for your average hoedown.

"My sister? No," I say too quickly. "You'd remember if you had."

They exchange glances but, to my relief, take the hint and don't pursue it. My sister has insinuated herself into enough areas of my life. I don't want my job to be another.

"Cool earrings," Daniel says. He has a tendency to use retro words, like cool, groovy, and peachy keen. "Where'd you get them?"

"I made 'em." I'd pulled my hair up into a messy bun, half-hoping he'd notice. But now I feel shy. I duck my head and paw through the pile of costumes to be restored, settling on a '30s floor-length gown with a raveled hem.

He cocks his head. "You got any more?"

"More what?" I mumble through a mouthful of pins.

"Earrings. Jewelry. You can't keep hiding your talents from us," he says. "We're bound to find out."

"Yeah, I do." I fib. Actually, I only have two more pairs, tops. My heart pounds from the lie—and the possibilities.

"I've got a friend in L.A." He polishes a pair of green cat-eye sunglasses thoughtfully. "If you make some slides, we could send them to him. See what happens." He hums the melody of "California Dreamin'."

"Yeah, right." I force a laugh, realizing he's joking. The Mamas and Papas are a dead giveaway.

He keeps a straight face, not that that means anything, coming from him. "I'm not kidding. Am I kidding, David?"

"He's not kidding," David pipes up. "The guy reps jewelry artists. He's good. And he likes our taste." He tinkers with a display of McCoy and Bauerware.

The Double Ds lived in L.A. for ten years before moving back to Butte. They're twelve years older than me. Daniel was a star wide receiver in high school, David a distance runner. They didn't hook up until they went away to college in Southern Cal and have been together ever since. When they returned as a couple, no one batted an eye, at least not outwardly. Some people might find that surprising, Butte being such a Catholic town, and they formerly such examples of the masculine ideal. But then, Butte has always had several sides to it, especially during the boom years when hell broke loose on a regular basis.

I blink at the Double Ds. "I'll think about it." I can barely thread a needle, my hands are shaking so much. My first collection. I'll stay up all night if I have to. I imagine my own store in New York, my name in gold letters.

Daniel nudges David, who's now tackling the mussed scarf boxes on the shelves next to the front counter. "She's seeing it."

"Seeing what?" I knot the threads. To my relief, the needle slips smoothly into the fabric. Rayon's tricky, and I'm wary of snags.

"The potential." He throws his arms wide, as if he's under bright footlights, not behind a cash register. "Fame! Fortune!"

"Who knows where I'll end up." I baste the hem carefully to take in the fullness. "I mean, no one would have expected you guys to come back here. Butte must be pretty dull after L.A."

David strokes his chin. "The dream doesn't have to be big to be worth having." He gazes at the dusty street.

"Ooh. Mr Philosopher. Look out. Next he'll be spouting Rimbaud." Daniel winks at me.

David puts his hands on his hips. "And what's wrong with Rimbaud, I'd like to know?"

"Don't get me started," Daniel drawls.

"You're insufferable." David rolls his eyes. "Sometimes I don't know why I put up with you."

Daniel shoots him a wicked grin. "I do."

David blushes. "Thank God." He waves as a customer pushes her way into the store, staggering under the weight of an over-loaded sack. "Saved by a delivery."

It's Grace Dean. With her frizzled red hair, gawky limbs, and prominent nose, she bears a striking resemblance to a puppet in a Punch & Judy show. When she speaks, it's hard not to laugh. Her voice reminds me of Julia Child.

Goofy appearance aside, Grace has an eye, a true gift. She brings in great stuff. Now that her children are grown, she indulges in her passion for collecting with a zeal that borders on compulsion. David calls her "Grace Dean, the vintage machine." He theorizes that she's trying to recover the past rather than something as tangible and practical as furniture. Surprisingly, "her little hobby," as she calls it, doesn't cause her financial hardship. Her husband has money and she prides herself on getting excellent deals. She accumulates new pieces with alarming speed so that, every month or two, Mr. Dean insists she winnow down her treasures—which is a good thing for us. After one of these episodes during which he tells her she has to choose between him and her treasures—the house isn't big enough for all of them—she arrives with a mountain of clothes and linens and the occasional sofa or chair. She says she brings her wares to us because we give them a decent home, patting them gently as if they're children being sent off to summer camp, not collectibles being put up for sale. But the real reason she patronizes Funkified is that the Double Ds give her the fairest price. As David says, "Underneath it all, she cares more about the bottom line than the hem line."

"What do you have for us today, Grace?" Daniel runs his hand along a length of green velvet that spills from her bag.

"This and that." Her sharp blue eyes sparkle. She elevates bargaining to an art form.

Daniel and David stopped trying to beat her to a deal months ago. They simply don't have the energy to head her off at estate sales. She rises in the early—and I mean *early*—morning to secure the first place in line. If a newspaper ad reads "Numbers at 8 A.M." she'll be lurking outside in her car at 4 A.M., a time when the less reputable members of our community are lurching home from the bar and the more upstanding citizens are snug in their beds.

Today Grace displays, among other things, a '40s shawl-collared red sweater with pearl buttons, a pair of rumba-print pedal pushers, and a rayon wrap-dress with palm-leaf-patterned fabric. Some of it needs my attention, a tear here, a split seam there, but really everything's exquisite. Then she holds up a ring, marcasite with a diamond in the center.

"H'mm. From the '20s, isn't it?" Daniel studies the piece. The diamond casts an erratic spot of light on the ceiling, like a miniature searchlight.

I narrow my eyes. The ring looks very familiar. I set the dress I'm mending aside and approach the counter. "May I see it?"

"Sure. Here." Daniel hands it to me.

I stare down at the ring. It has to be Ginga's. All the memories come rushing back from that brief period in our lives when we were innocent and everything seemed possible: mornings spent at Ginga's house before my sister and I were old enough to go to school—and for some afternoons thereafter—when my parents were at work, and we'd page through photo albums, looking at stills of Ginga when she had the lead in every Little Theater production, of my grandfather in his Butte Rats baseball uniform, staring down a batter from the pitcher's mound, of the Dirty Dog Racetrack where they bet on greyhounds that chased a bunny on a stick, round and round the oval. Ginga dressed impeccably. No jeans and T-shirts for her. She had style. She had élan. Even now, she is my inspiration. Her mother had a flair for fashion too. Both of them were teachers and amateur actresses, experts at acting like things were better than they were, at rein- venting and distancing themselves from the deep vein of alco- holism and depression that ran in the family. Ginga taught Meghan and me to read. We learned our numbers and letters, to add and subtract and write, from her. We learned to pretend, the most valuable—and dangerous—skill of all.

"Where did you get this?" I turn to Grace.

For once, she doesn't act coy about a source. She probably senses my mood. "A girl sold it to me outside the mini-mart. Guess she needed the money. Didn't drive a hard bargain, that's for sure."

I slip the ring on my finger. Size four. A perfect fit. "When?"

She shrugs. "This morning."

My sister inherited the ring after Ginga died. It was a slow, quiet death; she'd been dying inside for a long time, though we didn't realize it until she took to her bed, too depressed to face the world any more. She pulled the curtains, blocking the view of the mines and the ragged hills beyond, and lay in darkness. Nothing we did or said could lift her spirits. It began after my grandfather retired, deepened after his death, and continued five years, five years of us visiting and cooking and caring for her, five years of her turning in on herself, lips caved because she refused to wear her dentures, because she'd run out of things to say. Then she was gone. We had an estate sale and sold everything. I wish we hadn't, but I was too young to know that I'd collect vintage clothing one day, that I'd want to have some- thing that had belonged to her for my very own. I kept thinking stray pieces might surface at Funkified some day. None had.

Until now. Meghan must have hawked the ring when she said she was job hunting.

A tremor of rage runs through me like an electric shock. The stupid bitch. Nothing matters to her. Nothing.

"It looks good on you," Grace observes.

I take the ring off my finger. It's never been mine, no matter how much I've wanted it. I was jealous when Ginga left it to Meghan—because she was the oldest. Because she came first. Because they both had a flair for drama. Because, because, because.

"Is something wrong? You look funny," David whispers.

I shake my head. No use saying anything. It's my sister's ring to keep or sell, even though I can't help thinking she betrayed our family. I'd never give a part of us away like that, not after all we've lost. Meghan sold Ginga's legacy for a hit. Why do people give her everything, when all she does is throw it away?

Daniel pays Grace and pops a lemon drop in his mouth as she closes the door behind her. He's addicted to the candy, he says, because he's such a tart.

"Want one?" He offers me the bag.

"No, thanks." I'm feeling sour enough as it is.

I'm not sure what I'll walk into when I get home. The sun glares down, hard and shiny as a fake metal poker chip. I listen for the sound of yelling to carry down the block, of Mama and my sister going at it. But it's quiet. A loose shutter bangs somewhere, pinwheels hum and flash from the fence line of the only home on the block with kids in residence aside—now—from ours.

Dust insinuates itself into cracks in the sidewalk. Everything has finally dried out after the storm.

I turn up the front walk, braced for the inevitable. To my surprise, the sound of laughter comes through the screen door.

The aroma of roast chicken and apple pie fills the house. "Hi, honey!" Mama calls. "We're celebrating."

I don't have to ask what. Everyone beams with joy, both forced and genuine. Teeny stands on top of a chair, helping Mama make gravy. Si-si rides on Mama's hip. Meghan lounges at the kitchen table, jaw stretched into a tight smile, leg jiggling slightly underneath the table, indications that everyone's trying too hard to keep things together, tap-dancing on ice.

The table's set with a rumpled fifties fruit-patterned table-cloth from Funkified I gave Mama for her birthday in March, and a bouquet of lupine and daisies Mama and Teeny must have picked from the roadside. I can't remember the last time the place looked so festive. Christmas would have been—if Meghan had showed up. (Mama and I had eaten the turkey—we ate turkey the entire week until we couldn't stand it any more and threw the meaty carcass in the garbage.) We deluded ourselves into thinking there was still hope even after Meghan's esti-mated-time-of-arrival came and went, tried to ignore the unopened packages and shreds of spent tinsel scattered over the carpet like silvery cutgrass. Close to midnight, we gave up on her and unwrapped presents. The paper rustled too loudly in the empty room, so we turned on Christmas carols and sang along, the way we used to years ago when my father was alive and my sister wasn't addicted. It didn't work. As we opened the gifts, we didn't tear the paper. We slipped our fingers under the tape to loosen it and folded the pieces neatly, intending to use it another time, as if that evening were merely a practice drill, and we'd be doing the real Christmas, the one that counted, later. Once we discovered what was inside the boxes—a velvet scarf I'd made for her, a carved cinnabar pendant she'd found for me—we acted even more pleased than we would have under normal circumstances, our eyes shining with false merriment and something else we didn't name, because it was too painful, like the sudden stab of a cold spot beneath the smooth surface of a lake. We took self-timed photographs, arms wrapped around each other, pressing more tightly than usual to hold it together, to make a happy picture—to convince ourselves and others that we had. We did our damnedest to pretend everything was all right.

We still are pretending, but at least there isn't an actual void to fill this time. Meghan's here. That's what matters. We'll have our Christmas in July. Meghan herself is the gift.

Without realizing it, Mama has adopted her perky nurse's demeanor. She bustles. She beams. I want to shake her. "How was your day?" she asks me.

"Grace Dean came in again. She finds the best stuff." I feel dull compared to her megawatt sparkle. I add, as a casual aside, "And Daniel is interested in my jewelry designs."

"He is?" Mama's voice is bright as sunlight on tinfoil. "That's wonderful. What did he say?"

"He knows an artist's rep in L.A. He thinks I should send him some slides." I glance at Meghan. She doesn't seem to be paying attention, staring out the window, chewing on her lower lip.

"They're pretty." Teeny chimes in. "Like princess jewels."

"Thanks, sweetie." I smile at her, then turn back to Mama, adding "It's a long shot," because I don't want to jinx it by getting everyone, including me, excited. It's too easy to believe your own fantasies.

"I doubt that." Mama carves the chicken. She distributes pieces according to everyone's preference: Meghan goes for wings, I like white meat, Teeny drumsticks.

"Are those a pair?" Meghan pokes at a wing with her fork. She tends to toy with her food rather than eat it. She toys with a lot of things.

I nod. After years of disappointments, I still want the big-sister stamp of approval. I've spent most of my life trying to impress her, to make her think of me as more than her dopey younger sibling. Even now, she hasn't completely fallen off the pedestal I set her on. I have to catch her and push her back up, because she's my sister, because if I don't, she's not the only one who fails: I do too.

"Cool." She licks her fingers with the delicacy of a cat washing itself.

Cool. The word seems smaller than it really is. I've always wanted more than she will give. I'm tempted to dangle the earrings in front of her face; then, perhaps she'll take a good look at them, marvel at the craftsmanship. At me.

The earrings jangle softly as I turn to Mama, my voice a half-step higher. "Did you have many deliveries today?"

"Three. One tiny woman had a ten-pound baby. And a young girl delivered a preemie. At least her boyfriend was there," she pauses, remembering, no doubt, that Meghan's hadn't been in attendance in either case, then plunges ahead, picking up speed to cover herself. "And a couple from the local amateur theater association had twins. You've never seen such drama. You'd have thought they were on stage rather than in a delivery room. I wanted to say 'cut'—and I don't mean the umbilical cords!"

Meghan and I laugh, hers low and throaty, mine rapid as gun fire.

"Were they girl babies?" Teeny pats her face with her napkin, all ladylike. Must be Mama's influence. Meghan hasn't exactly had time to work on manners with her. "Girl babies are best."

"As a matter of fact, they were." Mama gets a glass of water at the sink. I've been trying to persuade her to drink bottled instead, not only because the tap water has a chalky aftertaste, but because I'm afraid that toxins from the Pit—a mile-deep open pit mine, now a Superfund cleanup site so polluted it kills any waterfowl stupid enough to land on the pond in the middle of it—have leached into the groundwater. She catches me looking at her and holds up her hand. "Hon, I've been drinking this stuff my whole life and it hasn't done me any harm," she says, adding, with a grin, "Besides, you can't say I'm not getting enough iron."

She does, however, get bottled water for the kids, though Teeny prefers milk and juice. Si-si isn't old enough to register an opinion yet. "What about you, Megs?" She regards Meghan over the rim of her glass.

Meghan raises her tumbler of tap water in a toast. No one says anything about her hand shaking so much, water slops over the side. "Lots of toxic substances have gone through my system. A little water's not going to kill me."

Teeny's eyes widen. The idea of death, particularly her mother's, frightens her.

Mama's smile stiffens. "I meant, how was your day?"

"O-o-oh." Meghan draws out the word, making it last three syllables instead of the standard one. "Well, it wasn't nearly as interesting as either of yours, though we did have a customer come in who said she found a ring in her bread. She wasn't real happy about it. She said it cracked her tooth."

"What kind of ring was it?" I watch her carefully, dying to ask about Ginga's.

Meghan doesn't take the bait. After all, how would she know that I know? "A class ring," she says. "Butte Central class of '85. It belonged to Ronnie, one of the bakers."

"What did you do?" Teeny asks.

"Well, the woman was like a tea kettle, steaming hard enough to explode. I told her it was her lucky day—that she'd won our monthly find-the-ring contest. I gave her a bag of free donuts as a prize. That lowered the heat of her temper right away. She even left me a tip."

"Quick thinking," I say between bites of broccoli.

"And a nice thing to do too," Mama adds, always one to promote selflessness and compassion.

"Not really." Meghan's eyes sparkle. "They were a couple of days old."

"Didn't she notice?" I can't help admiring Meghan's ingenuity.

Meghan shakes her head. "They still taste good. I've eaten some. Matter of fact, she'll probably be a more loyal customer now, trying to win again. Carl was real pleased." Carl's the owner of the bakery, Carl's Colossal Cakes. His agreeing to hire Meghan probably had something to do with the fact that he used to have a crush on Mama in high school. I bet he still does, though Mama denies it.

"I'm sure he is." Mama smiles.

"Isn't anybody going to ask about my day?" Teeny pipes up.

"Sure, honey." Mama gives her a piece of pie a la mode. "We'd love to hear about it."

"Well," she pauses dramatically, her eyes wide, "I found gold—in the back yard!" She takes a piece of pyrite from her pocket and sets it on the table for us to admire. It's the size of her fingernail and shines so brightly, you can understand why people mistake it for the real thing, though it doesn't have any market value. It's a trickster rock, fool's gold, masquerading as something it's not. Yet it can make a little girl feel she's on top of the world.

"Aren't you the lucky one? Better take good care of that. You don't want to lose it." Meghan doesn't ruin the illusion for her, as she did for me when we were young. She touches the stone with her finger, then turns and smiles at me, an eyebrow raised teasingly. "Guess there's gold in them-thar hills after all, huh?"

"Yeah." I start clearing the plates and stacking them in the sink, my usual balancing act. "What d'ya know?"

After the girls go to sleep that night, I find Mama in my father's study. She's sitting in his chair, looking at his picture. When he was alive, he didn't keep a picture of himself in there. He kept pictures of her, of us. But now that he's gone, she stands his portrait on the desk to watch over her while she's writing grocery lists, paying bills, missing him.

"He's slipping out of his frame," she says. "He won't stay put."

"Did you try using tape?" I open the window to let in some air, but it doesn't do any good. The night is hot and leaden.

She nods. "Nothing works. It's as if he's trying to tell me something."

"Like what?" I ask. My father smiles brilliantly, happy that day. Hard to tell if he was sober.

"To get on with my life." She twists the wedding band on her finger. She's never taken it off. She still visits my father's grave every Thursday after work, because it was their date night.

"Maybe you should listen." I touch an Italian glass paperweight on the desk that looks as if a multicolored explosion has occurred inside. "It's Joe, isn't it?"

She sighs. "That obvious, huh?"

"I figured things might be getting serious." I turn the paperweight over in my hands. "It's hard, when you live with someone, not to notice things. Does he call and hang up if you don't answer?"

She laughs. "He might. He's pretty shy. Why?"

"We've been getting a lot of 'wrong numbers' lately." I set the weight back down on the desk.

She toys with a button near the hem of her shirt. "I'll tell him he can call freely now."

"Just not in the middle of the night, okay?" I say. Lover-boy will have to wait until morning.

97

"He wouldn't call then," she replies. "He knows I'm at work or asleep. He's very considerate."

I pause for a moment. "Then maybe the calls have something to do with Meghan."

"There are plenty of drunks in this town who misdial. It happened before she came home, too." Mama runs her hands through her hair. Now that Meghan is home, she's quick to make excuses for her. "She seems to be trying this time. Really trying."

"She does, doesn't she?" *Seems* being the operative word. It's tempting to tell Mama about the ring incident, but I don't know the full story, so I keep quiet. I'll corner Meghan later and get the truth out of her. I hope. "Does Joe know about everything?" I ask. I wave my hand in the direction of the bookcases, but I don't mean my father's outdated encyclopedias, I mean our general situation.

"Meghan and the girls?" The chair creaks as Mama leans back. I nod.

"Yes. He's careful not to offer advice—not the way some of my girlfriends do," she says wryly.

"Yeah. Pen's pretty opinionated, isn't she?" Mama's oldest and dearest friend, Penny, is one of the most melodramatic, loyal, exasperating women in town. Her full name is Penelope Corcoran, but she's always gone by Penny, on account of her coppery (now dyed) hair and her bright—some would say glaringly bright—personality. She and Mama have known each other since they were three years old.

Mama laughs.

"He hasn't gotten spooked yet?" I stare at the citations for valor on my father's wall. He was in line to make assistant chief of the fire department before he died.

"I guess he doesn't scare easily."

"He hasn't met the rest of us," I tease. "By the way, when *are* we going to meet him?"

She twists a curl of hair around her finger. "Well, I invited him to be my guest at Lisa's wedding reception."

"Thought it would be less awkward with more people around, huh?" I grin at her.

My father smiles too, from the St. Paddy's bash picture next to the commendations, him hanging on the arms of his friends, hair dyed green, raising a glass of green beer. The biggest party you've ever seen—shamrocks painted on windows and sidewalks, Irish language classes, pipers and bands, and the bishop parading down Main Street in a jalopy along with representatives of the Ancient Order of Hibernians—which sometimes degenerates into a free-for-all. People take the wearin' of the green too literally, throwing up copious amounts of shamrock-colored beer. It doesn't even matter if you're Irish. Once everyone gets good and drunk, lines tend to blur. A punch gets thrown, doesn't matter who does it or why, setting off a chain reaction, calling up frustration or boredom or desire, the need to feel skin beneath fists, to bleed, to kid yourself into thinking you can fight your inner demons. My father would be there every St. Paddy's Day he was alive, brawling through the night, staggering home at dawn when I was in the living room watching cartoons and eating a maple bar. He smiled at me, the love he had for us still apparent in his broken face. Mama would shake her head as she tended his wounds, her nursing skills coming in handy yet again. For the next few days, some members of the male population—and a few women too—walked around town bruised and battered, sheepish, yet proud. It had always been about fighting everything—the mines, the fires, each other.

It's up to us to carry on the tradition, but the only one who comes close is Meghan—and she takes it too far.

Alex's dad, Mike Brewster, otherwise known as Brew for his ability to drink anyone under the table, is in some of the pictures. Everybody knows everybody in this part of town—which is simultaneously comforting and claustrophobic. There's a shot of Dad and Brew playing Fockey, which sounds more like a sex act than an amateur sport—though sex is kind of an amateur sport for some people, come to think of it. Anyway, they played rec-league football year-round, calling it Fockey when the field froze over, because they'd slide across the ice in tennis shoes. The injuries were frequent, worn with pride. Even as the years went by and their bodies got more mileage on them, the guys refused to stop playing. My dad was still at it around the time he died. The old pigskin sits on the shelf. His teammates gave it to Mama at the funeral, the way a flag is presented to a soldier's widow.

Mama must sense that I'm dwelling too much in the past. Suddenly she wads up a piece of scratch paper and throws it at me. I bat it back at her and we have a play-fight, our laughter laced with hysteria, which ends too soon because we don't have the energy to sustain it.

Mama glances at the clock. "I'd better get to bed." She'll catch a few winks before she has to go to work. She kisses the top of my head as she walks by, the way she used to when I was a little girl. "Nite, hon."

"Nite."

After I'm sure Mama's asleep, I decide to have it out with Meghan about Ginga's ring. Meghan's in the living room, watching a movie on the Sundance channel, one of Mama's few indulgences, since we don't exactly have access to cutting-edge cinema here in town.

Meghan continues to entertain the idea of being an actress some day. She has a gift for that sort of thing—at least as far as her personal life is concerned.

"Hey." I plop down beside her. She has the lights off. The glow of the TV screen casts a gray-blue shadow over the room, blurring edges and dimensions, encompassing everything in it, including us. One of Mama's half-completed puzzles is on the coffee table. She has a couple of them in progress, a rose window at Notre Dame, and Picasso's Guernica. No cute kitty pictures for her. She likes high art, the more complicated the better. A piece or two always gets lost, preventing her from finishing them. When she's in a practical mode, she says, resolutely, that it's a reminder to take things one step at a time. When she's feeling pensive, she'll say *If only the puzzles of life were as easy to solve.*

Yes. If only. If only.

The phone rings. Meghan stares at it, as if it's a rattler that's crossed her path. She's closer to it than I am.

"You going to answer that?" I ask.

She doesn't say anything when she picks it up.

"The word is 'hello,'" I remind her.

"I know that." She puts the receiver back on the cradle. "It was a hang-up."

"There've been a lot of those." It's irritating to the point that I wish we could afford to get a better phone system—say with Caller ID.

Meghan shrugs. She doesn't have any answers for me.

Not a good sign. I face her, my back against the arm of the couch. "Thought you had an early day tomorrow, you being the Pillsbury Dough Girl and all."

She yawns. "I have trouble getting to sleep before midnight." Her voice is raspy, as though she's coming down with a cold. Or maybe she's started smoking again. It'd be nice if it were only nicotine for once.

I pull my knees to my chest and lock my arms around my legs. "Old habits die hard."

"Some of them." Her smile stiffens. "Guess I don't need as much sleep as most people."

"Yeah. Your needs are different from a lot of people's."

She sighs, a sound with substance to it, heavy and long. "Why don't you say what's on your mind, Erin?" she says evenly. "It's obvious that something's eating you."

I point at her bare fingers. "What happened to Ginga's ring?"

She presses her hands together, like a prayer, except she doesn't have one this time. "I feel terrible," she says, her voice soft. "I lost it."

"When?" The word crackles. I narrow my eyes, keeping Meghan in my sights.

"A while ago." She picks at a hangnail and swears under her breath when she pulls too hard and makes herself bleed. "Why?"

"A woman brought it into the shop today." I flick a tassel, hanging by a thread from a brocade pillow. "She said a girl sold it to her this morning, someone who really seemed to need the money."

Meghan turns toward me, folding one leg under the other. "Are you sure it's the same ring?" she asks eagerly.

"It had to be. It's pretty distinctive." My eyes don't leave her face, alert to the slightest hint of deception. I can't detect any, though that doesn't mean she's on the level.

"That's lucky." She doesn't miss a beat. Her eyes gleam in the dark. "I thought it was gone for good."

I don't say anything. There's no sound except the murmur of the TV and the drip-drip of the leaky kitchen faucet, each drop gathering into a tiny mass on the nozzle until it becomes too heavy and splatters into nothing in the sink.

"Oh, I see." Meghan sighs. "You think it was me, don't you? I can understand why you'd believe that after everything we've been through, Erin." She gives me a sad-eyed look. "But do I seem high to you now?"

I admit she doesn't. Wrapped in a star-patterned quilt, she appears small and vulnerable. Nevertheless, I can't shake the feeling she's up to something. She knows how to play me. She knows how to play all of us.

She strokes the pale tan-line on her finger where the ring used to be. "Are we going to have to buy it back?"

Sure, I could get it back—for a price. But there's a distinct possibility that it'll only stay on her finger for an hour before she sells it again. If that's what happened. "I don't know."

I don't know a lot of things—mainly, if she's being straight with me. We're playing chess with our words and although I initially thought I'd found a way to beat her, I'm discovering I was wrong. She's the master. I'm still an apprentice.

On the television, black-and-white images flicker on the screen. Little girls, speaking Polish. English subtitles tell only half the story. The older one, Kara, yearning for her own perfect family because her mother neglects her, lures away a young neighbor girl. Kara's face is lean and hungry for love, for a place to start over again.

Her face is the face of my sister, looking at me and then away. Hungry for our father's love, which in her anger and pain she tries to satisfy with men, heroin, crack, meth—everything under the hallucinogenic sun.

"Is it a good movie?" I ask.

"Yeah," she says as the girls dance over sand dunes, screeching like crows, their steps fierce, their faces filled with quiet desperation.

My throat gets tight from the beauty and sadness of it all, but I'm not going to cry. I have things to say that won't be served by an untimely outpouring of tears.

I open and close my mouth I don't know how many times, to find the words that won't come. The grandfather clock ticks relentlessly in the hall, its pendulum swinging back and forth, its movement hypnotic, its sound getting into my head, measuring hours and minutes the way I measure my sister's words. Truth-truth-truth-truth. Lie-lie-lie-lie.

I want something to happen. I'm spoiling for a fight, something to show that I've gotten through to her.

Meghan doesn't say anything. Her skin is tinged blue from

the light of the television, her brow beaded with sweat from the heat and the struggle to stop using. She doesn't look at me, waiting me out, which is something new. I don't know how to react. After a few moments, she spreads the edge of the quilt over my legs. Though the space remains between us, we huddle beneath the quilt that Mama made from bits of clothing we out-grew years ago—a pale green shirt, a daisy-patterned sun dress, a pair of red gingham shorts. I almost feel as if we're children again, revisiting the times we'd sit together like this and giggle and tell each other secrets.

But I don't allow myself to succumb to nostalgia, don't scoot closer or rest my head on her shoulder. I don't laugh or confide. That type of intimacy is a thing of the past.

Still, something survives. An ember that glows among the ashes and insists that it's enough to feel the warmth of her nearby, to hear her quiet breathing. And for a moment we breathe together in the silence, in the blue-gray shadows, until, finally, one of us has to get up and move away to our separate rooms and separate dreams.

CHAPTER 6

A week passes. By all accounts, my sister goes to work every day, arriving home late in the afternoon, her hair and clothes dusted with a light coating of flour. She travels on foot, because she claims to enjoy the exercise. After washing up, she heads to her AA meeting, announcing "home again, home again, jiggety jog" upon her return. They're the most regular hours she's kept in years, maybe ever.

Mama's pleased. She says we should go on a picnic to Divide on our day off, which is Sunday. I'd rather hang with Alex & Co.—it's going to be hot enough to raise blisters today and they're going tubing on one of the rivers west of here—but Mama wants us, her daughters and granddaughters, to be together in a semblance of normality so bad, I can't bail on her.

We even go to church as a family, something we never do any more. Mama's the only one who attends regularly, mostly because she sings in The Heavenly Voices choir, a misnomer for everyone but her. The group sticks to the same tired repertoire because there isn't enough money in the church budget to purchase new music. Some of the singers veer so far off pitch that they sound like squealing tires before a wreck. As we sit in one of the back pews, Meghan stares straight ahead, her gaze vacant. I wonder what she's thinking, if she's praying. Yo-ho's in the opposite pew, a rosary dangling from his shaky fingers, lips moving soundlessly. If you ask him, he'll say the ship's chaplain sent him. That he's petitioning God for fair weather, smooth sailing.

I do the same. *Please, God, or the Patron Saint of Addicts and the Ones Who Love Them, let us have a good week, a good year, a good life.*

No, that's asking too much. How about a good afternoon in Divide, the place we used to visit when my father was alive? The cabin my great-grandfather built might not have been much to look at, but it was an escape from the mines and the city. His little piece of paradise where he could fish and breathe clean air, as it was for my grandfather, father, and us—until it burned down one night after my dad died. We can't afford to rebuild.

All that remains is the square foundation with front steps that lead nowhere and blackened timbers that rise from the earth like a row of broken teeth. Heaven has become its roof. Black-eyed Susans and red-plumed grasses sprout from ash-enriched soil. Shards of glass lie half-buried in the dirt, transformed by the heat into lopsided hearts and open hands. I have a collection of them in an old cigar box. I keep thinking I'll use them some day, strung on necklaces with beads, but I haven't done it yet.

When we were young, the cabin smelled of wood smoke and earth. There were only three small rooms, with barely enough space for a bed. To say it was Spartan was an understatement, and yet it was as if the cabin knew better than to compete with the landscape, which is everything that beautiful should be. The country is the complete opposite of the town where we live, which, though it has abundant character, possesses little in the way of aesthetic appeal, a battered pugilist vowing to fight until the final bell, unwilling to admit defeat.

I've zoned out through most of mass. The end catches me by surprise. I troop to the altar for communion along with the rest of the pious and devoted, choke down the host (why can't they make the body of Christ taste better?) and plop down in my seat. As I'm kneeling there, trying to pray, a guy I've never seen before walks by. Our eyes meet for a moment and I have to catch my breath, not because he's incredibly good-looking—he's tall and tan, with deep-set, wounded brown eyes, and swarthy skin—how is it that guys can make acne scars look sexy?—but because there's something that passes between us.

Then a mournful dog howls—no, it's one of the choir members singing the closing hymn, spoiling the moment. I sit on my hands so I don't use them to plug my ears.

"Man," Meghan whispers. "That was painful."

The priest gives the final blessing, and we're released into the retina-searing morning. Everyone files out silently, no sound except the shuffling of footsteps and the occasional sneeze, because the caretaker's fighting a losing battle with the dust. Once outside, we chatter like kids freed from detention. I search for the cool church dude, but he's gone. Not that I would have known what to do if he'd stuck around.

"Looking for something—or someone?" Meghan asks, amused.

"Just the car." I hop in the front seat, set the picnic basket on my lap, and close the door as they pile in. With Mama at the wheel, we take to the highway, the mile markers whipping by, away from everything—except the past.

The place at Divide sits on the bank of a quiet, meandering river of the same name. Wind rushes through the grass, making it ripple as if it's alive, the muscled form of a mountain lion running across the plains, all sinuous movement. Dragonflies in startling hues of orange and red and blue drone over the water, like miniature floatplanes. Painted lady butterflies nest in milkweed bushes. Teeny delights in seeing them land on her outstretched hands and arms, a fascination Meghan and I shared when we were children. First one, then another, until ten of the creatures rest on Teeny, their fluttering wings tiny stained-glass windows, amber, red, and orange, as they mate in the palm of her hand.

"St. Francis has some competition," Mama says as she unpacks the food: turkey sandwiches, homemade potato and fruit and bean salads, lemonade, and chocolate chip cookies.

Since Meghan's return, Mama has been knocking herself out at the stove. I heard her clattering away at six this morning, getting things ready. Now and then, she'll become a culinary whirlwind, baking up a storm as a way of working through a problem. Sometimes she just cooks to keep things interesting. "Life is short—why eat boring food?" she says. This time, it's different. She's doing everything she can to satisfy my sister's appetites, to entice her to stay.

Teeny holds her breath, not wanting to disturb the butterflies or Si-si, who's sleeping in the Moses basket at her feet. "Can I take them home?" she whispers.

"They wouldn't like it." Meghan tucks Teeny's half-eaten sandwich into the hamper in case she's hungry later.

"I'll put them in a special jar." Teeny touches a wing with her fingertip. "I'll poke holes in the lid. I'll get them grass and all their favorite things to eat. I'll make them happy. I know I will."

Meghan shakes her head. "They'd die cooped up like that."

I suppose she knows what she's talking about. She's an expert at not wanting to be confined, at flying away.

The butterflies seem to agree. Within seconds, they take flight, their wings making animated v's as they swirl into the air and vanish from sight.

Teeny's eyes fill with tears as she stares after them. "Why did they have to go away?"

"Sometimes things just do." Meghan selects a sandwich and adds lettuce and tomato. "They can't live like us."

I cast a sidelong glance at my sister. Most of the time, she can't live like the rest of us either. The butterflies have their nectar, their migration patterns. And she has hers.

To get Teeny's mind off the loss, Mama leads her down to the riverbank to search for frogs. Teeny all arms and legs and a tangle of honey-colored hair. Mama nearly twice as tall, a small woman striding purposefully toward the river her husband used to fish. Sunlight dapples the water's surface with diamonds and makes their hair shine, lustrous as bolts of silk, Mama's highlighted with glints of obsidian, Teeny's with gold, blending with the colors of the grasses and the hills.

I recall standing that way when I was a little girl, drinking up the sun and water and scent of switchgrass. Nothing was ever too hot or cold for my sister and me back then. We were impervious to discomfort, shrugging off our coats in the snow, forgetting our hats on purpose in summer. Everything seemed simpler, probably because I didn't pay attention to troubling details at that stage of my life. Teeny sees things more clearly than I did at that age. She doesn't have a choice. But right now, she's being a five-year-old looking for frogs with her grandma.

"Do you remember when we used to hunt for frogs?" I ask Meghan. "One was bigger than my hand." I hadn't been able to hold onto the moss-green monster that looked as though it had lived at the bottom of the river since the beginning of time.

"It wasn't that big." Meghan extends a twig, rather than an entire olive branch. "But it was big enough."

Frog hunting was something we did with my father when we were young. We splashed through the shallows, clenched our toes on slick river rocks, feeling for footholds, peering into the shallows for our quarry. The tiny ones could be beautiful, their skin green as jade, the large toads, with their warty snouts and low-slung bellies, ugly. We prized them not for their looks, but their size. Most of the time, the frogs proved too slippery for us. It didn't matter. It was more about the chase than the capture, more about spending time with my father than having something tangible to show for it.

The river was my father's territory. He'd spent many summer days there in his youth. He loved to fish. Sometimes we rose early to accompany him, dressing in pint-sized waders and sweaters to ward off the early morning chill. We sipped hot chocolate and ate cinnamon toast and whispered quietly among ourselves, so as not to wake Mama. She wasn't as interested in fishing as the rest of us, though Meghan and I didn't have my father's patience and couldn't put in the hours he did while the light in the sky shifted from soft lavender to gold to blue. Even then, Meghan couldn't stand still for long. She had to move, to splash and sing. And my father, the essence of silence at those times, would send us in the opposite direction, because we were scaring the fish.

There are a couple of old rods back home in the basement, but we didn't bring them with us today. We're trying to catch other things that have nothing to do with fish or bait. But as my sister and I sit eating sandwiches, I think I glimpse my father, hip-deep in the water, casting for trout. He looks so real, I almost call his name before I remember he's been dead six years and can't hear me, though part of me wants to believe that he can.

When I blink, he's gone. A ring radiates from the spot where I saw him, cast by a trout flicking its tail.

My sister glances at me. I wonder if she saw it too. She wouldn't admit it if she did. She hasn't said his name since the day he died. We stopped talking about him, because it hurt too much.

My sister was the one who found him. He sat in the den, watching sports on TV—there was a small, portable TV in the room in those days—the way he always did when he got home from work. He'd watch anything related to sports, didn't matter what it was. I think it was a hurling match that afternoon. My sister went in to give him the drink he'd asked for. Homemade lemonade, slices of fresh citrus fruit floating in a hiball. He'd start with that and move on to hard liquor later. Ice clinked and snapped as she walked past. Water beaded the outside of the glass and dripped onto her bare legs and feet. She wore cut-offs and a wife-beater. She'd painted a flower on her big toe with nail polish, the blue petals chipped, as if something had taken a bite out of them. She smirked at me as she went by, pleased with herself for having beaten me to it. She wasn't getting him the lemonade to be helpful. She wanted to go to the movies with her friends and was trying to get on his good side, so he'd give her permission—and money.

I sat in the porch swing, reading a book. I'd started out in the living room, but it was too hot and noisy in there, what with the televised crowds roaring for their team in the next room. I needed quiet in order to concentrate.

Then I heard my sister scream. I remember the sound of the glass breaking when it hit the floor, ice shattering and skittering into corners. I dropped my book, losing my place, and pulled open the screen door as Mama rushed past. I followed her, listening to her speaking to my father, her voice soft, yet insistent. *Patrick, I'm here. Stay with me.* Him sprawled on the floor, his legs bent at a sickening angle. The door to the study closing. Me stuck on the outside. Them not letting me in, not wanting me to see. Phone calls made from inside that room. Muffled voices. I couldn't see any more, couldn't hear. *What's happening? Somebody tell me.*

Our neighbor, Mrs. Sullivan, seemed to appear out of nowhere—Mama must have summoned her—and took me by the hand to her house where I ate popcorn and watched *Bambi* resentfully, because I was too old for it, but not old enough for my mother and sister to let me into the room where something was terribly wrong. The two Sullivan kids were toddlers then, snotty-nosed and chewing Cheerios with their mouths open. Meghan baby-sat them on occasion, claiming they were brats but she needed the money.

Bambi's father was telling him what a brave little deer he was when a siren wailed outside. Distant at first, then close enough that I thought the ambulance was going to crash into the room. Even though it was the hottest day of the year, I'd never felt so cold in my life, a cold that penetrated to the bone. I ran past Mrs. Sullivan—I remember her rising from her chair in the kitchen where she'd been looking at a lingerie catalog that had come in the mail—and toward the house as the medics brought my father out on a stretcher.

"Daddy!" I cried.

He didn't answer me. His eyes were glassy and fixed on a single cloud in the sky, a cloud the same pale gray as his skin, the color of angels, the color of heaven.

There's a cloud very similar to that one in the sky this afternoon over the river in Divide. At least it seems that way to me. It's a flat, gray little cloud, a rectangular shape with rounded edge. It's all by itself up there. The heat will dry it to nothing as the day wears on, or it might only take a minute or two. It's too small and doesn't have enough company for making major weather. It can only play at rain, then disappear. Still, it's as though we sit under our own invisible cloud, one we can't get out from under, one that won't vaporize.

I can't eat any more of the sandwich. It's delicious, but my stomach won't settle.

I pull out a small bag of beads and begin to string them. I always carry a supply with me, like an old woman with her knitting. It gives me something to do with my hands other than pick at my nails when I'm restless or uncomfortable, as I often am when it comes to my sister. "How's the job going?" I ask her.

"Good," she says between bites. Possessed of a high metabolism, she eats steadily, with purpose, like a runner carbo-loading for a race—or another drug binge. "As long as they don't make me wear one of those damn hairnets, I'll be fine."

"Who knows?" I bite off a length of thread with my teeth. I've forgotten my small scissors. "It might turn into the latest style."

"Yeah, right," she smirks. She's never eaten her crust. My dad ate it for her, claiming it would give him curly hair. Now, she crumbles bits of crust, as if she's feeding a flock of invisible birds.

"Don't be so sure," I tease. It suddenly becomes important for me to know that I can still make her laugh. As she's grown less dependable over the years, I've grown more serious—too serious. "You could decorate yours with rhinestones."

Meghan gives me a crooked smile. "If you put it that way, maybe I'll have to get one after all."

Teeny stands on the bank with Mama. They're done with frogs, it being mid-afternoon and, if not hotter than hell, close to it, which drives the amphibians into deep water. Instead, she and Mama race reed boats down the river, seeing which ones make it past a snag and over a small waterfall created by a rock ledge beneath the surface, without getting swamped. None have managed to run the course cleanly yet, though one came close.

Si-si doesn't stir. She clutches the edge of her blanket as if it's a life raft. I reach over and touch her hand.

"Don't wake her up." Meghan rolls a bite of bread into a ball and pops it in her mouth.

"I won't. I do that all the time. It doesn't bother her." There's an awkward silence, filled with the idea of me knowing something about the baby she doesn't, or worse, knowing more than she does.

My sister snaps off a piece of red licorice rope, which Mama packed because it's Meghan's favorite. I can't help thinking that in a pinch, she could use it to tie off and shoot up. Willie Wonka and the Heroin Factory.

She holds out a rope to me. I take it, not because I like licorice that much, but because she doesn't offer me anything that often and it'll give me something to chew on.

Meghan turns the conversation to a topic at which she's always had more success than me. "So, you got a serious boyfriend these days?" She gnaws on the tender white shoot of a blade of grass. Her eyes stay on the river, not near Mama and Teeny, but the open stretch downstream where it runs fast and free.

"I'm eighteen." I knot beads into place, one after another. "What do I want with a serious boyfriend?"

"Exactly," she says. "You're eighteen. Why don't you want one?"

My chest tightens. "I never said I didn't. It's just not a pressing concern for everybody. Some people have aspirations."

She looks away, acknowledging my verbal checkmate. As a girl, she'd cut her head out of wallet-sized school photos and pasted herself into thrilling fantasy scenes—Meghan on top of Mt. Fuji; Meghan's name in lights on Broadway; Meghan in a rocket ship. Not any more.

"Oh, yeah. Those." She pauses. "I only meant you should get out more. You don't have that much experience."

"How would you know? You're never around," I snap. Okay. I've slept with a grand total of three guys. One was a friend I got overly friendly with one night at a party; we tried to pretend we were too drunk to remember the encounter the next day. Another I really liked, my summer of love, when I was sixteen, but he moved to Chicago; we wrote for a while; I don't remember who stopped first. And the other one, well, he turned out to be a jerk—he cheated on me with my sister. I'm glad he's at college. I hope he never comes back.

"I don't need your kind of experience," I tell her.

Whenever we talk, it's as if submerged snags trip us up. Sometimes we see them coming and change the course of the conversation. Other times we don't.

The thing is, I care about the boyfriend issue more than I let on. A lot of people in my high school graduating class are getting married. The battered church at the top of the hill is booked solid through the summer months, weekends filled with the sound of the bell tolling hollowly. Brides stand on the front steps, buffeted by the wind that peppers their lovely white gowns with grit. Grooms duck their chins into their collars, everybody wondering what they've gotten themselves into, but determined to be happy, because it's supposed to be the best day of their lives.

Except for one notable exception (Jimmy, the Chicago boy), the guys I've been with haven't lived up to my expectations. My sister isn't as picky. She likes men the way she likes candy, the way she likes drugs. She can't resist them, even if they aren't hers to have.

"And if I did have a boyfriend, I wouldn't tell you," I add. "You'd steal him."

I've lost a guy or two because of her, though it probably speaks more to their lack of character than hers. If we got into it, she'd claim she was smashed—that's why she went down on my boyfriend-at-the-time, the aforementioned jerk, in a bathroom at a party. I know, because I walked in on them. I closed the door fast and I went outside and threw up. Because I'd had too much to drink. Because he'd told me to do it and I hadn't wanted to.

Meghan blinks as if she has something in her eye. She knows what I'm thinking. Even though she insisted she was too wasted to have a memory of the incident, she hasn't forgotten. "I don't steal from people," she says.

"Yeah, you do." I tie the last knot. "You steal lots of things."

She's famous for her temper. I wait for the flash, counting, the way you do between thunderclaps and lightning bolts, to judge how far away the storm is. The hairs rise along my arms as if there's electricity in the air.

Si-si cries. She feels it too. She kicks her legs, trying to keep it away.

Or because she's messed her pants.

Meghan checks her diaper. "Guess she's registering her opinion about the way this conversation is going." She smiles at me, a smile that's real.

Teeny skips up to us. "There's the ship that didn't sink." She points downriver, where a reed boat bobs in the current. For as far as she can see, it appears the crew of that miniature vessel will emerge victorious.

She notices we've fallen silent. "Were you talking about me?" she demands.

"No," Meghan says as she changes Si-si. When Meghan's clean, she does it expertly, no torn tabs or loose leg openings.

"Yes, you were," Teeny insists.

"Though you are the center of my universe, I don't only talk about you." Meghan throws a handful of grass at her.

Teeny squeals and runs away.

There's the universe of family, which is where we are now, and there's the universe of drugs, which is the one I hope we've left behind. It makes such a pretty picture, my sister the young mother, caring for her children. At moments such as this, she plays the role so well I think it's possible for her to reform, that she's finally hit bottom and is ready to enter recovery. And yet a part of me has doubts, considers that, for Meghan, perhaps there is no bottom—that all she can do is keep falling and falling.

We're quiet, no sound except the baby gurgling and cooing, her chubby legs and arms punching at something invisible. The sky over the distant mountains goes smudgy, resembling the black stuff football players smear under their eyes to cut the glare.

Meghan follows my gaze. "Another fire."

I nod. We're approaching the height of the season when forests burn. Alex has fought them. She describes the experience as a party with cute soot-covered guys. Maybe that's because she's never had to battle a big blaze before. Even here, in this valley, we see the scars the fires have left in the charred single trunks of trees and the burned-out cabin that used to hold our dreams.

A piece of charcoal crumbles between my fingers. It isn't the type you can draw with. It's too fragile for that. But if I could, I'd make a portrait of my father. Meghan gives me a piercing look, as if she knows what I'm thinking. She tucks Si-si back in the basket and gets to her feet. "Come on," she says. "It's time to go."

I dust off my hands, fingertips stained black, and follow her, as I did when I was a child. The sun slinks down toward the hills as if it has a guilty conscience and is trying to sneak out of the sky. The insects along the river hum in the cooling air, and a trout backflips over a log. "Daddy would have loved that one," I whisper.

Meghan doesn't turn around. She heads to the car, acting like she didn't hear me. Mama and Teeny honk the horn, not with impatience but mischief. Teeny can make Mama seem younger or older, depending upon whether Mama is playing with her or worrying about her.

"It was a good day, wasn't it?" Mama declares as I slide into the passenger seat next to her.

I steal a glance in the rearview mirror at Meghan, who stares out the window at the sun, which is veined red as a blood-shot eye on account of the fire smoke. She looks at Mama, whip-quick, and snaps on a smile before anyone except me notices something else is on her mind.

"Yes," she says. "It was."

We close the windows against the bugs and dust as Mama drives the dirt track to the main road. She turns the wheel rhythmically, right, left, left, right, guiding the car around pot-holes deep enough to bust the axle or bite a hole in rubber. The last thing we need is a blown tire. She reminds me of a conductor, with the wheel her baton, directing the orchestra through a particularly challenging piece of music. She prefers the road this way, because that's the way she remembers it. To change it would be to take another step away from the past.

A wide plume of dust fans out behind us, obscuring the place we've been. When I look back, I can't see that section of the river or the valley or the ruined cabin. They're lost in a great brown cloud of our own making. It won't dissipate until after we've gone.

I pull down the visor mirror and attempt to get a speck of grit out of my eye. In the background, I see Teeny slumped against Meghan's shoulder, hair in damp strands against her forehead, breath soft and steady. Meghan appears outwardly calm until you look closer and realize her muscles are rigid from the effort to contain whatever's boiling up inside her.

"You okay, honey?" Mama asks as we pull onto the highway. Glancing from me to the road and back again.

"Yeah, there was something in my eye, that's all." I flip the visor into place. My face is reflected in the side mirror, the one that says objects may be closer than they appear. Behind me, dust and tumbleweeds and the swath of green recede, a mirage shimmering in the heat.

"We'll have to do this again soon," Mama says. "Remember how we'd head out here every weekend?" She floors the accelerator to build up speed.

We crack the window since we're free of the dust now and the air conditioner is broken and we're starting to bake, rivulets of sweat snaking down our necks. The wind whooshes, like an animal that's been panting to get out of the house, whipping our hair into a frenzy, making too much noise for us to talk. We're too tired and pensive to compete with it, each of us wondering if we're happy or sad or both, but unwilling, or unable, to give our feelings a name. The wind is the only thing we don't try to shut out. We let it go ahead and stir things up.

CHAPTER 7

All that week, Ginga's ring calls to me from the display case at Funkified. It sparkles next to the coral rosary, the Kewpie doll salt 'n' pepper shakers, the mercury glass Christmas ornaments, and the gold heart-shaped necklace with a lock of flaxen hair curled inside the pendant, which David refers to as the Locket of the Unknown Baby. It's disturbingly personal, like the scores of black-and-white family photos filed in a box on one of the shelves. The women in their corsets, hair pulled back from their faces, everything about them constricted, the coiffures, the clothes, the expressions. The men in their black suits and pocket watches that ticked off the hours once upon a time. No one ever smiled, not for the camera anyway. Finding these things in the shop makes me uneasy. There's a nakedness about them, a rawness that's unfathomable, like a shirt button unwittingly left undone, letting people see the skin, the wounds, of a family. Why would someone want to buy them?

Why would someone give them away in the first place? The selling seems worse than burying, than burning.

Ginga's ring doesn't possess the hint of abandonment, of reproach, in the obvious way the locket and photos do. As I gaze at the faceted setting, a plan forms in my mind, of rescue, and, less nobly, of possession. If I buy it, it'll technically be mine. There's nothing that says I have to return it to Meghan.

"You've got a thing for that ring, don't you?" Daniel spritzes the case with Windex and wipes away the smudges. The cloth squeaks against the glass. He takes perverse pleasure in the sound, because it makes David wince. "You can have it if you want," he offers. Spritz-spritz. Spritz-spritz. "Consider it a bonus."

"Oh, no. That's all right." I shrug.

"Look." He puts his hands on his hips. "It's not like it's the family jewels. We wouldn't be able to sell it for that much anyway. The setting is marcasite, the diamond's not even real, and there are flaws on the face. Right, David?"

"Right," David chimes in from the loft where he's sorting vintage luggage and hat boxes.

"It looks real," I murmur.

We always thought it was.

"A lot of things do, honey. Doesn't mean they are." Daniel pats me on the shoulder. "You still want it?"

I nod. I mean, it's the sentimental value that makes the ring priceless to me.

"It's settled then." He takes the black box from the case. "Do you want to wear it?"

"Not right now." I don't want Meghan to see it on my finger. I tuck the box into my purse, feeling like a thief, as if I've stolen from her, though it's not as if I've done anything wrong—or that she doesn't deserve it.

"Hey, are you coming to the luau?" Daniel asks.

I look at him blankly. He leaps from topic to topic like a flying squirrel.

He taps his foot. "Remember, we asked you last week?"

And then I recall the conversation—and the card with the dancing pineapple on it. "Oh, right. I don't know. I've got family stuff going on. My sister and her kids are still staying with us."

"Bring 'em," David calls from the loft. "The more, the merrier."

"I'm not sure what their plans are." I have an image in my head of a nightmare evening involving my sister and tiki lamps and mai tais and hula skirts, her yelling "aloha" at the top of her lungs.

I don't tell them this, but I'm not going to invite Meghan. I'll go into avoidance mode. Sometimes it's better to let things slide, to forget. I'll hook up with Alex and the rest of our crew instead. It's karaoke night at the Fillmore. I'll have a beer or two. Maybe I'll even take the stage and pretend I'm someone else for a while, someone who doesn't have a sister like mine.

When I pass Yo-ho's house late this afternoon, he's rocking on his porch swing. The chains creak, timbers of a ship at sea. "All hands on deck!" He waves a cardboard paper towel tube—he insists his daughter buy Bounty because of the name—that he uses for a telescope. "Pirates on the horizon, closing fast."

I look in the direction he's pointing. All I see are white skid marks of jet stream in the sky.

"They have their cutlasses drawn." He narrows his eyes.

The only Cutlass I see is a car, bumping down the road. At least that's what I think it is. It's too far away to know for sure. Probably not the kind he means. But who's to say? His mind works in mysterious ways, making roses into knots, cars into weapons. Nothing's a stretch for him.

"Where are they from?" I play along.

"California!" he barks. "The worst kind."

I suppress a smile, wondering what else he's woven into his buccaneer fantasy. There isn't much to work with, not that that stops him: tumbleweeds bouncing over the potholed road, the angular remains of the ironworks, a house with a caved-in roof that looks like a giant sat on it. Perhaps it's the hulk of a rusted-out Buick that inspired him, sprawled face down in the dirt without tires or prayer of repair.

His parrot, Methuselah, hops along the railing. "Pirates! Pirates! Help! Help!"

Yo-ho salutes me. "You take care now, Missy!"

"I'll keep an eye out." I consider the dirt and gravel roads that lead nowhere and figure we could do with a visit from the pirates of California. Maybe they'd liven things up. As I push open our front gate, I hear Yo-ho singing sea chanties, his voice lusty, if off-key.

Teeny's busy digging in the garden, a garden which isn't about to win any awards, isn't, in fact, more than a scrubby lawn with a couple of bone-dry beds. One literally is a bed. Mama took an old frame and headboard and filled them with topsoil. She planted flowers where the mattress should be, a horticultural joke, which she embellished with a hand-painted sign: "Life is a bed of roses."

Never mind that the roses are barely alive.

Teeny has a smear of dirt on her chin. "Hi, Auntie Erin."

"What are you doing?" I hitch my bag up on my shoulder. The jewelry box containing Ginga's ring knocks against my hip bone.

"Looking for gold." Teeny grunts as she pushes a rock aside.

The bed bears evidence of her excavations, an archeological site in miniature, holding fragments of our past: a cat's-eye marble, a rusty jack, a clip-on earring with the stones missing, and a copper penny worn so smooth it appears Lincoln's features have been erased.

"Seems you're having some luck." I sit next to her on a patch of brown grass.

"Not really," Teeny admits. "Just those things"—she gestures with an impatient wave at the small mound of losses she's unearthed—"and some icky bugs."

I nod. "There go the big beetles." With their hard shells and stiff gaits, the insects resemble a military convoy. They lumber off to conduct maneuvers in the dead leaves beneath the euphorbia by the front porch.

Overhead, starlings scrabble in the eaves, destroying parts of our home to make rooms of their own. The sparrows are more like masons, applying mud and wattle to the crooks of downspouts.

Teeny points at a speckled egg smashed on the ground. "Why did the mama bird kick the baby out?"

"I'm sure it was an accident," I assure her.

Teeny frowns at the bird in the nest. "She doesn't even notice the egg is gone. She doesn't care."

I touch her wrist. "Do you want me to bury it?"

She nods.

"Here?" I indicate a shady spot underneath a withered Gallica rose.

She nods again.

I scoop a handful of dirt to make a shallow grave. The top layer of soil has the consistency of sand. The strata below are more impenetrable. I put a piece of granite on top to serve as a tombstone and anchor the dirt.

Teeny lays a rose petal on it. "Little bird, rest in peace," she intones. "Your mama didn't mean it." She looks up. Wisps of cloud scribble a message which dissolves before we can read it. "Is there a heaven for birds?"

"I suppose there's a heaven for everything," I reply, "as long as you believe in it."

"I bet an angel bird will take better care of her." She stabs at the dirt with her shovel. The metal pings against something hard. "She'll have a nice nest with the best twigs and every-thing." She sits back on her heels and wipes her forehead.

"Maybe you should take a break," I suggest. "How long have you been working anyway?"

"Since Scooby-Doo ended." Hers is a child's life, ordered by a sequence of cartoons, at least when Meghan's in charge.

"You want some lemonade?" I ask. I could use a glass myself. The mercury's pushing ninety today.

"Uh-huh." She jabs the trowel into the soil again. She sticks

128

her tongue out slightly, something she does when she concentrates hard, a trait she shares with Meghan. I can see a lot of Meghan in her, now that she's getting older and I'm spending more time with her. I hope she only inherits the good. Who knows what's she's gotten from her father, other than her turquoise eyes.

I hold the scuffed world of the marble in the palm of my hand. It's cloudy inside; the cat's eye looks as if it has cataracts. I don't remember losing it. One of us must have, long ago, in this yard that once wasn't merely something to walk through on the way to the front door, but a place to play and dream. It's as if the marble—and the garden itself—had been waiting all these years for a child to rediscover it.

The yard hasn't changed much over time. There's the walk where Meghan and I hopscotched and raced tricycles, the posts on which we carved our names in minute script so Mama wouldn't see and get mad at us. The marks have been painted over, but I can make them out, because we cut deep enough that the paint hasn't totally filled the grooves but lies slightly below them, like the low water line of a lake during a drought. Meghan M. Erin M.

"What'cha doing?" Teeny looks over my shoulder.

"Your mom and I wrote our names here when we were little." I touch the letters.

She shakes her head. "I can't see."

I take her hand and run her fingers over them. "There. Feel that?"

"Yeah." She strokes the letters as if she's rubbing a genie lamp. "Can you write mine?"

"Sure." I scratch her and Si-si's initials in the paint with a stick. Maybe the girls will do better at the sibling thing than Meghan and I have. "Where's your mom, anyway?"

"Inside." Teeny jerks her head toward the house. "Si-si started to cry. She's too little to be a prospector."

My footsteps sound hollow and tired as I climb the stairs. One of the rockers, whose finish gives a whole new meaning to the word distressed, ticks back and forth like a metronome. Maybe it's the breeze. Maybe Meghan had been sitting there. Just because I didn't actually see her keeping an eye on Teeny doesn't mean she hadn't been doing it. After all, it isn't like you have to be supervised to play in your own front yard.

Though, these days, you never know.

The house has the heavy airless atmosphere it sometimes gets on summer afternoons, despite open windows and drawn shades. It holds the heat inside as if nursing a grudge. The refrigerator gags and gurgles as though something is stuck in its throat. The kitchen faucet drips a version of water torture. I move toward the living room, where I hear the sound of breathing, my sister and her baby asleep on the couch beneath the portraits of our ancestors and the remnants of her golden past. Si-si is on Meghan's chest, head tucked underneath her mama's chin. Their bodies, the pieces in their peculiar puzzle, fit together perfectly when they're unconscious. There's no impatience, no resentment, no desperate grasping and rooting. Meghan's arm hangs limp, grazing the oriental rug that's so used up, the pattern's nearly worn off. She has on one of Mama's button-down shirts, the costume of a more conventional character than she's ever been. It's the kind of shirt that can be worn over anything—a black lace bra, a Devil Girl T-shirt, fresh needle tracks, a fickle heart.

If you didn't know Meghan and Si-si's history, you'd think you were viewing a portrait of maternal love and child's innocence, their cheeks pink, faces soft and peaceful. I slip out of the room and stand in the cold draft of the fridge, where the pitcher of lemonade waits in frosty silence and the hard light cast by the bare bulb hurts my eyes and obliterates the lingering image of those simple things: the mother who wants to love, the baby who needs sleep, the little girl who needs a drink.

"Grandma makes the best lemonade in the world!" Teeny gulps the liquid without taking a breath and belches.

"Wow." I laugh. "I'm surprised there's any of you left."

"I can burp up to the letter L in the alphabet," she informs me.

I help Teeny dig. She's gone down ten inches. She calls it level 1, as they used to in the mines. She picked up the lingo somewhere. "What an accomplishment. Where did you learn how to do that?"

"Greg taught me." She shapes a mound of dirt into a pyramid. "He can get all the way to Z."

The infamous Greg. Who is he anyway? Her father? No. He's a more recent acquisition.

The phone rings, once, twice, then stops. Either Meghan answered or the caller hung up. Wrong number. Wrong number. It's driving me nuts. I've had wild ideas about tapping the phone, installing surveillance equipment to spy on my sister, but then I realize I'm overreacting.

"What happened to Greg, anyway?" I sift dirt through my fingers, letting it fall like grains of sand in an hourglass.

Teeny shrugs. "He made somebody mad. He had to go away."

The story of Meghan's life. Somebody gets mad. Somebody shoots up—or runs short—or gets shot—or—

Meghan comes outside and sits on the bottom step. She's twisted her hair into a messy bun. "Made a strike yet?"

"No." Teeny shakes her head. "But I'm not giving up."

"That's a girl." She pulls a pack of Marlboros from her pocket, going for the heaviest hit of nicotine she can find.

I pick dirt from beneath my nails. "Who called?"

"David from Funkified." Meghan lights a cigarette and blows smoke toward the sky. "He invited us to the luau. I told him we could go."

Teeny looks up. "What's a luau?"

"It's a Hawaiian party." Meghan grins. "Cool, huh?"

"Yeah!" Teeny exclaims. "Can I wear a grass skirt?"

"I told him I'd mention it to you." I sit down next to her and wave the smoke away. A splinter pokes into my thigh, making me wince. I'd better pick it out before it goes too deep.

She grinds her cig on the step slowly, as if she'd like to do the same to my face. She knows I had no intention of telling her about the party. "Maybe he thought you'd forget."

I take a deep breath. "You could have asked me before you accepted the invitation. I'm not sure I even want to go. I have other plans."

"Really? What?" She leans forward, elbows on her knees.

I draw back. "I was thinking about going out with Alex."

"She left a message earlier." Meghan stares at me. "She can't make it. She has to pull a shift at the Perkatory."

"Oh." Great.

Meghan smiles, her eyes cold. "Not feeling embarrassed by our relatives, are we?"

"Of course not." I gaze through the warped boards of the picket fence. The peeling white paint looks as if it has a severe case of dermatitis.

"You're a bad liar, Erin," she says quietly. "You always have been." She wipes her hands on her jeans and goes back inside.

"I mean, it's not as if I have anything to feel embarrassed about, do I?" I can't keep the sarcasm out of my voice.

The porch screen yawns open behind her, exposing a sliver of dim house before it slams shut.

"Are you and Mom fighting?" Teeny asks. "She fights with a lot of people. I don't want her to make you so mad that we have to leave."

"Don't worry, Teens." I run my hands through my hair. "You're not going anywhere."

She pauses for a moment, then asks: "Can we go to the luau, though?"

The luau. I don't say anything. I wish I'd never heard about the damn thing.

"We have to go, Auntie Erin." Teeny's determined. "It'll be fun."

Fun. Sometimes I wonder if I know what that means any more. I look at the sky and sigh. I can be such a bitch sometimes. "Yeah. You're right. It will." I force a smile.

I mean, what's the worst thing that could happen?

• • •

Daniel and David live in a restored revival-style house in what used to be considered Uptown. It isn't quite on a par with the mansions of the Copper Kings, the big bosses of the mining industry, whose sumptuous abodes have been preserved for posterity as museums where Important People Once Lived, but it's close. My ancestors inhabited eyesore shacks too flimsy and grim to withstand the years. They got plowed under a long time ago.

Not the Double Ds' place. It's a beauty inside and out, the sort of home that suits people whose lives and dispositions are orderly. It's the last spot you'd expect to find a luau. But the Double Ds are expert at defying expectations. Cars jam the streets. Either someone else on the block is having a party or David and Daniel invited nearly the entire population of Butte. We have to park a couple of blocks away to find a slot. I wish Alex could have come, but she couldn't ditch her shift. She was bummed.

Meghan hasn't spoken to me since the phone call incident. She enjoys having something to be mad at me about for a change. She's going to get as much mileage out of this as possible. She begins by almost slamming the car door on my leg.

"Hey!" I cry.

"Sorry," she says without a backward glance. I want to trip her but restrain myself for Teeny's sake.

Since it's a costume affair, Mama unearthed a hula skirt one of us wore for a painfully bad middle school production of *South Pacific*. Teeny parades down the sidewalk, wearing it on her head, wig-style. I've got on a Hawaiian shirt with hula girls printed on it from the shop and a pair of capris. Meghan saunters along in short-shorts and a halter to prove she still has it despite being the mother of two. Va-voom. And Mama, she slipped into a bright red muumuu, establishing again just how brave and beautiful she is. I asked her why she didn't ask Joe to come along, but she said it was too last-minute and besides, it wasn't his kind of scene.

The door's wide open, which is a good thing, because Don Ho tunes blare so loud no one could have heard the doorbell ring. The music makes the floors vibrate and the dishes rattle. There are people everywhere—where did the Double Ds find them all?—people eating pu-pus ("Don't you just love the name?" someone giggles), dancing in the grand hall, lounging on the staircase, singing at the top of their lungs. Meghan dives into the center of things, champion of the party circuit. I want to run for the exit, but Daniel swoops out of nowhere and drapes a lei around my neck.

"Here. Get leied!" he yells over the noise. From the glassiness of his eyes, he's been throwing back as many drinks as he's mixed.

The joke's so bad I can't help laughing.

"Isn't it amazing?" He raises a toast to the room at large. "Butte's party of the year!"

I blink at the spectacle. It must have taken days—no weeks—to put together. They've made columns into palm trees, tacked hula-skirt grass on the walls, hung fake hibiscus flowers from the chandeliers. "Who are these people?" I ask.

"I don't know!" He puts his hands to his face in mock dismay. "They won't stop coming."

David appears at my elbow. "You'll never get a straight answer from him now."

"Of course not, because there's nothing straight about me!" David howls.

I glance at Teeny to see how she's taking this, but she's already tearing up the dance floor. Mama chats with a woman who has a pineapple-shaped hat on her head. Meghan's deep in conversation with a guy playing a ukulele. She has a thing for musicians as well as bikers.

David's eyes sparkle, but he isn't as far gone as Daniel. "So that's your mom over there? And your nieces and sister?" I nod.

"Good genes," Daniel says. "Your sister's a dead ringer for that actress. Damn it, I'm not good at names. Who am I thinking of, David?"

David toys with his pirate-sword-shaped swizzle stick. "Um. Jennifer Jason Leigh?"

"No-no-no."

"Winona Ryder?"

He shakes his head. "What do the two of them have in common, I'd like to know?"

"It's in the eyes." David nods sagely.

"You're not helping. It'll come to me." Daniel puts his fist to his head, The Thinker pose.

I keep an eye on Meghan, waiting for her to head for the open bar, for everything to spin out of control. But she chats away as if a drink is the last thing on her mind. People often think they know her, or mistake her for a celebrity, because she has a way of taking over a room with her megawatt charm, which blinds people to her less attractive qualities.

While the Double Ds continue their debate, I slip out a side door and onto a porch that must have once been part of the servants' wing, a place where overworked, disillusioned maids could contemplate the scarred hills and smoke a precious cigarette or two. I think about how much I hate crowds and big parties and being in my sister's shadow. I don't have her allure. I sit on the lower step overlooking the garden, wild with grasses and flowers. Either the Double Ds have one hell of a water bill or the plants are drought-tolerant.

I'm not. I feel like I'm withering. The ice inside my drink cracks loudly, a calving iceberg, and I imagine myself breaking away and floating across the Arctic Sea.

A step creaks behind me and I glance over my shoulder, startled.

"Sorry. I didn't know anyone else was here."

It's the guy I saw in church before we went to Divide. I choke on my drink.

"You okay?" he asks.

I nod, sputtering. "Wrong pipe." God, how embarrassing.

"I saw you in church the other day, didn't I?" he says. "A good Catholic girl, huh?"

"Not exactly," I rasp.

We're quiet for a moment. I'm too aware of the silence, of my heart beating loudly.

"I just came out to get some air." He laughs at himself, because it's one of those remarks people make when they're not sure what to say.

I rest my chin on my shoulder. "Not much of a Don Ho fan, huh?"

"I guess not." He leans against the railing, hands in the front pockets of his jeans.

"So, what's the Hawaiian part of your costume?" I raise an eyebrow.

"My tan." He grins.

Before I can add anything else, Meghan appears. "There you are," she says to me. "Daniel needs you for the limbo contest." Then she notices the guy with the wounded eyes. "Oh, hey. I didn't think you'd be here."

He's mine! I want to shout, suddenly, inexplicably possessive. But I can't because I don't even know him and she apparently does and I'm at a party where I feel like I need to behave myself or at least not get hysterical because I don't need any more sister-induced mortification. Wait a minute. It's possible—very possible—that I misunderstood the dynamics of our first encounter in church—that he and I hadn't shared a special moment after all—that he'd been looking at Meghan, not me.

"So how did you two meet?" I break in, a Chihuahua dancing on its hind legs for a doggie biscuit.

"My crew goes in for donuts," he explains.

I bet. "Crew?" He doesn't look as though he works construction and there isn't enough water around here for sailing.

"We're doing a groundwater study at the Pit." He nods toward the hills.

There'd been a write-up in the paper. "Oh, yeah. I read about that," I chatter away, wishing I didn't sound like such a nervous idiot. "Are the results scary?" Scary. Jesus, what's happened to my vocabulary?

"We're not done yet," he says.

"Don't get all serious again, Erin," Meghan interrupts. "This is supposed to be a party."

Great. Now my reputation—according to her anyway—as a

boring-downer-social misfit gets cemented. *You just have to get to know me better*, I want to tell him.

"Erin!" Daniel calls from the hallway. "Limbo!"

That's right. That's where I am. I have to find a place to hide before Daniel corners me. "It was good to meet you." I shoot the guy a smile, then bump Meghan harder than I have to as I squeeze past. I don't want to do the limbo. All I want to do is go home.

"Erin!" Daniel's voice gets closer. I duck into the kitchen, where David's putting a bag of ice on his head.

"What happened to you? Did you walk into a door?" I ask.

"No," he moans. "I have a headache."

"Too much Don Ho?"

"Too much everything. This is our big blow-out of the year. But honestly, I'd much rather have a salon evening. You know: wine and cheese and erudite conversation. It would be in keeping with the era of the house—and a lot quieter. Daniel's more of a party animal than I am." He puts the ice back in the freezer and rubs his temples.

"Better?" I ask.

"*Un peu*." He nods toward the porch. The guy is still out there, talking to Meghan. "Cute, isn't he? He's Puerto Rican or something. Makes me think of the dancer in *West Side Story*. God, I loved that movie—"

"Is he a friend of yours?" I pinch a passion-fruit tart from a tray.

"We met him at the Fillmore last night and Daniel invited him. Daniel would invite the whole world if he could," he sighs, adding "He seems nice."

"I guess. What's his name?"

"You didn't even ask his name?" He looks up at the ceiling as if appealing to God to help me with my social skills. "What am I going to do with you? It's Ray. Short for Ramón, or something like that."

"I was going to. My sister butted in, as usual. Turns out she knows him."

"The dreaded sister," he says in a sinister tone. "Knows him well?"

"I don't know." I shrug. "Apparently, he likes her donuts."

He giggles. I glare at him but can't hold onto the mood and end up laughing in spite of myself.

"C'mon. Let's limbo." David links arms with me. He smells of sandalwood and musk and the pineapple he's been slicing to accent drinks. "If Ray has any sense, he'll see right through her."

I'm afraid sense doesn't have much to do with it.

As it turns out, I don't have to join the limbo line after all. Daniel holds Si-si as Teeny and Mama battle for the title of Limbo Queen, the prize being one of David's luscious coconut cakes. Teeny's lower center of gravity wins in the end, but Mama puts up a good fight, despite being hampered by the muumuu. Downward-facing dogs and proud warriors—God, it sounds as if she joined the Roman army, but I mean yoga—keep her flexible.

I went with her to yoga once but giggled almost the entire time at some of the women in the class. There was Kitty Shirt, who wore T-shirts with small furry animals and her name in patchwork gingham letters on the front, and the Princess, who looked like a mini-me Barbie, performed every pose perfectly, and couldn't talk about anything but herself.

"How does this make you feel?" the instructor asked as we huffed and puffed.

"Like Darth Vader," I replied.

Only Mama thought it was funny. Everyone else stared at me as though I'd sworn in church. What really got me was the whale-song of stomach growls and vaginal farts that reverberated after inversions. I laughed so hard I cried. It was suggested I not come back. Expelled from yoga class. Now, that was an accomplishment.

"Coconut cake isn't Hawaiian!" a party-goer protests.

"Who cares? Coconut is!" Daniel licks frosting off his finger and presents Teeny with her award.

I don't see Meghan or Ray. They're probably plying each other with mai tais, or going at it in a closet. I try not to think about it. I chat with Grace Dean, who's wearing a truly hideous skirt with shells all over it, and meet the bespectacled, round-faced Mr. Dean for the first time. He clearly adores his wife, even though she's turned their house into a perpetual jumble sale. I discover he's the unlikely scion of the Dean family, who made their fortune in beef jerky. "Don't eat the stuff myself." He winks. "Too salty." I talk to a bunch of other people whose names I can't remember, talk until my throat's scratchy and my cheeks ache from smiling, until I have to sit down on the bottom step of the staircase and catch my breath.

Teeny plops down next to me. "Make a wish." She holds up the piece of cake.

"There's no candle." I point out. "And it's not my birthday."

"So?" She frowns, making me feel like a spoilsport. And maybe I am. I've gotten into the habit of expecting the worst.

"I wish for you to have the best day ever," I finally reply. "What do you wish for?"

"I wish for angels to come down and guide us so that nothing bad will happen ever again." She says this with utter conviction.

"Did you make that up?" I look into those breathtaking eyes of hers, angel eyes some might say.

"Uh-huh." She mumbles through a mouthful of cake.

I wonder where she learned about angels. It's not as if Meghan's big on church. Probably the TV again. THE 700 CLUB. Oh, well, it doesn't matter. I smile in spite of myself, because it's a message that's hard to top.

Teeny offers the plate to me. "Want a bite?" She lifts the fork to my lips.

The cake's so sweet it makes my teeth ache, but we can't stop eating it, because it's light as clouds. We swipe frosting on each other's cheeks, threatening to start a full-fledged food fight, but someone turns up the music just in time and we're dancing, crazy dancing, Teeny and me and everybody else, so crazy I tell myself I didn't see Ray leave, or my sister, crazy until it's time to stagger to the car and go home, just Teeny and Si-si and Mama and me, because Meghan has already left without us.

"Where is she?" I yawn. Teeny slumps against my shoulder, snoring lightly. Si-si sleeps in her car seat.

"She was tired and called it a night," Mama says. "I told her she could leave the girls with us. She's been working so hard. I wanted to give her a break."

I'm too tired to ask her just how many breaks Meghan needs, how Meghan got home and where she might have gone beforehand. I feel Teeny's warm breath on my arm, and I wonder if she's dreaming of angels, with that sweet smile on her lips and her little hand in mine.

CHAPTER 8

At first, in the days following the party, I drifted around Funkified, unable to concentrate, thinking about missed opportunities, about Ray.

"You know," David whispered in my ear, "he frequents the Fillmore on Thursday nights."

I feigned ignorance. "Who?"

He gave me a knowing smile and shook his head.

I never did find out the story with Meghan and Ray. Meghan said there wasn't one. We found her asleep on the couch when we came home after the party, which seemed to substantiate her claim, though it made me wonder if she'd hit the bottle when I wasn't looking. I leaned over and smelled her breath. Her eyes fluttered open, then closed, giving me a scare, as if I were a cop whose cover had been blown. She didn't remember me being there; at least, she didn't say anything about it the next morning.

By the end of the week, the memory of the party fades. I have new concerns about my sister's behavior, relating not to stealing men but actual goods. Hints of deception fall like rain. Not a downpour, but a few drops here and there. The type of furtive precipitation that makes you pause and try to catch the sky in the act of pulling a fast one, which is harder than it sounds, because when you hold out your hand to catch whatever falls, you have to be in the right place at the right time.

I begin to suspect that certain items have gone missing. At first, I think they're merely misplaced. *Oh, it'll turn up. Or, what did I do with that hairbrush, anyway?* There isn't any logic to it. It's as if an invisible vacuum is sucking things up without regard to taste or need. A fork, a pair of socks, an earring. All of it going to fill a void. Or a pawn shop.

Then, suddenly, the clouds of doubt get heavy enough and it rains. I'm drenched, in the thick of it again. I suppose I knew it was coming, somewhere, down inside. Or that's what I tell myself, when I look around, bewildered, itemizing all that's been taken. It's a clean sweep, including Ginga's ring, even the jewelry collection I've been working on.

Meghan had left early that morning, ostensibly for her shift at the bakery. She wore a baggy barn coat, because she said she was cold. Now I wonder what she'd crammed in the pockets, if she had headed to the addict's fall-back money source, the Hock It to Me, to get what she could, making us the pawns in her pawn game. As I wait for Mama to return from her shift, the usual graveyard, it's hard to act as if everything's normal. I want to call her at work. I want to scream and yell. Teeny steals glances at me as we play another round of Go Fish, then Candy Land, the game that lasts forever. I'm beginning to hate Grandma Nut.

Mama doesn't walk in until lunch time, as I ladle out alphabet soup, Teeny's favorite, into bowls. I set them on the table hard enough to cause mini-tsunamis, liquid slopping over the rims and onto the plates.

Mama drapes her cardigan and purse over the back of a chair. "What's wrong?"

I eye Teeny slurping broth and motion with my head for Mama to follow me into the hall. "Meghan's been stealing from us."

Mama doesn't say anything. She's either blind or in denial.

I feel the anger that's been simmering in me all morning come to a boil. "Don't tell me you haven't noticed."

Mama shakes her head. "She wouldn't, not this time. She's getting better." She wants it to be different, because she knows we're reaching the end of the line and she can't bring herself to find out what that means.

"That's what she wants us to think," I say. "Have you checked your credit cards lately?" Meghan has swiped them on previous occasions.

Mama goes into the kitchen and gets her wallet. Her hands tremble as she opens the clasp. "It's got to be in here somewhere."

"What are you looking for, Grandma?" Teeny asks.

"Nothing, hon," Mama says. "Enjoy your lunch. You don't want your soup to get cold."

I cross my arms over my chest.

"Maybe she borrowed it," Mama says weakly.

"That would be one way of putting it," I say. "F.Y.I, my jewelry collection is gone too."

"She wouldn't take that. She knows how much it means to

you." Mama's shoulders slump, and I feel bad for dumping this on her, but not bad enough to stop. "Someone must have broken in," she continues, talking more to herself than me. "It couldn't have been her."

"Maybe. Maybe. Listen to yourself." I clench my hands into fists. I want to hit something.

Mama gives me a sorrowful look, like a saint on a prayer card who's about to get burned at the stake or endure pain, making the ultimate sacrifice, for someone else's salvation. "You don't have to take that tone with me."

"Grandma—" Teeny calls.

"Just a second, hon."

"Somebody has to do something," I hiss like a cornered snake, spewing poison. "We can't go around with our eyes closed. We can't let her walk all over us. She has to be held accountable for once."

Mama rubs her forehead. "You shouldn't be so quick to judge."

"And you shouldn't be so quick to make excuses for her," I lash out.

She gives me a cold, measuring look. "You think you have all the answers, don't you?"

"I never said that."

Her eyes shine. "I do the best I can."

Oh, Jesus, not tears. "I know."

She takes a long, ragged breath. "I'll go to the bakery and talk to her. I'm sure it's a misunderstanding."

"Grandma. Did I spell a word?" Teeny's spoon clinks against the bowl as she fishes for the right letters.

"You've had a long night," I say. Which is true. But I also don't trust her to say what has to be said. "I'll go."

"Grandma—"

In the kitchen, we stand over the soup bowl as if it will give us an answer to our problems. A fly lands on a piece of bread, buzzing dully, scavenging. The clock on the wall hums louder as it makes a final push to the next minute.

"What does it say?" Teeny takes a sip of milk, licks the white mustache off her upper lip.

"XLICKSA," Mama replies.

"Oh," Teeny nods. "That's a new city under the sea, kind of like Atlantis, but older. I think Mama's been there."

She probably has. Drugs can take her—the ultimate frequent flier—anywhere.

I drive Mama's VW Bug, not the most serious car for this type of undertaking, but it's all we have, to the bakery in such a fury I almost take out a parking meter—and Ray as he walks along the sidewalk.

"Couldn't get enough, huh?" I taunt, still thinking he'd made a move on her. Everybody wants Meghan—wants to love her, wants to forgive her. Me? I want to wring her neck.

He looks down at the bag of donuts, with its bull's-eye of grease on the bottom, then back at me.

"You know what I mean." I want to grab the bag and trample the cakey morsels to crumbs.

"No, I don't." He stares at me, bewildered. "What's the matter?"

"Never mind." I push past him. "I need to talk to my sister."

"I don't think she works there any more," he says. "Hasn't for about a week."

The sympathetic smile he gives me is more than I can bear. I crumple on the curb and put my head in my hands. God damn her anyway. God damn her to hell. "I suppose you'd know."

"Not that it's any of your business, but I came for the donuts, not your sister," he tells me.

I kick a lipstick-rimmed cigarette butt—hers?—down a storm drain. "That's what they all say."

"Listen. I don't need that kind of shit in my life." He sits next to me. "I have a brother like that already."

"Congratulations." Why is it that people want to trade on their misery as if it were a baseball card? My Jackie Robinson has more value than your Joe DiMaggio. My brother's addiction is worth more pain than your sister's. "Don't you have somewhere you need to be?"

"Yeah. Right here." He bends himself, as if he's a folding chair, into the spot next to me.

I can't sit still. "Look. I don't have time for this right now. I have to go. I have to find her."

His eyes don't leave my face. "You can't keep rescuing her."

His scrutiny unnerves me. "I'm not going to. I just want my stuff back." I'm tired of her stealing from me.

I expect him to leave.

He doesn't.

We face each other, not speaking. A loose strip of metal clangs against the ironworks at one of the abandoned mines. The hot wind blows pale dirt down the sidewalk into shifting sand paintings, scouring, eroding. It tugs at his shirt, at my hair. It won't let up.

Neither will he.

"Why are you still here?" I snap.

He's unflappable. "Because you need me, Erin."

"Like hell," I growl, adding "I never told you my name."

He doesn't move. He seems to have all the time and patience in the world. "Your sister called you that at the party."

I roll my eyes, anger fizzling to a puff of smoke. "Well, get in." I jerk my head toward the car. "If you're coming." I figure he'll back off. Who'd want to ride with a ranting bitch like me?

But he slides in beside me, knees nearly touching the dash, and holds out the bag. "Donut?"

I spy Bone in his usual spot. "Wait here," I say to Ray. I don't need an entourage. Bone won't like it. He'll clam up or skulk away. He's selective about who he talks to. "I'll be right back."

"Whatever you say." He takes a pair of mirrored sunglasses from his pocket and puts them on. The lenses reflect my face. I look terrible. Maybe I'll blame that on Meghan too.

The soft light of dawn has been gone for hours and hours. The sun bleeds the color out of everything, singes the tender skin of our scalps. The street's empty, which is nothing unusual. Most people conduct their lives, their business, down on the Flats, where discount stores and new housing developments spread like a bad rash. In this part of town, the bugs don't even have enough energy to move, not on a day like this.

Bone has a new cut above his lip. Someone must have jumped

him. Or it could have been the other way around. He's got some fight left. "She didn't settle down, huh?" he asks. He smells worse than usual, a combination of the rankest b.o. imaginable and booze. He doesn't bathe much, claims he's being European. Besides, personal hygiene costs money. Money he doesn't have, because whatever he gets goes for another bottle.

"You knew she wouldn't, Bone."

He glances at the car, his eyes reptilian. Ray taps his fingers on the door, watching me, watching him. "Who's the dude?" Bone flicks a cigarette butt in Ray's direction.

"A guy." I shrug. Someone had spray-painted a tag on the bricks, J-Zee, someone else the words "Flyin' High." A smear of red paint, like blood. The work of some of my buddies, proba-bly. I keep wondering when they'll get caught.

"I figured that out." Bone chews the inside of his cheek, med-itative. "You should marry him."

"What?" I pull back. "Where did that come from?"

"I didn't mean now. Some day." Even though he has a bottle of Olde English Malt protruding from his army coat pocket, he has a way of speaking that makes him sound like a prophet. Wisdom and disillusionment bound together, a two-for-one sale. "You can't stay mad at the world forever."

"You should heed your own advice." If you look hard enough, you can still see the potential in him. I can't stop myself from saying it this time: "You're better than this."

He takes a long swig and wipes his mouth with the back of his scarred hand, fingernails dirt-encrusted, broken. He doesn't have much left in the bottle, only an inch or two. He starts early, never stops. "So they say."

Bits of dirty paper lie scattered on the sidewalk. Someone's old receipts for dry cleaning and groceries, vestiges of the life he doesn't have, that he uses for scratch paper.

"You writing again?" He used to let me read his work once upon a time. It was out there. But it was beautiful. You couldn't say he lacked for talent.

Bone stuffs the papers in his pockets before I can see what he's written. "Chicken scratch, mostly," he coughs. He always has a cough. "Tends to sound profound when you're wasted. Like crap when you're not."

I shift my position. Broken glass crunches underfoot, a kaleidoscope of brown and green and blue. "The college would readmit you." He'd gotten a scholarship. They said he was brilliant. Like an exploding star.

He gives me a weary smile. "How many life preservers you got with you today?"

I look at him quizzically.

He lights a cigarette. It takes him a couple of tries before he succeeds. He has a bad case of the shakes. " 'Cause it's hard to save more than one person at a time."

"Stubborn bastard." I take a deep breath of the alley, the stink of urine and garbage. "Just tell me what you know."

"Not much more than you." He blows smoke. He's good at that. "She doesn't hang with me any more. She runs with the big boys, the ones with the right connections, who can get her what she thinks she needs."

I tug at his sleeve. "She took some of my stuff."

He raises his eyebrows. "Uh-oh. Stealing from family. That's about as low as you can go."

"Well?" I don't blink.

He stretches his arms in front of him, a sleep walker, lets them fall slack at his sides. "Word is, she's hanging with some out-of-towners."

I wait a couple of beats. "Who?"

"Don't know much about 'em. I'm not one for mixing, at least not when it comes to people, present company excepted," he says. "But I suspect they aren't exactly gentlemen, if you get my drift. You'd best stay out of it."

I wait a couple beats more. It isn't wise to rush him. "Where?"

"You ask too many questions." He pulls his hat down lower on his head, retreating from the world, from me. "They're the types that if they want to, they'll find you. Not the other way around." He clamps his mouth shut. He's done.

I wait for a minute, but he shuffles away, steadying himself against the brick wall. I know better than to follow him. I'm shut out, for now. All I can do is stalk off in frustration.

"Go on home and forget about them," he calls after me. "Forget about her."

It isn't as simple as that. I wish it were.

"You look like a cop with those things on," I harp at Ray when I get in the car. The vinyl seat burns through my pants. My wet rag of a shirt clings to my back. It's one extreme or the other around here, too hot or too cold. There's no in-between.

"They keep out the glare." He touches the rims. "Any luck?"

"Nada." I start the engine, which pings and misses like a washed-up mariachi band.

"Who was that guy?" Ray gestures toward Bone as he rounds the corner and disappears.

"Someone my sister knows. Or used to know." I wipe the sweat from my forehead with the back of my hand.

He glances at his watch.

"Need to get back?" Part of me wants him to go, part of me doesn't.

"Probably. The guys will wonder what's happened to me."

The steering wheel sears my hands. I steer with my fingertips until I get used to the heat of it. "You should probably do a lot of things."

"Careful you don't cut yourself with that sharp tongue of yours."

Out of the corner of my eye, I see he's looking at me with amusement. "Where can I drop you?" I ask.

"Why does that sound like a rejection?" He rests his left hand on the back of the seat, not quite close enough to touch me, adding: "At the mine."

"What about your car?" I remind him. He must have driven one to the bakery. It's too far for him to have walked.

"I'll get it later." He sprawls on the seat. It's a small car and he takes up a lot of room.

We drive in silence. The tiny dice on my keychain tick against the dashboard. The engine rattles again.

"You need a tune-up." He lays his other arm on the edge of the open window. He makes himself seem as if he belongs here next to me. He has long, supple limbs, the type that could wrap around anything.

I narrow my eyes.

"I meant the car." He shrugs. "Someone as young as you shouldn't be so cynical."

"You an expert on everything?" I blink. Something's gotten in my eye. I don't want him to think I'm getting emotional. About her.

About him.

"Nope. Just toxic waste."

There's plenty of that around here.

I crank the wheel hard to the left, throwing him against the door. He grins sheepishly as we roar up the chalky, gnawed hills to the site. I guess I'm trying to shake him up or get him mad, but he won't bite, not even a little nip. "Here?" I stop alongside the precipice. Any closer and we'll go over. Another test.

He doesn't flinch. "This'll do. I'll take the shuttle down. The guys are waiting for these." He shakes the donut bag and motions toward the truck idling at the top of the service road that spirals a mile deep to the bottom. "You'd better watch it when you leave. You're pretty close to the edge."

He's got that right.

"I can handle it," I reply.

He gets out of the car and surveys the pit with a pair of binoculars he's taken from his backpack. "Another goose has been cooked. Look." He pokes his head back in the passenger window and hands the binoculars to me.

I sweep the lenses down the side of the pit. I feel as though I'm falling without a parachute. Everything's blurry until I hit the bottom, where a white-feathered body floats on the dull orange surface. It isn't the only one. "Are you going to fish them out?"

"No point. The chemicals will do the job in a couple of days," he sighs. "Where else will you look for her?"

I stare at the binoculars in my hands, as if they'll help me spot my sister more easily. Then I turn my gaze to the raw-cut hills. "Maybe Bone's right. Maybe I should stop. It's not as if it'll change anything."

He stays quiet. Perhaps he knows better than to reply. Bits of grit sting my arm. A tumbleweed rushes by en route to oblivion. *Tell my sister I'm looking for her,* I almost call after it. *Tell her there's nowhere to hide.* When I finally do speak the wind nearly carries my words away. "We could cancel the Visa card." That would be easy. Canceling other things wouldn't be.

The guy driving the shuttle truck honks. A light on top of the cab revolves and flashes, lending the vehicle a sense of urgency and importance. The driver has a flushed, fleshy face, like a lump of Teeny's Play-Doh, beneath a yellow hard hat that won't provide enough protection if something big falls on him. He honks again.

"That's my cue." Ray hesitates, then, when I don't reply, pats the door and pushes off. "See you around."

I don't trust myself to say anything. I reverse, forgetting to look where I'm going, and it's pure luck I don't slide into the Pit. Ray starts toward me, then stops. From the expression on his face, I guess I scared the heck out of him. But he realizes I'm in the clear and he grins as I speed away, gravel flying out from the wheels. I steal a glance at him in the rearview mirror, see him staring after me in the haze of dust I've kicked up. He isn't my type at all. He wears plaid, button-down shirts and jeans and cowboy boots. He's too old and too bossy and he seems to think he knows things about me that I don't even know myself.

I turn the corner as he raises his hand to wave.

By the time I get home, Meghan and Mama are chatting at the kitchen table as if nothing's happened. My sister's got guts to come back after robbing us blind, I can say that much for her.

"How was your bakery shift?" I say acidly.

"Fine." Meghan takes a sip of coffee, not that caffeine can give her much of a jolt. She's used to stronger substances.

I press my lips together. "I didn't see you there today."

"Honey—" Mama seems to sense where this is going.

"That's because I'm working in the back now," Meghan explains.

"Ray said you haven't been there for a week."

"Honey—" Mama says again, more sharply this time, letting me know she's the mother and she'll handle it.

I ignore her.

"What, you've got spies following me now? Who the hell is Ray?" Meghan's eyes narrow as she drums red-painted finger-nails on the table.

I'm not letting her off this time. "The guy from the party."

She looks at me blankly.

"Tall. Works at the mine?"

"Honey, that's enough." Mama folds her lips into a thin line.

"Oh, the rock guy." Meghan adopts Mama's expression, a united front, as though I'm in the wrong, not her. I hate it when they mirror each other like that. "What does he have to do with anything?"

I don't appreciate the way they're looking at me. It makes me feel shut out. "You didn't answer my question."

"Geez. I got promoted last week." She picks up the telephone receiver. "Here. You want to call? I'll dial the number for you."

"Are you done now?" Mama takes the phone from Meghan and sets it down hard enough for the ringer to make a pinging sound. She's talking to both of us, but mostly to me.

"What about our stuff?" I direct the question to Mama.

"The card was in the bottom of my purse. If you look around more carefully, I'm sure the jewelry will turn up. It wouldn't be the first time we've misplaced something."

Yeah, we misplaced something all right—our trust.

I cast a sideways glance at Meghan. She has an innocent expression on her face.

Maybe she really hasn't done anything.

Maybe it's me who's wrong.

That night, Alex comes over while I'm watching the kids. Mama's at work. Meghan's supposedly at her AA meeting. Si-si snoozes in her cradle, which I put in the half-closed closet so Teeny can play quietly in the bedroom. Alex and I are in the living room, munching Bugles. She's wearing a T-shirt that says "No, and that's final" and a pair of cut-offs. My top has a rodeo queen with the words "Rhinestone Cowgirl" on the front. I like

Alex's better. I should wear it when Meghan's around, or better yet, give it to her. She's the one who needs to *just say no*. What a stupid phrase. As if it's ever that easy.

Alex slips Bugles on her fingers like claws and wiggles them at me. "I forgot how good these are. I haven't had them since I was a kid."

"Me neither. But now that we have kids in the house, we have lots of fun food. Fun everything. Fun-fun-fun."

"Are you going crazy?" She tries to stick a Bugle on the end of her nose. It falls off.

"A little. A lot. It's them. It's Meghan. It's how my mother acts. It's everything." I put Bugles on each side of my head and make devil horns. "It's hell."

"You need to get out of here." Alex crunches.

I buzz my lips, attempting to play reveille on a cracker without success.

"You've got the best shot of any of us," she reminds me. "You should take it." It's not as if Alex doesn't have talent. She takes a camera with her wherever she goes, documenting our lives. Someday, she wants to have her own studio. But she's going to open it here. I mean, she got homesick whenever we went away to camp as kids. She still does, even when we hit the road for concerts. A week is her limit. Then she has to come back.

Me, though. I could actually leave—if Meghan and the girls hadn't crashed into our lives. "I don't know. Things are so mixed up. I feel like Meghan is all I ever talk about. Blah-blah-blah." I put a pillow over my head. "Next."

"How about the wedding?" she snickers. "That's what

everyone else can't stop talking about. Or Lisa anyway. She's totally freaking."

I peek at her and groan.

She raises an eyebrow. "You get your shoes dyed yet?"

"Yeah. But I'd rather die than wear that stupid outfit." Pepto-Bismol pink everything. Yuk.

"You're gonna have to on Saturday, or Lisa will disown you." She laughs. "Hey, I know. We'll burn them afterward, have a big bonfire up at the 'M'."

"I was going to give them to Teeny for dress-up clothes." I rest my feet on the coffee table, next to issues of *Lucky* (mine) and *National Geographic Traveler* (Mama's—she likes to dream about traveling, even though she never goes anywhere).

"Lisa better not find out. She'll go ballistic." Alex tosses a Bugle in the air and catches it in her mouth.

"She'll never know." I wind a curl of hair around my finger and let it spring loose. "She never comes over any more. She's too tangled up with Dillon."

"Speaking of romance, Lisa said she saw you with some guy on Main the other day." Alex shoots me a sly look.

"Meow. You guys are such gossips." I smirk. "Who? Bone? You know what a hot love life I have."

"N-o-o-o." She draws out the word, her voice high and musical. "An out-of-towner with mirrored shades."

"Oh, him." I scoff. "Ray."

"Tell." She turns to face me, legs folded underneath her.

"He's just some guy I met at the Double Ds' party." I shrug. "I ran into him again while I was trying to find Meghan."

She grins at me. "Then why is your face turning red?"

"Look. He's too old——" I shake my head.

Alex doesn't give up. "What? Like 28?"

"I don't know." I'm getting flustered. "And besides, he'll be leaving."

"Even better. Go with him." She claps her hands.

"What's gotten into you?" I throw the pillow at her.

"I'm trying to help you see the possibilities." She rests a hand on my arm, serious now. "Geez, if I didn't know better, I'd think you wanted me to leave."

"Are you kidding? You're the only person around here who keeps me sane. It's just that you could really do something, Erin. The rest of us don't have the prospects or the talent. Don't get me wrong. I'm at peace. This is the place I was meant to be. But I'm not sure it's the place for you."

"Sometimes I feel like I'm an airplane taxiing down the runway and I can't lift off," I admit.

"You will," she says. "I know it." Then, "Did you get his number?"

"No."

She rolls her eyes. "What am I going to do with you, girl? Does he hang out at the Fillmore? You should go down there later, when you're done baby-sitting."

I crunch another Bugle. "Maybe I will."

Alex leaves at nine. She's meeting the guys for another attempt to climb the Mary statue on the ridge. I go upstairs to tuck Teeny in. I want to get some work done on the collection. I bought new beads and wire this afternoon.

Teeny must not have heard me coming, because when I open the door, she acts guilty and hides her hands behind her back.

"What you got there, Teens?" I ask, my voice low. I don't want to wake Si-si.

"Nothing." Her lower lip trembles. She nudges something under the bed with her heel.

I crouch down, and there, jammed under the frame, is my jewelry box. Teeny also has a strand of beads in her hand and Ginga's ring on her finger. I grit my teeth, trying not to get angry. "How long have you had these?"

She shrugs and stares at the floor, drawing invisible circles in the carpet with her toe.

"I've been looking all over for them." I think of how I accused Meghan. "You can't take things from people like that."

"I wanted to make something pretty." She still won't look me in the eye.

"Then you should have asked me. You don't understand. This is my life. This is my ticket out of here." My pulse pounds in my temples, face reddening from the effort of keeping my voice down.

Teeny considers the box of beads, probably wondering how somebody's life could fit inside. "Where are you going?"

I don't know what to say. Her eyes. God, her eyes, so wide and hopeful and innocent, in spite of everything.

"Can I come with you?" she asks.

I need space. I need room to breathe. "Just give me my stuff back, okay? I have lots of work to do. Some of us have to work, you know."

Teeny looks down at the small noose of elastic thread onto

which she'd strung three cerulean beads. "I wanted to make Si-si a bracelet."

I don't acknowledge the thoughtfulness of the gesture, only the stupidity of it, which is unfair, given that Teeny is only five, but I'm so annoyed I can't stop myself. "Si-si's too little for bracelets. She'll choke on the beads."

Teeny's eyes fill with tears. Feeling bad now, I follow her down the hall as she goes to the bathroom, but she doesn't turn around. She drags her footsteps, a criminal headed for the electric chair. She brushes her teeth without my having to tell her, then scoots past me and crawls into bed, making herself as small as she can beneath the sheets. She doesn't ask for a story. She doesn't ask for anything. She pulls the ring on a musical toy, one of those ducks that's really for babies. She asked Mama to buy it for her at Wal-Mart. The sweet tinkle of its music carries down the hall: *These are a few of my favorite things.*

I hover outside the room, wanting to go in, wanting to stay out.

Meghan's favorite things are drugs.

I don't know what mine are. Something intangible. Like freedom.

And Teeny?

She's not telling. She closes her eyes and pretends to sleep.

CHAPTER 9

Just past 1 A.M., the phone rings. Night after night, it rings in my dreams—the call that came from the hospital, the one that informed us my father was dead. Is it all in my head? Who could it be? My father? One of Meghan's druggie friends? A battalion of telemarketers raising funds for the Fireman's Ball or offering something for free—oh, those hidden costs—or promising snake-oil cures or requesting donations for Community Services for the Blind. What they don't know is that we're blind too, because we refuse to see what's right in front of us.

Sometimes I open my eyes to that ringing and realize yes, it really *is* happening this time. By the time I get to the phone, whoever it is has already hung up—or they do, once they hear the sound of my voice. No one else stirs. Mama doesn't notice. She sleeps so deeply it's like she's underwater. Me, I've always been a light sleeper, attuned to every change in the atmosphere, every ghost.

Bring. Bring. Bring. Tonight I'm fully awake. I have my chance. When I slip down the hall, I pass by Meghan's open door, see her rumpled bed sheets. I tiptoe downstairs, avoiding the creaky spots, as if I'm walking on coals, not carpet. The door to my father's study is ajar, and I see a slice of my sister— her profile, a bird-boned hand gripping the receiver, the sharp line of her shoulder. Her hair tumbles over her shoulders like bits of frayed rope, ends split and dry. Once, everything about her had been smooth—her skin, her life. Eons ago. We might as well be talking about the Pleistocene Epoch.

"I know. I know. I don't have it. I told you. . . . No. I don't care." She gnaws her fingernail. "Look, don't call me here any more, okay? It's not— Yeah. Tomorrow. . . . I won't."

I push the door open with my toe. "Who was that?"

She whirls around. "Shit. You scared me."

"Sorry," I say, my voice flat.

She glances down at the phone, then back at me. Phone, me, phone, me. Trying to come up with a likely explanation. "It's not what you think."

"Uh-huh." I stare at her, waiting.

She goes for the defensive feint. "Aren't I allowed some privacy? It's my life."

"Now that you're back here, it's ours too." Our lives keep intersecting, like a convoluted freeway interchange, all of us tearing around at a hundred miles per hour, screaming at each other to get out of the way.

"I'm clean. You know I am." Yes, her eyes are clear. Yes, she doesn't have the shakes any more. Yes, she seems to have pushed down her need, her rage, whatever it is that drives her, so we're lulled into believing that we aren't in the middle of a hurricane any more. The thing is, I suspect we're in the eye—where it's deceptively quiet and you think you're safe, until you try to get out. Then, everywhere you turn, it's a tempest. It's hell.

I sigh. I'll be convinced when her sobriety lasts more than a week, a month, a year.

She takes a different tack. "You like this, don't you?"

"What do you mean?" I lean against the door frame.

"Sitting in judgment." Spit flies from her mouth. Flecks of it gleam, briefly, in the lamplight before falling to the floor. "Maybe I'll give you a big ol' throne for Christmas."

I consider the Christmases she hasn't shown up. "Are you planning on actually coming this year?"

"I told you. I got stuck in the snow."

"Yeah. I bet you did." The type of snow she gets stuck in has nothing to do with the weather.

"I don't like what you're insinuating." She narrows her eyes. "It's not as if you're an angel, kegger-girl."

"I never said I was." The difference being, I apparently haven't inherited the addiction gene. I never get completely wasted. My body won't let me. It has built-in limits. A guy once told me that I had the most non-addictive personality of anyone he'd ever met, one of those backhanded compliments you're not sure how to take. At the time, it almost seemed like an insult. Now, I'm not so sure. "You haven't answered my question."

"It was a friend from California, wondering how I'm doing." She picks at the torn hem on her T-shirt, a souvenir from a metal concert. She's a head-banger all right. "I didn't have a chance say good-bye."

"Why not?"

"We didn't cross paths. He was out of town." She yawns. "Look. It's late. If the interrogation is over, I need to get some sleep."

I make a sweeping gesture with my arm, as if I'm directing traffic, thinking, *you've made your bed, go ahead and lie in it*, and *why don't you tell your fucking friends not to call so late*, but I only say "Good night," because I can't handle another argument.

I follow her upstairs.

"Nite." She closes her door, which still has the porcelain sign with "Meghan" on it, decorated with flowers, from when we were kids and liked to have our names on everything, to establish ownership, to show we mattered.

I think about knocking, because I'm not satisfied. I suppose when it comes to her, I never will be—which is my problem, not hers. The strip of light at the bottom of the door disappears. Within minutes, she'll be breathing heavily.

And me, I'll lie awake until dawn, listening for the phone to ring.

I stumble through the next morning in a fog. Meghan's used to keeping late hours. She isn't as dragged-out as I am. Playing the perfect mother, she says she's going to take the girls to the park. Whatever.

After I get dressed, I head for the Perkatory Coffeehouse. I need a shot of espresso. I feel like a zombie.

The Perkatory is home of the Hellfire Roasted Bean and the best devil's food cake this side of the Rockies. The interior is painted red and the décor includes such artistic touches as devil-horn and pitchfork coat hangers. The morning rush, such as it is, has dropped off by the time I drag my sorry ass over there.

"Hey, girl." Alex grins when she sees me. "Late night, huh?"

"You could say that." I yawn.

"You go down to the Fillmore?"

I shake my head.

"Jesus, Erin." She rolls her eyes. "You got to be more proactive."

"Big word."

"It's the word of the day." She has one of those rip-off-the-page-as-the-day-goes-by-and-improve-your-vocabulary calendars at home. "What'll you have?"

"A double tall." My usual.

"I bet you will." She laughs. "C'mon. Something must have happened for you to look this wiped."

"Nothing exciting." I fill her in on the phone incident.

"What does your mom say?" she asks as she cleans spills around the machine.

"She's either working, dead to the world," I run my finger around the rim of the cup, "or in denial."

"Bummer." Alex tosses the rag into the sink and grabs another. She has to look busy or the owner, Eric, will chew her out. "Where's she now?"

"We all have the day off. She's walking with Pen." They power-walk the hills of Butte most Sundays after mass, talking non-stop the entire way. (I overslept and missed mass. I wonder if I would have seen Ray if I'd gone.) Pen has had a lot to say lately. She's been working through a nasty divorce with her dentist husband, who'd left her for his dental hygienist. Pen made a series of balloon faces from condoms and tied them to the fence line of their love nest. She called the balloons the fuckheads— because he was one. He didn't like the housewarming present and told her to get rid of them. So she brought a knitting needle and popped each one, leaving their deflated sacs behind.

"And the Meg-ster?" Alex swipes the cloth over the counter.

I blow on my espresso and take a tiny sip. "She went to the park with the kids."

"Sounds like something a good mother would do."

I lick the foam from my lip. "It does, doesn't it? And now I'm going to be a good auntie and check on them."

"You going on the climb tonight?" Our buds continue to undertake climbing expeditions throughout the greater metropolitan area. The guys usually do one a week. "Matt thinks there's treasure down shaft 16. It's probably an excuse to leave another tag." He's still in a graffiti phase, the goal being to leave his tag on as many places as he can before he leaves to fight fires in Idaho.

"Dunno. Maybe. Call me." I pass the display of Perkatory T-shirts with "The Devil Made Me Do It" and "Hotter Than Hell" printed on the front.

Shaft 16. The one I tried to go down when I was a kid.

The one Meghan saved me from.

They've fancied the playground up since Meghan and I were little. The place used to consist of a slide that clattered like a tin pan and seared our skin on hot days, a rusted cage of a monkey-bar set, and a couple of half-splintered swings kids used to fight over, because they were better than nothing, even if they gave you splinters in your butt. There are six swings now. The slide is molded plastic, part of a climbing structure with a pirate motif. Yo-ho would approve.

Teeny's swinging, stretching her toes to the sky. Si-si cycles her arms and legs in a baby swing. She can't make herself go, and her face is turning red. She'll scream any minute.

Meghan is nowhere in sight.

I run across the field, stirring the dust. "Hey, girls."

"Hey, Auntie Erin." Teeny grins at me. She seems to have forgotten about me being mad about the beads, thank God. I'm still feeling bad that I lost my temper.

"Where's your mom?" I ask.

Teeny clutches the chain with one hand and points to an alley with the other. "Over there."

Okay, I'm pissed off. I don't know what to do. Si-si's contorting her face, ready to blow. I give the swing a push to calm her down. Her face relaxes and she coos. That's all she wanted—the pressure of a hand on her back, to fly, with the knowledge that someone would be there to catch her.

I don't want to leave them alone while I go yell at Meghan. I don't want to grab the girls and stomp over and make a scene. I guess that means I'll wait until she's done with whatever she's doing. I can't see what that is, other than she's talking to a couple of guys, who I can't see clearly because they're just far enough away for me not to be able to make out their features.

Teeny soars higher, higher. "Are you sad, Auntie Erin?"

She's too intuitive for her own good. "No," I lie. "Why?"

"I don't know." She kicks her legs, forward and back, forward and back.

I get seasick watching her. Yo-ho would be disappointed. I wouldn't last a day on the high seas.

A sprinkler head spits a thin stream of tepid water, which the grass ignores, determined to die. Or maybe the grass has a talent for playing dead, and if we ever get a good, hard rain, it'll spring back to life, exclaiming over the joke it played on us. Ha-ha. Gotcha. But it never rains enough, and if grass could talk, its voice would fall to a terrified whisper, considering the endless blue sky overhead, the sky that refuses to give it rain, that remains, fixedly, far away and unattainable. The dying grass, like my sister, dry to the point of desiccation, a lifeless husk, beaten to the ground, so that you think she's finally done it, that she's checked out, but she grabs your wrist and rasps, red-rimmed eyes wide enough to pop straight out. Ha-ha. Gotcha. Then a flicker of awareness, a terrified whisper, *Where am I? What happened? Don't let me die!* Like my father, reaming his insides with drink until he passes out and you think he's dead, until he mutters and snorts and sits up. Ha-ha. Gotcha. *Where am I? What happened? Don't let me die.*

But in the end that's exactly what he did.

"Can we go to Disneyland again?" Teeny interrupts my thoughts. "They have big rides."

"Sure. Some day." I squint. If only I were more farsighted, I could see what Meghan's doing.

"I wish there were big rides around here," Teeny says.

Once upon a time, there were. Once upon a time, there were a lot of things. Once upon a time, Mama was a girl and the Columbia Gardens had flowers and a midway. But the mine ate those too.

Dust devils chase each other around the deserted baseball diamond before running out of gas. "Meghan!" I yell finally. "Yo, Meghan!"

She turns and sees me, gives a friendly wave, like there's nothing wrong. The guys melt into the shadows, down the alley, back to wherever they came from. Meghan saunters across the field with that loose, loping gait of hers, the type supermodels use, all hip and swivel, taking her own sweet time. I'm here to watch the kids. She doesn't have to hurry. Mine is the hand on her children's backs, steadying them, being there for them.

As the kids swing, I approach her, getting close enough so that only she can hear. "What the hell were you doing?"

"Chill." She wards me off. "I was talking to some board-heads. They can do amazing tricks."

Skate punks. "Yeah? What kind?"

"Flips and stair descents." She mimes the moves. "They rock."

I suppress the urge to pat her down, to search her pockets for baggies. "You can't leave the girls alone like that."

"I was keeping an eye on them," she says. "It was only for a minute."

Anything can happen in the space of a minute. A child can cry. A child can fall. A father can have a heart attack and die. "You need to be there every second."

"I am, Erin. I am."

"Are you guys fighting again?" Teeny jumps, catches air, tumbles, dusts herself off, adding, "I'm okay." She's a tough little thing.

172

"No." It's the only word Meghan and I say in unison, that we agree on—shielding Teeny from just how mad we can get at each other.

Above us, there's a crack in the sky, a jagged line of white powder, a remnant of jetstream.

"Look. A ship's sailing in the clouds." Teeny indicates a galleon cruising west to join an armada and make rain somewhere else. "It's going to an island in the sky."

Si-si cries, the only moisture we'll see for weeks. She's had enough.

We all have.

It's time to go home.

Mama says I need to get out more, so when Alex drops by—she doesn't call first, because she knows if she does, I'll bail—she practically pushes me out the door. Maybe she wouldn't have if she'd known what we were going to do.

Alex has on jeans and a stained Perkatory T-shirt.

"You're stylin' this evening," I say as we climb into her Volvo, one of those Flintstone bubble models from the '60s with patchy green paint.

"I figured I might get dirty," she explains. "Remember, they're going down shaft 16 tonight."

The more I think about it, the stupider it sounds. I mean, I was a kid when I tried it. That was my excuse. But these guys are older. They should know better. We all should. "You going with them?"

"You're not?"

"Nah." I shake my head. Ever since that day I got trapped, I haven't liked dark, enclosed places. I'd never have made a good miner, not that it would have been an issue, since the women stayed above ground in those days. They were laundresses and seamstresses, scrubbing away the dirt, mending the holes.

"Me neither," she backs off. "We can sit there and make fun of them—and if we get bored, we can leave." She has a thing for this guy in our crew, Matt, has for years, that's why she accompanies them on raids. They'd make a good couple, I guess. He's rambunctious as an overgrown puppy, though he can be thoughtful and philosophical if you catch him in a quiet moment. Plenty of girls throw themselves at his feet, he of the shaggy brown hair and ice-blue eyes, he who could have lettered in four sports if he wasn't such a lazy-ass nonconformist. Alex stays on the sidelines, watching him go by with another babe on his arm. I keep telling her that as long as she presents herself as a buddy, he won't see her as girlfriend material, but she doesn't listen.

The engine spits like a popcorn machine. The sky's clear. We might see shooting stars if we stay up late—and stay sober— enough. We pull onto a narrow gravel road, past snarls of rusted wire and empty oil drums to the hoist house that's on the verge of collapse.

"Maybe we shouldn't go in." My heart's already pounding from the memory of the dark.

"The guys checked," Alex insists as she slams the driver's-side door. "They said it's sound."

That's not exactly reassuring. "How do they know for sure?" I ask as I get out of the car.

She stops and looks at me. "They don't. That's part of the thrill. You didn't used to be so timid, Erin."

"I'm not timid," I protest, "I'm being realistic. I mean, I don't want to die. I've got too many people depending on me."

"Listen to you. You sound like a married woman with a bunch of kids," she exclaims.

"That's what I feel like." We step over scraps of twisted metal on our way to the entrance. "Without the benefit of sex."

"We've got to do something about that." She grins.

We slip through a hole in the fence with a NO TRESSPASSING sign over it, avoiding broken glass and beer cans. Apparently, we're not the only ones who've visited this scenic spot recently.

The guys are almost ready to make their descent. "You bring the crampons, Matt?" Josh asks as he fastens his harness. He's been Matt's sidekick since kindergarten, the straight man, the hanger-on.

"Naw, the snow's gone," Matt says.

"Tampons? Is it that time of the month, Josh?" Alex teases.

"Girls," he snorts. "Don't you know anything about climbing?"

"We're social climbers, hon," I say airily.

"What's that supposed to mean?" He misses the joke.

"Skip it." I roll my eyes. "So why this shaft anyway?" There are plenty of others riddling the hillside like bullet holes.

"My great-granddad went down this mine," says Matt, "said he hit the prettiest vein he'd ever seen."

"And?" I ask. He must have squandered his wealth, because his name isn't written among those of the founding fathers.

"The shaft collapsed before they could haul the ore out," he says. "I'm telling you. This is one ass-kicking mine."

Yeah, it almost kicked my ass. But that isn't a story they remember. For them, conquering the mine isn't about family or riches, it's about balls. They like to brag that they have plenty. That's why they call themselves the Danger Rangers. They thrive on the rush, hungry for another tale to add to their personal mythology.

This time, they've had the foresight to bring headlamps, though the illumination they provide is minimal. Hitting bottom is a very real possibility, all the more unnerving because they can't actually see it. Matt isn't bothered by the risks. The others, particularly Henry, are.

"This is fucked, man," says Henry, nicknamed "Hen," as in chicken.

"Brock-brock-brock," Matt clucks at him. "Look. It's cool. We'll tie our lines and slide down, just like in *Mission Impossible*—"

"Or *Spiderman*," Josh interrupts. He saw the movie five times, as much for Kirsten Dunst as the special effects.

"Yeah, that too. Anyway," Matt continues, "then we'll leave our tag and we're out. Should take fifteen minutes, tops."

"I dunno, man. I get claustrophobic." Henry tries to cover a shudder by coughing. He's spooked bad.

I know how he feels.

"So don't go." Josh shrugs. "One less tag for you."

"Asshole." Henry doesn't back down. Preserving his pride is more important at the moment than self-preservation.

"What about us?" Alex steps forward. "Where's our gear?"

I jab her with my elbow—I'm fine where I am and don't, under any circumstances, want to go down—but she doesn't listen.

"You can watch." Matt fiddles with a carabiner.

Okay by me.

"You mean watch you make fools out of yourselves." Alex's not ready to let him go.

"Save it." He ties his line to a joist.

"Don't you mean 'save our asses'?" She's got her hip thrown out, as close to flirting as she ever gets.

He waves as he goes over the side. The others follow, cans of spray paint in hand.

"What if we get bored?" she calls after him.

"Do your nails or something." His voice echoes.

"Nobody's even going to be able to see the tags," I add. "What's the point?"

"Doesn't matter," his yells back. "We'll know it's there. We'll have made our mark."

And have something else to boast about over a keg of beer.

Alex and I sit on a rotting piece of wood. "Aren't you glad you came?" she says sarcastically.

"Like you said, at least we can give them a hard time." I swat a mosquito away. Too late. One already bit me. Hope it doesn't carry West Nile. I clench my fists in an effort to resist scratching.

"I guess." She blows a strand of hair out of her face. "So what about that guy Ray?"

"What about him?"

She nudges me. "I know you like him. When are you going for it?"

I pause for a moment, thinking of her and Matt. "When are you?"

She presses her hands between her knees. "It's not the same. He doesn't like me like that."

"It's not as if you've given him the chance to," I point out.

"I know," she says in a small voice.

"Hey!" Matt shouts before I can ask her anything else.

"What?" We get up and stare into the black pit. Headlamps glow below.

"The cords jammed." He shines his lamp in our faces.

"Turn your head." I put a hand over my eyes. "You're blinding me."

The light swings away. "C'mon, haul us up," he says.

"We're not strong enough." Alex winks at me. "We're just girls, remember?"

He groans. "I was wrong, okay? You're superwomen. You're amazons. Now, help us out."

"I dunno." Alex yawns. "Our nails aren't dry yet."

"Give us a break." Josh chimes in.

"That's tempting." I snicker.

"Please," Henry says.

He's someone I have sympathy with. I tap Alex on the arm and nod my head.

"You're pathetic, you know that?" Alex tells them. She takes one of the lines. I stand behind her. I feel like we're playing tug-of-war.

"Whose line is this? Use your feet or something," Alex grunts. "You weigh a ton."

Once Matt's grinning face appears, it's hard to resist the impulse to push him back over.

"Don't even think about it." He plants his elbows on firm ground for insurance.

"Okay, Mr. Muscle." I step away. I've had enough excitement for one night. "You can help the other guys. We're out of here."

"Where are you going?" he asks.

"Some place you're not," Alex replies.

"Oh, yeah. I'm sure he knows you like him now," I say to Alex as we head to the car.

"Some days I like him more than others—and I'm pretty sure the reality won't live up to my expectations. Love is always better in my imagination," she muses.

"You should have your own radio show." I roll down the window, hoping that the bugs won't get in once we pick up speed.

"That's me," Alex sighs. "Dr. Love."

The sky is black as a bottle of spilled ink with a few swirls of cloud spray-painted across it. Celestial graffiti in honor of the occasion. Lights shine in the houses down the hill, darkness concealing their decrepitude. As we descend, warm air blows in our faces and insects kamikaze into the windshield.

By the time I get home, it's almost midnight. "How did it get to be so late?" It wouldn't be that bad if I didn't have to work tomorrow.

"You sorry you came?" Alex asks.

I shake my head. "I always have a great time with you. Besides, I didn't realize how badly I needed to get out of the house."

"Yeah. You didn't talk about Meghan once," she says.

"Must be some sort of a record."

"I know you're trying to help her, but you have to live your own life." The radio spits static. Alex turns it off. "This town needs a new station."

"This town needs a lot of things."

"Looks like the house didn't burn down while you were gone." She grins.

"I hid the matches before I left," I joke as I slam the door.

"I'll call you tomorrow." She waves as she pulls away.

"See ya." I turn toward the dark house filled with my extended family, sleeping soundly, safely.

As I enter the hallway, the phone rings. I dash into my father's study, determined to answer it, to discover who it is.

All I get is the hollow whine of the dial tone. *Hello? Hello? Is anybody there?*

I'm never in time.

CHAPTER 10

When I walk into Funkified the next morning, David and Daniel exchange secretive smiles. They're definitely up to something. There's an unmistakable sense of anticipation in the air. Even the mannequins seem to cock their heads, listening.

After a few minutes, I can't stand it any longer. "All right. Spill." I know they want to.

"Guess who came into the store yesterday?" David can hardly contain himself. He does that flutter-lace-flutter-lace thing with his fingers, one of his nervous tics.

"I don't know. Hugh Grant." David has a huge crush on him.

"I wish." He puts a hand over his heart.

"Easy, boy," Daniel smirks, then to me, "No. As a matter of fact, it was Ray."

I blink. "How did he——? I mean, I didn't tell him where I work."

"I did." Daniel grins. "We saw him the other night at the Fillmore, and it seemed like a good opportunity to set you up."

"Set me up?" Yeah, for a fall. They wouldn't mean to, but— "You were talking about me? What did you say?" Daniel, in particular, is one of those people who has verbal diarrhea, especially once he's had a drink or two.

"Only good things." David smiles.

Ray was here. I gaze around the shop, as if it might reveal evidence of his presence. The feather boas and vintage photographs give nothing away. The mannequins, well, they're designed to look coy; it helps sell the clothes.

"When a button-down guys goes vintage to get the girl, it's gotta be love," Daniel says.

"He probably just needed a new shirt. Cheap." I head for a box of damaged garments, of which there are plenty, thanks to people who try to cram themselves into dresses that don't fit.

Relationships that don't fit.

"Nah." David flicks a duster at a display case filled with turn-of-the-century bead purses, fans, and opera glasses, accessories needed for a night on the town, from an era when people still dressed up.

If I ignore the Double Ds, they'll eventually lose interest, but I have to admit I'm curious. "What did he buy?"

"A '40s plaid shirt, natch." Daniel indicates a rack of menswear at the back of the store.

I wrinkle my nose. "Not much of a departure from his usual style." I'm trying to find things wrong with him. That he's too conservative. Too old. Too unconventionally handsome. Too—

"Maybe not," Daniel admits. "However, the choice, though safe, demonstrates taste."

"He has a good eye," David adds. "He picked you, didn't he?"

"You guys should work for the tabloids." My face is getting hot, as if I'm inside a toaster oven. The Double Ds are definitely roasting me—and enjoying every minute of it.

Daniel sings the matchmaker song from *Fiddler on the Roof*. The Double Ds are big theater fans. They hit Broadway every year and love revivals.

"I'm sorry, honey. We can't help ourselves," David says. "We want to see you happy."

"I'm not ready for a relationship right now."

"Who said anything about a relationship?" Daniel snorts. "Get out there and have some fun."

"He took one of your business cards." David taps the stack on the counter.

I'm not getting my hopes up. I mean, he was probably thinking of getting a gift for his sister or mom or something. "My jewelry designs aren't exactly his style."

"Unless he goes in for drag." Daniel strikes a pose worthy of *The Birdcage*.

"Ooh. That would be interesting." David giggles.

"Knock it off, guys." I wiggle my fingers through the split seam of a full-length velvet evening gown and shake my head. There are holes in everything today. I've got my work cut out for me.

"I doubt it's your chandelier earrings he's interested in," Daniel says.

"He's not going to call me, if that's what you mean." I dig around in the mending basket for a needle and thread.

"Five bucks says he does."

"Your loss, Mona Lisa." I smile.

• • •

An hour later, the phone rings. Daniel answers, his voice sugary, sure he knows who's calling. "Funkified. Yes, she's right here." He holds out the receiver, mouthing, "Show me the money, honey."

I throw a wadded-up bill at him and snatch the phone from his hand.

The Double Ds beat a hasty retreat to the second floor, where they pretend to sort the latest shipment from an estate in Helena. I can tell they're listening. It's too quiet up there.

I keep the conversation short. My voice is higher than usual. I'm having trouble sounding normal. I wish I could come across as nonchalant, but I'm such a bad actress I can't pull it off. Ray wants to pick me up at the house later, but I insist on meeting him at the corner of Galena and First at 5:30 P.M. instead. He's already had a snapshot of my complicated home life. I don't want to burden him with the entire family album just yet.

"So?" David peers over the balcony after I hang up.

I feel like I'm on stage. "What?"

"He asked you out, right?" Daniel asks. Both of them are beside themselves with excitement.

"Uh-huh."

"Such an impressive vocabulary you have, Miss Mulcahy," David says.

"Let's see." Daniel rifles through a pile of lingerie and unearths a black lace bra with red bows and ribbons, and tap pants. "You could slip into these. Perfect for a special occasion."

I wave him away. "That looks like something a hooker would wear."

"Exactly." He winks.

"Jesus. It's not like I'm going to sleep with him on the first date," I exclaim.

"Pity." Daniel fingers the strap. "This'd be great. If it were bigger, I'd wear it."

I frown at him. "I don't want him to think I've got this whole seduction thing planned."

"Why not?" Daniel puts his hands on his hips. "You're way too Catholic for your own good."

"It has nothing to do with religion. It's just not me—and you know it." My voice gets quiet, my old insecurities bubbling to the surface.

"Oh, honey," David sighs. "You know we love you just the way you are. We're having a little fun, that's all."

"Yeah. Yeah. Yeah."

"Hey, that's the name of a New York band." David takes the opportunity to change the subject, so we don't get dangerously maudlin. "I've got their CD around here somewhere." He searches through his music collection. Good. Something to keep them occupied, other than bugging me.

The bra lands on my head, followed by the tap pants. "In case you change your mind," Daniel calls. "It's not like he has to see them. It's enough for you to know they're there. Trust me, sport bras don't cut it on a night like this."

I sit on the stoop of a boarded-up hotel, waiting for Ray. I'm early. I had to get away from the Double Ds. I love them, but they were making me nuts.

Bone limps up like a character in a silent film and sets to work constructing a rock cairn on the corner.

"What are you doing?" I ask.

"Making a tower to mark the way," he says. Whenever we talk, it's like we're continuing our conversation, each of us holding the opposite end of an endless strand of thread.

"To where?"

He looks at the hills. "Wherever I'm going. Wherever I've been."

"You're making even less sense than usual."

"And you're being even more of a smart-ass." He tips his hat back on his head and squints at me. "Got a hot date, huh?"

"What gave you that idea?" I'm wearing a lacy tank top and jeans, not exactly dressed-to-impress.

"With the du-u-ude." He gyrates his hips.

"Beats building cairns." I kick a pebble at him.

"There are many ways to get lost and found." He folds his hands in front of him like a circuit preacher.

"So you're finding yourself?" I shouldn't give him such a hard time, but I'm nervous about seeing Ray and it makes my sass-factor go off the charts.

"Or keeping myself from getting more lost than I already am." His hands cup dusty air.

"Is it working?" I pick at a piece of flaking paint on the door frame.

He stares at me a moment. "What do you think?" He shambles away, humming "Papa Was A Rollin' Stone" under his breath.

"Hey, Bone," I call after him, feeling bad about being such a bitch. "You rock."

He turns toward me, flashes a smile before he moves away, silhouetted against the blood-red sky. "You too, girl. You too."

A few minutes later, Ray rumbles up in a beater Land Cruiser. "I came straight from the mine. Sorry about the dust."

"Comes with the territory." I grab the Jesus bar to hoist myself inside. This isn't going to be the cushiest ride. The springs feel as if they'll pop through what's left of the upholstery, and the loose suspension jiggles me around like a pocketful of marbles.

Ray's wearing the shirt from Funkified. I can't decide if he looks cool or ridiculous. The colors do bring out his eyes, though. "Want to have a beer at the Fillmore?" he asks.

I shake my head. "My friends might be there." Certain disaster. Josh can be such an asshole when he's drunk. They all can, depending on their mood and the amount of alcohol they've consumed and what they're trying to prove.

"Don't want to be seen with me, huh?" he teases.

"No. It's not that. They can be like leeches."

He looks at me questioningly. Can't say I blame him. It did sound like a description of a scene from *Night of the Living Dead*. "What I'm trying to say is we could be stuck with them for the rest of the night."

He gives me a slow smile that lets me know he's happy I want to be alone with him. My face heats up and I have to look away, and I really wish I hadn't put on that lace bra, because it's too much too soon and it's making my boobs itch.

"How about dinner at the Great Wall?" he suggests.

I nod. Walls are good. Walls are safe. Walls keep him on one side, me on the other—where I can't make an ass of myself. I hope.

It only takes few minutes to get there. The place is busy, though not fully booked. The hostess shows us to our table, a booth shaped like a half-moon. Ray slides in next to me. My hands shake. I can barely bring a glass of water to my lips without spilling. We order beer. Maybe that will steady my nerves. I don't usually care about making a good impression, but this time, I do. I want him to think I'm smart and pretty and interesting.

Soon I'm talking, talking like I've never done before. I give him my life story—my dad, Mama, Meghan, the girls, art school, wanting to stay and needing to go. Everything recedes into the background. There's just us in this tiny Chinese universe, as if we're curled inside our very own fortune cookie. We talk as if we've known each other a long time, as if we're resuming a conversation we've been having since before we met, which doesn't make sense, logically, I know, but that's how it feels to me.

"Funny, isn't it?" he says, taking a bite of kung pao chicken.

"What is?"

"People used to come to Butte to make their fortunes a hundred years ago. Now they feel they have to go somewhere else."

"It isn't just a feeling. It's a reality," I reply. "A lot of people of my grandparents' and mother's generations left because the mines started to die."

"But your family stayed—and some people, like the Double Ds, are moving back," he says. "The town has character, a perfect sense of itself. That's hard to find these days."

"Yeah," I laugh. "It's like living in a museum. I can't imagine why someone would want to be here if it weren't in their blood."

He shrugs. "It's a good place for a rock guy—and a change from New York."

"I've always dreamed of living there." I sigh.

"It's an amazing place, but I like being somewhere I don't have to worry about locking my doors or scraping to pay the rent. Somewhere I have more room to breathe—literally, maybe because I grew up in such a big family in the Bronx." His leg is right next to mine.

"How big?" I edge closer.

"I'm one of ten kids. My room was in the closet until my older brothers started moving out of the house."

I laugh. "So how did you get interested in geology, living in the city and all?"

"We used to go to Cape May sometimes. I had a rock and shell collection I kept in a shoebox."

"So do I." Mama tried to get rid of it once when she was cleaning. I had a fit. "My sister and I kept thinking we'd find the gold our ancestors never did. We didn't have any luck, but we found a bunch of other specimens. We'd check out books from the library and go to the mining museum, trying to identify them."

"Me too. I was fascinated with learning about the way the world worked. No one else was into it, except me. A couple of my sisters are nurses. Another two are cops. Three brothers are firemen." He bit his lip, quiet for a moment.

Firemen, like my father. Ray's so pensive, something bad must have happened to them, and then a terrible thought occurs to me, one I hope isn't true, but I fear is. I rest my hand on his shoulder, ask the question, my voice hushed, even though I already know the answer. "They were part of 9/11?"

He nods. "We lost my brother, Manny. I took a leave of absence from graduate school in Colorado and moved home for a while to help my parents and get my brother Carlos out of a tailspin. He'd been closest to Manny when we were growing up, and his death hit him hard. It hit us all hard. Carlos is the one who reminds me of your sister. My parents are raising his son, because he and his girlfriend—well, you know the story."

Yeah, I do.

"We kept waiting for him to hit bottom," he continues. "We hit bottom first."

"What do you mean?"

"He set the house on fire. He didn't do it on purpose. He rarely does anything on purpose, except score. That was months ago. Now my mom refuses to let him in until he's clean." He takes a sip of beer. "It's better for me to be here. I don't know if I could shut him out."

We haven't been able to turn Meghan away. I don't know if it will come to that—or what it will take before we can.

"I'm sorry." He touches my hand. "I should be making you laugh, not making you sad."

"No. It's all right." I press his fingers. "I understand."

The waitress makes another circuit of the dining room. Even the bar is nearly deserted. We're the only ones left. It's nearly closing time.

"I should be telling you have the most beautiful eyes, the most beautiful ears." He traces my lobe with his finger.

I giggle. "Now you *are* making me laugh. My ears look like Dumbo's." I've always been self-conscious about the way they stick out. No one, and I mean no one, has ever complimented me about them before.

"They're delicate as shells." He sees beauty in places I haven't fully appreciated before. In Butte's scarred visage. In me.

After paying the tab, he takes my hand and guides me to the car. We sit in the shadows, half-lit by a street-lamp. I don't want to go home, don't want the night to end. I'm wearing seductive lingerie, but it isn't making me feel as bold as the Double Ds would have liked. "Ray—"

He puts my fingers to his lips, then releases them. "It's getting late. I should take you home."

I turn away and gaze at the sputtering neon signs. My fingers tingle from his touch. The bra itches terribly. He's such a gentleman, I don't know what to do. What would he think if I threw myself at him? That I'm a slut? Or would he be pleasantly surprised?

"When will I see you again?" he asks.

Tomorrow, I want to say, but I don't want to appear too eager, or worse, desperate. Then I think of the wedding, for which I still don't have a date. "Actually, a friend of mine is getting married this Saturday. You could come to the reception. If you want to."

He gives me an apologetic smile. "I wish I could. I have to go to Helena for a survey tomorrow. I'll be gone until Sunday morning."

"Oh." I look down at my hands, unable to hide my disappointment.

"But if you're free Sunday afternoon, we could go on a picnic," he offers.

"Around here?" Butte isn't exactly known for scenic spots.

"A secret place," he says as we pull up to our gate. "You'll like it." He starts to get out of the car, probably with the intention of walking me to the door. Even though the house is dark and it appears everyone is asleep, I don't want to risk another encounter with my sister, not yet. I lean over and kiss Ray before he can step outside. He settles back on the seat. His lips are softer than I expected. He strokes my face gently, as if I'm made of glass. "You'd better go," he says, his voice huskier this time.

"Sunday," I whisper in his ear before slipping into the night.

CHAPTER 11

The wedding day arrives. Whoopee. We, the bad-assed (or is it big-assed?) bridesmaids, cram into a meeting room at the back of the church, which is so historic it's ready to fall down. The cooked-liver smell of incense hangs in the air, the scent of unanswered prayers mingling with layers of dust. It makes me want to gag—that and the fact that we look like wads of cotton candy in our pink taffeta dresses and updos. We were planning to go to Missoula for cool off-the-rack dresses instead, something we'd have half a chance of being able to wear after the ceremony. But there hadn't been time, and the bride's mother wouldn't have gone for it anyway. She's one of those just-so people. Candy dishes filled with petrified mints on the coffee table. Not a pillow, not a hair, not one thing out of place.

"So, when are you going to see him again?" Alex says, referring to Ray.

"Tomorrow." I smile whenever I think about him, which is just about all the time, including now.

She nudges me in the ribs. "I've never seen you like this before. You've really got a thing for this guy, don't you?"

I shrug, but I'm still grinning. "Why would you say that?"

"Well." She puts her hands on her hips. "Because you've been kind of spacey lately—and you haven't been dissing him like you have every other guy you've ever gone out with. When's he meeting the family?"

"God, I don't know." I mean, in his line of work, he deals with poisons so he ought, in theory, to be able to survive such an event, but still. "What about you? Are you going to ask Matt to dance?"

"Maybe." She bites her lip. "If I get drunk enough."

"I hope the ceremony's quick," I whisper. "I don't know if I can stand for very long." The shoes—pointy pumps with four-inch heels—pinch my toes.

"Don't count on it." She snaps her gum. "They're going for the full-meal deal, remember?" She means a complete Catholic ceremony. Mass, homily, Eucharist, the works.

It's tempting to skip it and go straight to hell.

"Why did they have to make me look like a milkmaid?" Alex touches the braids wound on either side of her head. Her usually sunny personality isn't much in evidence today. She has a hangover from partying too hard last night. I went home early, wanting to dream about Ray.

"I guess they didn't know what to do with all your hair," I offer. It reaches her waist.

"We should have gone to a different salon. I mean, they made Darla's hair look like shag carpet, for Christ's sake." She frowns in the mirror. "That does it. I'm going to take this stupid hairdo out."

"Better not. Lisa will freak." I blast myself with hair spray. The nozzle's blocked. I end up pressing too hard and getting myself in the face. Great. Now my expression will be locked in place too.

"Watch it," someone says behind me, "that stuff'll blind you."

"I wish. Then I wouldn't have to see myself. I *look* like a freak." Alex takes the hair spray from me and spritzes the braids.

"You do not," I assure her.

"I've got to do something. Maybe I'll cut it off after this." She adjusts one of the pins.

I raise an eyebrow at her. "That'd be pretty extreme."

She glares at her reflection. "Well, I'm feeling pretty extreme right now."

So is the bride, but for entirely different reasons.

"I'm gonna be sick." Lisa, who's a pasty pale rather than blushing bride, grabs a wastebasket and heaves. The photographer's shutter whirs. He specializes in capturing the wrong moments. It should be quite a wedding album by the time he's done.

"You can stop taking pictures, dude." Lisa wipes her mouth with a tissue. "This is one memory I don't need preserved."

"Oh, honey." Her mother wrings her hands. She wears one of those fake Chanel suits in a hideous pale green that complements the wedding's sherbet color scheme. She keeps offering us mints, making us paranoid that we have bad breath. "Do you have a bug?"

Not the kind she thinks.

A flurry of whispers ripples among us: Is it nerves? Morning sickness?

Probably the latter. Everyone knows. It happened after the basketball championships, when we got totally wasted. Amazing more people didn't get knocked up.

"Ow!" Someone cries when a curling iron gets too close. Ringlets come at a price, usually a singed lobe. "You don't have to burn my ear off!"

We're all on edge today. Lisa's the first one of us to get married. We're sure there will be a domino effect. Some girls find the prospect exciting, determined to snag themselves a guy—any guy—as though they're storming the doors of a department store clearance sale. Me? I used to think it best to get out of the way, that it was better not to need anybody, because then nobody can leave you. After meeting Ray, I'm not sure how I feel.

One thing's for certain: I'm definitely not ready for this type of commitment.

The organ pipes its dirge. We'd better get our puffy pink butts out there. The ceremony is about to begin.

"I don't see why I had to get paired with Andrew Slack," Alex says ruefully. Andrew Slack is the center for the basketball team, and is heading to community college in the fall to improve his grades before he transfers to a university. Former Big Man on Campus. Or, as Alex says, Biggest Moron of the Century.

" 'Cause you're the tallest," I say. "It was nothing personal. It was a matter of aesthetics."

"Whatever. It's still a drag." She tucks her bra strap, which keeps slipping off her shoulder, back in place. "If he tries anything, I'll punch him."

"He won't—not on the way down the aisle in front of a hundred people." I give my skirt a yank. It won't stop riding up. Grr.

"I wouldn't put it past him." She dated him once and has despised him ever since. (She calls it a classic case of date-and-hate.) Something about him making it with another girl in the bushes when he said he was going to the bathroom. Our friend Julie saw him, because she'd been out there too—with someone else. There isn't much vegetation in Butte. Bushes are at a premium, and gossip spreads fast.

As I try not to twist my ankle in the torture-shoes, I glance at the faces in the congregation, thinking about the different pairings that have gone on over the years and that will no doubt continue for years to come. I'd never have predicted that Lisa would marry Dillon. But here they are.

And here we are. Looking like royal, dolled-up idiots.

The fact is the guys in this town don't want to get married unless they have to. They'd rather race their cars and sit around and drink beer and have sex with whoever they want, whenever they want. They're having too much fun to make a vow to somebody till death do they part.

I hold my bouquet of baby roses, their buds in tight little knots, against my chest. Lisa wanted something more exotic, but the florist botched the order and these were the only thing she had left.

"They're so pedestrian," she fumed.

They're also white and scentless, and they have the appearance of wadded-up Kleenex.

Stiff mint-green bows adorn the ends of the pews. A flower girl in a white dress whose skirt sticks straight out like a tutu, making her resemble a ballerina in search of a music box, romps down the aisle and pelts people with blossoms that have wilted in the heat and make the air smell like stale tea. She nails a lady, who's wearing a straw hat, in the eye.

The church is over a hundred years old. Some of the panes in the stained glass, which detail the Stations of the Cross, have small cracks in them. The statues of Jesus and Joseph look like they've been in a fight, their noses chipped off. The red carpet has faded to a dull salmon color in the center, marking the passage of scores of the devoted, receiving the body of Christ. Confessionals, where people have gone seeking forgiveness for over a century, flank the pews. I wonder which of my ancestors knelt behind the grill, how many Hail Marys and Our Fathers they uttered. What good it did. Maybe Meghan should try it. She's the biggest sinner in our house.

Or is she?

I wipe the sweat off the back of my neck with a tissue. The church doesn't have much ventilation. Perspiration spots wet the underarms of summer shifts and dress shirts. Older women dab at their foreheads or the shiny pates of their husbands with hankies. Others fan themselves with the program, rippling the

edges with damp fingers and warping the names of the cele-
brant, singers, and readers.

Meghan, Mama, Teeny, and Si-si sit at the back. Things have
been more strained between us lately. Meghan knows I'm
watching her and she doesn't like it. She insists she's the best
she's ever been.

Maybe she means it this time. Maybe she really can get clean.

The bakery thing's the longest she's stuck with a job. In fact,
she decorated the wedding cake, a triple-tier affair with white
icing and chocolate filling, of which she's justifiably proud. She
has talent—I just hope she didn't accidentally mix cigarette ash
in with the frosting.

Mama made the arrangements. She's known Lisa's mother
for years and suggested they use Carl's Colossal Cakes, the bakery where Meghan works. She and Mama are more acquain-
tances than friends, but close enough, I guess, for our family to
receive an invitation and Meghan a cake commission. Me being
a bridesmaid didn't hurt either. Lisa's mother has always
thought I'm a good influence, though that's almost more of an
insult than a compliment in my crowd and I begged Lisa not to
tell anybody.

The wind kicks up outside, which would be a blessing except
for the fact that it hurls fistfuls of dirt through the open windows like a dusting of light-brown face powder. The ushers
spring into action and batten the hatches, making the air inside
even more stifling. With each passing minute, the interior of the
church smells more strongly of cheap perfume, old people, and
dirty diapers.

We sashay past a constipated-looking statue of the Virgin Mary. It's tough being holy. She gazes heavenward, hands clasped.

Get me out of this church, God.

Get me out of this town.

Step together. Step. Step together. Step. Walking down the aisle seems to take forever. I'm conscious of every movement, the effort needed to adjust my balance so I don't fall on my face and ruin everything. The shoes don't help. I'm like a child playing dress-up in her mother's pumps.

My escort's Dave Brown, a local wrestling champ who aspires to become the next World Wrestling Federation champ. After the wedding, he's heading to a tryout. "I'm gonna get in my car and drive." His eyes have a faraway look. Or maybe it's the weed he smokes. He shifts his body horizontally when he walks, the way people with bulgy muscles do. It's a challenge to stay in step with him.

Alex snags her heel on the edge of the carpet and almost bites it. "Fucking shoes," she mutters under her breath.

I stifle a giggle with a coughing fit. I'm hacking and laughing so hard, tears come to my eyes. Alex's too. Everyone stares at us. I guess they think we're overcome with emotion, because some of them dab at their eyes. Oh, the memories, the memories.

The organist plays the opening chords of the bride's song. The organ sounds as if it has a sinus infection. I bite the inside of my cheek to keep from laughing again.

Everyone turns to watch the grand entrance. Lisa wrestles with her veil, which doesn't seem to want to stay on her head.

Her updo is dangerously close to coming undone. She doesn't look radiantly happy. She looks scared to death. Or maybe she's trying not to be sick.

My eyes travel over the guests, people I've known my entire life, people who've settled down. Husbands and wives and kids. Lisa's mother in the front pew, her father walking her down the aisle. Her father. We were part of a family like that once. We're a different type of family now.

Till death do you part.

In our case, death did do the parting, didn't it?

The reception lasts for hours. And hours. And hours. Weeks maybe. That's how it feels. Dry weddings are frowned upon. Same thing with funerals. Any excuse to throw a party. To raise hell. We're happy there's an open bar. Lisa's parents are blowing a bundle on this one. She's their only daughter. They're going to make this a day they'll remember. She's going to be happy forever and ever.

I'm hanging with my friends, swaying my pink-clad behind to the music of the cover band. People are getting drunk and making strange requests. *Play the one by what's his name. Hey, I just saw Elvis, I'm not shitting you!* Meghan's found a guy she likes and busts a move on the dance floor. As far as I know, she hasn't had a drink yet. I'm keeping track.

Teeny and Si-si are curled up underneath one of the tables, at Mama's feet, sleeping, while Mama jaws with Pen. Their voices hum without pause, a freeway of words. They can talk for hours without interruption once they get going. They never lack for things to say.

"Lick and Din seem happy," Pen slurs. She means Dick and Lin, who are locked hip to hip as they glide around the room, in a bizarre tango/waltz, out of step with the music and everyone but each other.

Pen's drink sloshes on the tablecloth as she sets it down. Her ex-husband and the hygienist are at the reception, a fact she pointedly ignores, except for moments, like now, when the hygienist—whom none of us are allowed to call by name— erupts with her distinctive, cackly laugh. Pen gives her a poison- dart glare. "What a fricking cliché," she mutters.

"But you're not. And don't you forget it." Mama pats her hand, charm bracelet jingling. "We should go to the spa for a weekend, just us girls."

She means Deer Lodge, where there's a hot springs resort, and a prison, though not together. Our part of the world is full of such weird juxtapositions.

Joe Flanagan approaches Mama's table. I didn't see him come in. She said he'd be arriving late, because he had to deal with a rock slide that had blocked a highway. He's freshly scrubbed and smells strongly of Irish Spring soap. His suit doesn't have the drape of an expensive, well-cut design, but it's serviceable enough to see him through the evening.

Mama introduces us, since we haven't formally met. Meghan manages to restrain herself from flirting or saying something inappropriate, which she has a tendency to do even when she isn't blasted, because she likes to make people squirm.

As for me, I have to admit that while Joe doesn't blow me

away, I can see how he might grow on you. He has a nice hand-shake, not too hearty, but not wet-noodle weak either. He smiles shyly, seemingly at a loss for words, then asks Mama to dance. I stand there watching them, sipping my drink. I haven't seen Mama look so happy in years. Her face is radiant—and not just because of the mixed drinks. Yes, there's something about that Joe Flanagan. He's like one of those plain-looking rocks people tend to overlook, though if you take the time crack them open, you find beautiful crystals inside. As he and Mama dance, Joe leads with a quiet, tender strength, the kind that lets Mama know that when he dips her, he won't let her fall.

I wish Ray were here.

"Come on." Meghan grabs me by the elbow as everybody gets increasingly punchy from the punch and starts to punch each other. I won't even try to say that three times fast. I've had one too many myself. Nobody's checking who's legal. Nobody's checking anything. A fight has broken out, beginning playful, then getting serious. Nobody can remember who started it or what it's about. They take it outside before they wreck the place. If you stand near the doorway, you can hear the thump of bodies hitting cars as the brawlers throw each other around the parking lot. Boys will be boys, someone remarks. Mama and Joe keep dancing, oblivious.

"Where are we going?" The wine I've sipped on the sly makes me let down my guard, though not completely.

Meghan twirls, a mini-tornado, creating a tiny weather system. The skirt of her dress, a sleeveless number a la Marilyn Monroe, fans out from her legs. Unlike her arms, which she hides underneath a lacy cardigan, her legs have only one bruise near the knee, like a kiss from someone who'd been wearing purple lipstick. "To get some air."

"Okay." I think she means fresh air, which, given how hot it's getting in the reception, I could use.

I should have known better.

It isn't until we're on the sidewalk that I see she has Mama's keys in her hand. "Get in," she says.

I take a step back. "I should stay. Alex's going to wonder where I am." Had Meghan managed to sneak a drink or toke? I can't tell.

"Like hell. She's making out big-time with that guy she's had a crush on for years."

So Alex's finally going for it. Good for her.

Meghan hops in the car. She's on. Is she ever on. "Besides. You need to spend time with your big sister." She guns the engine and leans across the passenger seat to open the door. "You're not chicken, are you?"

The magic words. All she has to do is say them, and I'll do whatever she wants, to prove her wrong. It's been that way since we were kids, one of those dynamics that never change. I'm still closing the door when she screeches away from the curb. I grab the Jesus bar to keep from falling out, my heart racing along with the engine. "What are you trying to do, kill me?"

"Maybe." She grins.

The hard edges of town soften as night comes on. Lights wink at us, downright flirtatious, but we're wise to their wiles. The statue of the virgin on the hill turns on her wattage, the local showgirl of Catholicism. She glows brighter with each passing minute. She's in her element when she's in the dark.

And as I look at her, I want to believe in miracles, I really do—that things happen for a reason, that redemption is possible, that dreams come true. But wanting something doesn't necessarily make it happen.

Meghan skids around a corner. The wheels lift off the ground, then touch back down, a lick of danger, like a nip of whiskey from a bottle.

I pull the seatbelt tighter. "Mama's going to kill you if you wreck her car."

"Since when did that ever stop me?" Meghan's face is all planes and angles now, harder, more determined.

"How much did you have?" I sniff the air for fumes, but all I detect is stale perfume and lingering effects of garlic prawns. I had one too many of those too.

"Not as much as you." She scowls at me. "Yeah. I've seen you watching me, waiting for me to fail. How do you think that feels, having people who're supposed to love you treating you that way?"

I stifle a belch. "After the shit you've put us through, we've got a reason to be cautious."

"Stop hiding behind 'we,' Erin. This is about you and me." Her lip curls. "It always has been."

Insects splat against the windshield. Their smashed bodies streak the glass with a nasty collage of still-twitching legs and greenish-yellow goo. The casualties mount as we speed through the night. Wings catch the breeze like little flags of surrender we don't acknowledge, because it's getting too dark to see clearly and hostilities are running too high.

"I don't know what you want me to say." Sweat slicks the

backs of my thighs. It's so hot I can't stand to be inside my own skin, much less inside a vehicle with a nutcase sibling. I keep waiting for things to change, for the temperature to cool. Even more snow would be better than this. But that won't happen. We're well into summer now, the time when everything heats up to the point that you can't stand it any more and you want to scream.

Mama's keys tap against the dashboard. Meghan doesn't say anything, but I can tell something's building up inside her the way she opens and closes her mouth without saying anything, a human bellows, fanning the flames of her own personal inferno. She floors the car, and we go into her version of hyperdrive. Words aren't enough tonight. She has to be a woman of action. Neon lights streak by in a wicked, liquid blur—Mai Tai, Streetcar, Bloody Mary.

This time, she's going to kill us both.

"Meghan, knock it off." I have to remain calm. If I let her think she's getting to me, it'll only make it worse. She can't stop herself when she senses weakness. The opportunity to tease, to torture, to get revenge is too tempting to resist.

"Pedal to the metal, baby." She smiles dangerously. "I want you to experience the shit-in-the-pants fear I feel every single day. Maybe then you'll understand."

"Okay. Okay. I get it." I reach for the keys. She slaps my hand away, hard enough to leave a red mark and make my skin sting. I rub my wrist.

"No, you don't." She hunches forward, as if she's going to hurl herself through the windshield. "But you will."

I'm tired of trying to placate her, to figure her out. I just want to get the hell out of the car—I want her the hell out of my life. I want—. "Why do you have to be such a human cyclone?"

"Psycho, huh?" She snorts. "You ain't seen nothin' yet."

"Cyclone," I repeat. "A raging tropical storm."

"I know what it is, Brainiac." A muscle in her temple twitches. It reminds me of a cat switching its tail before it bites. "But I ask you this: what's better, to release the passion and pain or bottle it up inside you?"

"I don't bottle anything up." How dare she try to psychoanalyze me? Her, the fuck-up champion of the world.

"Oh, yes, you do, Little Miss Perfect," she sneers. "For once, I'd like to see you scream. I'd like to see you admit how you really feel. To expose that seam of pain you've got buried inside you."

"What would that prove?" I put a hand on the steering wheel to straighten us out, but she won't have any of it and pushes me away. My shoulder slams into the door. The rusted-out lock rattles, but holds.

"That you're no different from me," she says.

We catch so much air I think we'll never come down, not in one piece anyway. My stomach drops and I scream and Meghan laughs maniacally—*See, see, that's more like it, that's what I'm talking about*—and I wait for the crash, because I know when we hit, we're going to hit hard. That's the point of the whole thing. Annihilation. Because then nothing will ever hurt again. We'll be in the great beyond. We'll be beyond everything.

When we finally do come down, I bounce up and almost whack my head on the ceiling. So much for the safety of seatbelts, the safety of anything. The undercarriage of the car scrapes the cracked road as we bottom out. We miss cars by centimeters, as if we're in a demolition derby. Then we screech to a stop by the mini-mart. And just like that, it's over.

"We're not dead." I echo the phrase we used to say when we were kids, up to no good, risking our necks for the thrill of it, to convince ourselves that we could survive.

Meghan doesn't seem to hear me. She gets out of the car as if nothing happened and saunters toward the store, heels tap-tapping, hips swaying, though there's no one around to whistle.

I stick my head out the window. My heart's still stuttering. "Where are you going?"

She looks over her shoulder. "To get some Cheetos. I've worked up an appetite. You want some?"

Laughter bubbles from deep inside of me. "You're something else, you know that?"

"Yeah, I am, aren't I?" She winks at me. In that look, I see all that she doesn't say, that we made it again, that the worst thing you can imagine is never the last word. That it's possible to live through almost anything. That it's possible to love and hate your sister at the same time.

Behind her, the neon lights of the mini-mart buzz and sizzle. Lars Stover's. That's what the letters should spell. Most of them are burned out, so what you see instead is L (space) ove. The letters aren't close together enough to actually spell the word, nor are the two of us close enough to be able to say it. They just hang there in the dark with no way to push them together. Somebody call a repairman. Too bad there isn't one who can fix our problems.

Meghan doesn't notice. She's not into making emotional declarations—none of us is. Nor is she given to analyzing things much, unless it involves how to score or find the biggest high or get back at me. She's a Nobel Prize-winning chemist, a fucking genius, when it comes to that.

No. She's already gone inside. When I look again, the sign says Stover's once more, and I wonder if I imagined the whole thing, the effects of shock and alcohol and adrenaline.

"Are you coming?" Meghan yells from the entrance. "I'm buying."

I stumble after her. "With what?"

"Dough," she snickers. She means bakery money.

"Careful with that sharp wit of yours." My legs feel wobbly for a moment, but I manage to walk without making a complete fool of myself. "You might hurt yourself." And I blink, hearing the words Ray spoke to me come out of my mouth.

Meghan cocks her head. We both know she's already hurt herself as deeply as anybody can.

And her wit has nothing to do with it.

She stands there, backlit by fluorescent lights, Our Lady of the Mini-Marts, to whom I pray: check yourself out, baby, check yourself in. Please. Please. Before it's too late.

Soon we'll return to the party and Meghan will slip Mama's keys back into her purse and we'll yawn and stretch and go home with Mama and the girls, to sleep in the place of our childhood, where everything should be right as rain, where love should be all we need.

But we don't want to leave this halo of artificial light just yet. Meghan grins at me, a flash of love and grace and mischief, and I laugh, laugh though the darkness waits outside and we know we have to return to it all too soon. Laugh, because we're here now, trying to forget the battles that wait beyond the sliding doors, trying to delude ourselves into thinking that this moment is the only one that matters, that it has to be enough.

CHAPTER 12

Sunday. My day off. We go to church again. This is a record for us. The priest must be in a state of shock. We'd been such C&E (Christmas and Easter) people before. Not Mama, the rest of us. We arrive a few minutes early—another big surprise—and light candles beneath the statue of the Virgin Mary in an alcove. We spark our matches with flames from already lit candles, a theological version of a chain letter, a pyramid scheme for salvation. We extinguish them by plunging them into the sand, itself a mini-Sahara—I almost expect to see a tiny troupe of wise men journeying across it on foot and camel, pursuing the star of Bethlehem. We bow our heads and try to decide what to ask for, what we need most.

Teeny waves her hand over the tongues of flame, making them flicker, until Meghan pulls her away. "Those candles are people's prayers. It's up to God to blow them out," Meghan whispers to her. "Not us."

"I wasn't trying to blow them out,"Teeny insists. She's wearing a sundress with blue flowers on it that bring out the color of her eyes. "I was making the prayers dance."

Meghan shakes her head. "This is church, not a disco."

Teeny frowns. "The angels like to dance. I can tell."

A woman in a hat with artificial cherries around the brim turns and stares.

Meghan puts a finger to her lips. Shh. She picks up Si-si's baby carrier and we find seats in the back pew—a good place to be if you have restless kids and poopy babies in tow.

Mama's taken her place up front with the rest of the singers. Looks like Joe sings in the choir now too. He does a solo with Mama during the offertory. I cringe, expecting the worst. I guess I'm thinking Joe's voice will be average like the rest of him. But man, can that guy sing. He's got this deep, rich tone. He could work for the opera or something. I'm not kidding. He reins his vocal power in, though, so that he doesn't overshadow Mama. They harmonize perfectly. Everyone watches them in amazement, their faces alight.

"Wow," I whisper. "I'm impressed."

Meghan shrugs. It's not her kind of music. Mine either. But I can still appreciate talent when I see it. She can't unless it involves cranked amps and feedback and screaming, something that gets her blood pounding, that makes her veins hum.

After mass, we go out for brunch, Joe included. This is our first excursion with him. We take separate cars, what with the booster seat and baby carrier and all—which also gives us the opportunity to talk about him. Meghan and Mama sit in front, Mama at the wheel. I'm in back with the girls. Si-si's blowing raspberries. Teeny's doing shadow puppets, a coyote, a bunny, a shark.

"Does Joe sing like that all the time, Mama?" Meghan asks teasingly. "Do *you*? La-la-la-la-laaaaa."

"Oh, my goodness." Mama widens her eyes, both mockingly prim and playing dumb. "Whatever do you mean?"

There's an edge to Meghan's teasing grin, like a sign flashing "DANGER AHEAD." She's been more irritable lately. Who knows what's bugging her. Teeny chimes in before she can follow up. "Who's Joe?"

"The guy we're going out to brunch with. Grandma's boyfriend." Meghan puts a hand over her heart and pretends to swoon.

"I thought you were the one who had all the boyfriends, Mom." Teeny makes a crocodile.

That shuts Meghan up for a moment. We pass a going-out-of-business sale at a furniture store. "Not any more. I'm on the wagon."

Teeny tries to peek at her around the head rest, but the seat-belt holds her back. "What wagon?"

Meghan doesn't look at her. "Never mind."

"Where're we going to eat?" Teeny asks. "My tummy's been growling since comm-onion."

We laugh. "Mine's been rumbling since communion too," I tell her. "It always does."

"I told Joe the 4Bs would be fine," Mama says.

Eggs and bacon and hashbrowns. I can't eat them every day. But they sound really good right now. We zip through the deserted streets of old town to the Flats, where everything's new and improved. The cemetery, the resting place of our ancestors—and my father—is sandwiched between a car dealership and the Wal-Mart. The restaurant sign juts out ahead, one of many jostling for attention. We take the last spot in the packed parking lot. Joe's waiting inside at a large, half-circle banquette in the corner. We slide in beside him and make a show of putting paper napkins on our laps and sipping water—which Teeny manages to spill, soaking her napkin. Joe gives her his as the waitress breezes to our table. She's a model of efficiency in everything but her make-up application, which is heavy-handed as a Halloween costume, a shame, the Double Ds would say, because she has a lovely smile. We're grateful for her promptness, not only because we're ravenous, but because she helps delay the awkward moment when we're actually going to have to make small talk and get acquainted. Teeny orders pigs in a blanket, Joe the American with eggs basted, Meghan a Belgian waffle with a mound of whipped cream, Mama the American (like Joe, how sweet) except with the eggs over easy (Meghan takes the "easy" part as a double entendre and stifles a laugh, causing Mama to shoot her an exasperated look). I get an egg dish too. But what I'm really after is the hashbrowns, not nouveau country potatoes, but the grated, greasy brown type that are molded into a cake in the frying pan, crisp on the outside, soft on the inside.

Once the waitress retreats to the kitchen in a cloud of drugstore perfume, Meghan, true to character, wastes no time volleying questions at Joe. "So how long have you two been seeing each other?" She already knows the answer, but she wants to put him through his paces. She's getting back at Mama for all the years she interrogated Meghan's boyfriends, until she stopped bringing them home—and stopped coming home herself.

"Oh, we've been friends for over a year." As she tells the story of their meeting, Mama puts cream in her coffee, something she never does under normal circumstances. I can tell she's nervous—she wants this to go well—and needs to have something to occupy her hands.

"And now you're more than friends. Sounds serious." Meghan turns to Joe. "Is it?"

I kick her under the table, hissing "bitch alert" in her ear. Meghan ignores me. I kick her again. She kicks back, hard enough to jiggle the table, creating a mini-earthquake that rattles the silverware.

Joe takes Mama's hand. "Your mother's a special woman."

Meghan snorts. "That sounds like something from a greeting card. You can do better than that, can't you?"

"Meghan." Mama frowns.

"Stop it," I whisper. Where does Meghan get off being so judgmental? It's not like she's ever made good choices when it comes to men. But maybe that's not what this is about. Maybe this is about our father, about missing him, making him better than he was, impossible for anyone to live up to.

Joe doesn't flinch. He keeps his gaze steadily on Meghan, and says,

> *What love is, if thou wouldst be taught,*
> *Thy heart must teach alone—*
> *Two souls with but a single thought,*
> *Two hearts that beat as one.*

215

"That more what you had in mind?" he asks.

Meghan pauses. She's hardly ever speechless. Joe doesn't realize what a coup this is. She's not used to poetry being used as ammunition, to declare love or anything else, though she should be, since she lived with Bone. I guess she was too strung out then to listen. "Score one for you." She flashes Joe a Cheshire-cat grin. "Did you make that up?"

"No, I only committed it to memory," he says. "It's from *Der Sohn der Wildnis* by Friedrich Halm."

"A man of letters. You fancy yourself something of a closet renaissance guy, huh, Mr. Flanagan?" Meghan isn't quite as aggressive now, but she's still watching him closely, her eyes glittering like a cat toying with a mouse.

"The only thing I fancy is your mother." Even though he's quiet, it would be a mistake to consider Joe a mouse. He appears to be one of those people who don't let anything bother them, even the semi-belligerent offspring of their girlfriend.

Whatever type of man he is, he might be the right one for Mama. And, for now, that's good enough for me. I just hope she doesn't get hurt. She doesn't need any more heartbreak in her life.

That evening, when I go out with Ray, I don't wear the infamous bra and tap pants from Funkified. I do, however, take the trouble to make sure the color of my bra and panties match (blue) and that they don't have any holes, just in case. I wear a pair of batik pedal pushers and a short-sleeved button-down bowling shirt. Tennis shoes keep the outfit casual—and hopefully ensure that I won't twist my ankle or make any other klutzy move.

"You look pretty," he says as he opens the car door for me.

I try to ignore Teeny, Mama, and Meghan, pressing their noses against the living room window. I race to the car when he arrives, so we won't have to go through yet another round of introductions. I don't want a repeat of Meghan's performance with Joe.

"Bye, Auntie Erin." Teeny can't resist darting onto the porch and exclaiming, "He's cute!"

"So are you!" Ray waves.

She squeals and runs into the house.

"You're such a ladies' man," I tease as I climb into the passenger seat.

He grins.

"What's in there?" I gesture to the basket in the back seat as we pull away from the curb.

"On this evening's menu, mademoiselle, we are featuring potato and bean salads, fried chicken, wine and chocolate cake," he says in a fake French accent.

"Sounds good." I'm getting hungry already. "Trixie's Deli has great take-out, doesn't it?" I add, thinking that's where he must have gotten the fixings for the feast.

He turns up Mercury. "Actually, I made it myself."

"Even better." That is, if he really knows how to cook. One time, a guy I dated (very briefly) tried to make dinner for me—his parents were out of town that weekend and he had the run of the house. It ended badly all around, including my getting food poisoning.

I run my finger along the armrest. Ray must have taken the Land Cruiser to the car wash, scrubbed it inside and out—though he'd left a mound of gravel in the cup holder. An occupational hazard, I suppose. "Bringing work home from the office?" I ask.

"Nope. They're for you."

He was doing so well with the homemade picnic and spiffy rig. But this? "Gee, thanks." I mean, flowers, though a cliché, would have been better. "Just what I've always wanted. A pile of rocks."

He laughs. "I found them when I was surveying. I thought they might inspire you."

I raise my eyebrows. I don't know what to say. It's got to be the most unromantic gift anyone has ever given to me. And that's saying a lot. I've been the recipient of a pineapple (no, not directly from Hawaii, but from the produce aisle at Safeway), a candy bar ("to make you sweeter"), and a Zippo ("c'mon baby, light my fire"), but never a cupful of stones. "To do what exactly?"

He puts them in the palm of my hand. "Haven't you ever thought about using local materials in your work?"

I gaze at the black and gray nuggets. Yep. These are sure to start the next trend. He must be color-blind. "Not really."

"Believe it or not, some of those are garnets." He pokes the gravel with his finger.

"You've got to be kidding." There's no red, no sparkle, no nothing.

"You just need to know what you're looking for. There are some exceptional minerals out there that would be perfect to use in your line."

That's me. Ms. Mineral. I stare hard at the stones, small and dark as bird eyes. "It might not be worth the trouble."

"I don't only mean these. I mean crystals—and copper. The possibilities are endless." His enthusiasm is kind of endearing.

H'mm. Maybe he's on to something. Copper. The prime ingredient in lucky pennies, in conducting electricity, the substance my ancestors mined from these gouged hills and valleys. "You're full of surprises, aren't you? What else do you have up your sleeve?"

"I'd be happy to show you." He rubs the back of my neck.

I slip the stones back into the cup holder, freeing my hands for other things, such as traveling up his leg. I behaved myself on the first date. Maybe I won't this time.

As we drive through the mining district, aiming for the hills of the great beyond, we can hardly keep our hands off each other. He pulls over near shaft 6 and kisses me so deeply I feel dizzy. You know how people say, when they're really into someone, that the earth moves? Well, I glimpse the sky streaking past, faster and faster—and then I realize that we actually *are* moving. We haven't stopped. "Ray!"

We stare through the windshield in shock. This can't be happening.

But it is.

"Oh, shit," Ray mutters.

We must have inadvertently knocked the car into gear—and we're headed straight for one of the strip mines. I can see the headlines now: YOUNG LOVERS TAKE TRAGIC PLUNGE. THE BEST SEX SHE ALMOST EVER HAD.

Ray stomps on the brake and brings us to a screeching halt a foot from the edge. We gasp, then burst into giggles.

"You know what they say," he says after we catch our

breath, curling a lock of my hair around his finger. "Third time's the charm."

"Now?" I ask, wondering how far he's going to take things.

He shakes his head. "Let's wait until we're out of the car."

We push onwards, past earth that's been peeled down to the bone, to hills where trees still grow and rivers snake through ravines and there's a semblance of beauty, rough and tumble-down, but pure. Here and there, abandoned miners' cabins brace themselves against ravines. Prospectors used to find silver and gold around here. That was the rumor, anyway, the one that kept people coming. The dream they clung to as they struggled to survive subzero winters and heat-stroke–inducing summers, the thought that if they hung on, things would get better——that they could dig their way to a better life.

Most times, they just got dirty.

The single-lane track narrows and hugs the hills for dear life. Even though I usually don't have trouble with heights, I have to remind myself to breathe. We climb up and up, the dropoff steep-ening until the roller-coaster-ride of a road crests and we careen back down. Then, when I least expect it, the rocky, barely dri-vable track opens into a river gorge, its stones burnished, veined red and gold, its waters deep green. I thought I knew all the hid-den places in the area. But this one surprises me. "It's beautiful."

"It is, isn't it?" He sets the parking brake. "Stay," he says, as if speaking to a dog rather than a car.

The dust settles as we get out of the Land Cruiser. It's quiet but for the rushing water and the twitter of birds in the trees. The air is clear and sharp. It's almost as lovely as the cabin site at Divide. "How did you find this place?" I ask.

"When we were surveying a few weeks ago." He takes my hand. "I come here sometimes to think and fish."

"Have much luck?" I trace the inside of his wrist where the skin is softest. "With the fish?"

He nods, pulling me closer. "I'm good at catching things."

"Oh, yeah? Can you catch me?" I dart away from him.

He lopes after me, anticipating my every move. Around the bend, there's nowhere to go. The cliffs jut down to the water, cutting off my escape. I duck under his outstretched arms, but he grabs me.

This time I don't try to get away.

I feel his hands on my back, his chest against mine. We don't hear the rushing river, the hawk crying overhead, only the sounds we make together, our clothes rustling as they fall on the narrow strip of sand, our cries and murmurs and breathing growing more rapid until we collapse, and the outside intrudes again, reminding us that we are still in this world. And I want to hurl myself at him again, because he has looked into my eyes the whole time, because no one has ever held me this way before.

"More?" he whispers in my ear.

"Yes." We make sand angels on the beach, the sediment holding the impression of our bodies after we've gone, a geological record of us, of the first time we came together.

We stop at his house when we get back into town. His apartment occupies the entire first floor of an Italianate Victorian. Books fill the leaded glass cabinets. An orange-and-white striped kitten, a stray who Ray says he named Webster because he likes to sleep on top of a large dictionary, mews a greeting. Ray scratches him behind the ears. He purrs and purrs. I know exactly how he feels. I crave the touch of those hands too.

Nothing about the place feels temporary. It's warm and lived-in, neat but not in an obsessive-compulsive way. Through the half-open door of the bedroom, I glimpse a bed with a forest-green quilt the color of the river by which we lay this afternoon, and I'm tempted to crawl into it. But Ray calls from the kitchen, offering me a drink—Sprite this time, since we've already had plenty of wine and he doesn't want to send me home drunk— besides, there's no Chianti left. On the side of the refrigerator there's a large wipe board, scrawled with a series of equations.

Ray notices my puzzled expression. "We used to have one in college. We'd stay up all night solving math problems and drinking beer," he explains sheepishly. "Old habits die hard."

"I have an equation you can work on." I smile.

"I really want you to stay the night," he puts his arms around me, "but I don't want to give your mom a bad impression." I'm not caring much about impressions at the moment, other than the one my body is making pressed against his. "I want to get to know you better, Erin. Really know you."

No one's cared about that before, most people being more concerned with getting into my pants as fast as possible, making me want to flee. I don't feel like that with Ray. If I feel like running, it's toward him, not away. I don't want to go home, but I realize he's right: that if we want this to last, to grow, I need to let him drive me back tonight, while, overhead, a shooting star falls, a cartwheeling, glorious spark, a star worth wishing on.

• • •

I drop my keys a couple of times before I manage to fit them in the lock. Guess the Sprite didn't do the trick after all. Or maybe I'm just high on Ray, more dreamy and distracted than I've ever been in my life. I can still smell him on me. I'm never going to change my clothes. I lick my lips, still sticky with the chocolate cake he fed me by hand.

The house is silent. Everyone's asleep—everyone, that is, except Meghan. "Got some, huh?" she says as I pass through the kitchen.

I throw a tea towel at her. "Shut up."

She catches the towel and tosses it on the counter, reflexes quick as a gunslinger.

"He feed you well?"

"You could say that," I grin, adding, "homemade everything."

"Yum. Yum." She smacks her lips. "When do we get to meet him?"

"You already have," I remind her.

"Formally." She tips her chair back on two legs, eyeing me. "As The Boyfriend."

"I don't know." I shrug. "I mean, we're not formally anything."

"Er-head, it's okay." She calls me by the nickname she hasn't used in years, a play on "air-head." "I'm happy for you."

I can see she means it, because she's got a wistful look on her face, one I've never seen before. "You're going to find someone too," I tell her. "You never have any trouble getting guys."

"Not the good ones," she says ruefully.

"You will." I truly believe that if she can only stay straight, things won't be perfect, but they'll get better.

She's quiet for a moment. "Was it good?"

I giggle. "Yeah. How can you tell?"

"You have that special glow—and your shirt's buttoned up wrong." She laughs.

"Oh, God." I fumble to set it right.

"Doesn't matter. You're among friends."

The sound of Si-si crying carries down the stairs. "I'd better get her before she wakes Teens. As you know, it can be murder getting her back to sleep." Meghan grabs a bottle that's been warming in a pan on the stove.

"Here. Give it to me." I take the bottle from her and grab the towel to use as a burp cloth.

"Thanks, Er. You're going to make a good mother some day," she says as she goes outside for a cigarette.

For once, I don't rag on her about the smokes, nicotine being one of her lesser vices. As I hurry upstairs, I think about what she said. About her being happy for me. About my being a good mother some day.

I push the door to the girls' room open, freezing for a moment when it makes that haunted-house creak, because we haven't bothered to oil the hinges. Teeny gives me a sleepy smile, then rolls over and goes back to sleep.

By the glow of the angel nightlight, I change Si-si's diaper. I'm gun shy about this, because once she shot a load of crap right at me, little Ms. Krakatoa, and ruined my favorite sweater. We make the switch safely this time. She performs binky tricks with her pacifier for our mutual entertainment, flipping it upside down and twirling it with her tongue.

I sit in the rocking chair, the same one Mama used when we were babies. Si-si nestles into the curve of my arm and holds onto my hand as she sucks away, stealing glances at me and smiling around the nipple. She has cradle cap, which I've tried to comb away, the flakes coming off, like continents breaking up and reforming on the world of her skull. I think I see a map there, a path in the pulsing veins that thread through her delicate fontanel, a record of where she's been, but I don't know how to read it, and soon it will grow over, sealing everything inside.

I touch her cheek, thinking that some day, when I'm older, maybe I'll have a baby, a family of my own, filled with love like this one, but less trouble, less strife.

After I put Si-si down, I'm too wound up to sleep. My mind spins with thoughts of Ray, with everything we talked about, everything we did. I open my bead case, push aside the fancy, expensive materials I special-ordered, and select spools of copper wire. I can't believe I haven't tried copper before. It seems so natural to me now. I'm drawn to the color of the metal, whose warmth reminds me of burnished skin—Ray's skin— and to the fact that it's something my ancestors once mined from the earth, something they'd given their lives for.

I retrieve my big box of rocks, the remains of my childhood collection, from the top of the closet. The thick layer of dust on the lid makes me sneeze. Some of the pieces are too raw and bulky. There's no way I can use them unless they're cut and polished. But the crystals, delicate as fairy torches, will do fine. My fingers work quickly, twisting, crimping, in a creative whirlwind. Before, I had agonized over the placement of every stone, but now everything seems to be falling into place. I make two necklaces and two pairs of earrings using white quartz and amethyst. I have so much energy, I could work through the night, but I'll have to wait until I have another batch of stones. I'll ask Ray to help me find more. He knows the best spots.

I pause, breathless, amazed by what I've accomplished. It's the best work I've ever done. My very own seam of inspiration had been inside me all this time, and I didn't realize it.

Thanks to Ray, maybe I've finally struck gold.

CHAPTER 13

There's nothing about the next morning to indicate that it'll be any different than the others. Outside my window, the sky's clear except for scuff marks of cumulus. Power lines cut across the blue like a music staff without notes, or the bars of a prison, the image of possibility and limitation all at once. The color's so saturated, it looks as if it should actually have a taste, like crushed mints or blueberries.

The pipes clank. Meghan must be doing a wash. She doesn't have to leave as early any more. She's acting more like a normal person, adopting regular hours and goals, at least on the surface. That's the easy part. It's what's underneath that's trickier. You never know if you're walking on solid ground, or if it's going to cave in.

I hear the shuffle of bare feet on shag in the hall, a pause outside my door, then clumping down the stairs and the tinny sound of the TV. Cartoons. Teeny's up. I should be too. I stumble over to look at the necklaces and earrings I made last night, hoping they'll seem as accomplished now as they did then. The earrings sparkle in the sunlight streaming through the window. It's as if magical creatures stole into my room and made them. But it was me. I put the pieces in a special case to take to work later. I'm both excited and nervous for the Double Ds to see them, wondering what they'll say when they do.

I consider getting dressed, but then figure I'll slum around in my cut-off sweat pants and tank top for a while. It's nice having Meghan home, so she can deal with Si-si's 6 A.M. feeding. So she can go back to being a real mom. Or start being one.

I drag myself downstairs. I'm suffering from sleep deprivation and post-inebriation, part of a new equation Ray could scribble on his wipe board: too much wine equals too much whine.

"Hey, sleepy-head," Meghan says. She's making eggs. Meghan making eggs. What a novelty.

"Hey, yourself." I yawn. "You giving the Naked Chef some competition?"

"Only if I take off my clothes." She wiggles her butt.

"Please no. It's too early in the morning." I groan. The eggs pop and sizzle. "Where's Teeny?"

"'Tooning out." She gestures toward the living room with a spatula. "Hung over, huh?"

"Yup." I press a palm to my forehead.

She grins at me but doesn't say anything, no doubt entertained by the role reversal.

I wander into the living room and rest my back against the wall, next to the picture of a pissed-off looking great-grandmother on my father's side I never knew. Despite my pickled brain, I feel too happy to possibly be related to her. "Hi, Teens."

"Hi." Teeny keeps her eyes on the TV. Scooby-Doo again, the same show Meghan and I watched when we were little. Mama watched it when she was growing up too. The cartoon that goes on forever and ever. Amen.

Scooby's begging for another Scooby snack when something whizzes past my head and blows out the screen. Wires sizzle and snap. The electrical current doesn't have anywhere to go. Broken glass hangs in the frame like monster fangs. Teeny screeches and covers her ears with her hands and dives under the pillows, but they're not big enough to hide her. Her arms and legs stick out and she looks more vulnerable than ever.

I throw myself on top of her and peer over the back of the couch, but I can't see anything. "What the hell—"

Another pop, and Meghan's old track trophy crashes to the hearth. The runner's leg breaks off at the thigh. Now it appears to be an athlete from the Special Olympics, the way we'll look if whoever's firing those shots gets a bead on us. And someone *is* firing shots.

I grab Teeny and bolt for the back door. Meghan's not in the kitchen. I don't see her anywhere. "Meghan, where the fuck are you?" She doesn't answer. Damn her. She ran again. She ran and left us to deal with the shit she left behind. Because there's no doubt in my mind that this has something to do with her.

Down the hall, I see a shadow behind the back door, and I think it's another guy with a gun, so I tear upstairs with Teeny bouncing on my hip, as if I'm a pony ride and she's my little buckaroo in a rodeo from hell.

"It's the bad guys," she whimpers in my ear. "Mom said we were playing hide and seek. That they'd never find us."

More like Meghan is the one we'll never be able to find.

"What bad guys?" I pant as we dash down the hallway. "Why would bad guys be looking for you?"

Teeny's lip quivers. "Because they're mean."

Because Meghan owes them money.

"They shouldn't be mean," Teeny whispers. "They're from Disneyland. They let me go on rides while they talked to Mom. They buyed me cotton candy and Coke. They showed me skate-board tricks."

Coke. Yeah. Disneyland. Board-heads. A pipsqueak voice starts singing in my head: It's a small world after all.

And with a chill of recognition, I remember Yo-ho's warning: The pirates from California.

Shit-shit-shit.

I push Teeny into the closet, wedged among the broken dolls and mildewed stuffed animals, the survivors of lost childhood. Nothing is innocent any more. Nothing is still sacred. If it ever was in the first place.

Si-si sighs from her cradle. Si-si. Please don't let her cry. I heft the cradle off the floor. It's so small I can hold it in my arms. She's so small. We're all so small. And they're so much bigger. The pirates of California. I imagine them as giants, giants with automatic weapons. Automatic everything.

I shove the cradle in the closet with Si-si still in it. She doesn't move. She snores in a blissful ignorance I hope lasts until the danger has passed. If it passes. She sounds like one of those rain sticks, filled with sand. Shhh-shhh-shhh.

"Why are you putting us in here?" Teeny bats at the skirt of Mama's prom dress. Mama had been saving it for us to wear, but Meghan's a drop-out and I didn't go, so nobody wore it except her. Now there's a chance nobody ever will—that it will be riddled with bullets and blood when those jerks come up here and blow us away. "Auntie Erin?"

I blink. I can't let Teeny know what I'm thinking. "Because it's safe. Don't worry. I'll get help."

"Don't leave us!" Teeny clutches my sleeve. She won't let go. I've never felt a grip like that before.

"I'm going to call the police." I pry her fingers away. "You need to let me call the police, Teens."

"Okay." She doesn't seem to believe me. Too many people have made promises they didn't keep.

My hands tremble so much, I drop the phone twice before I manage to put it to my ear. No dial tone. Nothing. They cut the line. Smart bastards.

If only Mama hadn't taken the cell phone with her to the hospital. If it were just me, I'd jump out the window and run. If it were just me—

But it isn't.

I look at Si-si, sleeping peacefully and Teeny, wide-eyed and pale, and I realize that I'm here for a reason. For them. "The game's not over, Teens. You need to stay real, real quiet."

That's what you do in hide-and-seek.

If you want to win.

If you want to live.

"What about Mom?" Teeny glances at the door, a wooden door with numerous coats of paint and a bad hinge that doesn't look strong enough to keep anything out.

What about her? What about her? I want to shout. She's the one who got us into this.

But I can't turn my back on her, especially now when she needs me the most. What if she didn't run? What if she's in more trouble than she's ever been in in her life?

I thought she was in the deepest, darkest pit of the soul before. I was wrong. She was standing on the brink, looking down. Now she's fallen.

And it's up to me to get her out.

Okay. I have to calm down. I'm still here. I'm still breathing. I'm standing in the hall. The kids are in the closet. There are homicidal maniacs lurking outside the house who want something from my sister and, by association, from us. We are witnesses to her self-destruction, to their crimes, and soon, perhaps, to our own deaths. I can't move. The thoughts paralyze me. I shouldn't even be here. I should be somewhere far away, attending art school, soldering bits of chain to make necklaces. I press my hands to my head. Maybe this is the moment I've been waiting for my whole life, the moment when I don't just dream about being brave, but when I actually am, a moment when I find out what I'm really made of.

Clay.

I hear two more pops, glass breaking. No sound from Meghan. Why doesn't she scream? For her kids? For herself? For me?

I hear male voices shouting. They'll break down the door any second, if they haven't already. It won't take much brawn to knock the screen off its hinges. They won't stop to ask questions. They'll shoot us and take what they can.

Sirens wail, closer, closer. Did someone call the police? Someone whose line hadn't been cut? Who had the right connection?

Sirens. Waa-waaing, like a baby crying. Helpless, alone.

Sirens.

From the good ol' days of mining disasters when men were trapped hundreds of feet below the surface.

Sirens.

From the day my father died.

They didn't get there in time to save him.

Somehow, I manage to make it to the landing. I see Meghan's feet sticking out into the front hall. That phrase from a western movie echoes in my head: *they died with their boots on*. She died with her boots on. The boots with the loose soles that gape like the mouths of hungry birds, the slack mouths of drunks begging for another drink.

I'd wished her dead. I never meant it. People say a lot of things they don't mean when they're hurting.

Not like this. Please, not like this.

"Meghan?" I stumble downstairs and fall to my knees beside her. She's on her back, eyes closed.

Stay with me. Stay with me.

She hadn't been here before. Had she run to the porch, either trying to confront them or make a quick getaway, then come back in? Jesus. Jesus. Who cares as long as she lives? The frying pan's on the floor next to her. The eggs aren't sunny side up, they're splattered all over the linoleum, an abstract painting, Study in Yellow.

The yolk's on you, my father's voice echoes from my childhood. He was fond of making stupid jokes and we laughed and laughed, until the last year before he died, when we thought we were too old for such things, assuming the aloof pose of adolescents.

The yolk's on you.

He never meant it this way.

That's why Meghan didn't say anything. Because they'd gotten her. Those California pirates. "Where are you hit?" I touch her cheek. Blood pours from a wound in the back of her head. I can't see how bad it is. There's too much hair in the way.

The sirens get louder, making the sound of women keening at a wake.

The medics didn't come in time to save my father. They won't come in time to save my sister either.

"You can't leave. You're not done yet. *We're* not done yet. Damn it, don't you die on me. Don't you dare die or I'll never forgive you." I put my head on her chest and sob. Images flash through my mind, as if I'm flipping through a scrapbook, the memories, all good now, the bad conveniently blacked out like a censored document, the focus on childhood, before everything went to hell. The two of us singing in our own girl band. Roller-skating down the biggest hill we could find. Her pulling me out of the mine shaft, saving me from certain death.

When had I ever done that for her? Without judgment? Without thinking about how much it would cost me? By instinct only?

Her skin pales to the color of clouds, to heaven, her soul taking flight.

No.

I press my lips to hers. She must have had a cig, because her breath tastes of ashes, which makes me shudder, not from the smoke, but from the vision of cremation it brings to mind: that she's already turning to dust.

If only Mama were here. She could save her.

"Breathe. C'mon. Don't be such a chicken." I throw the words back at her.

She's a stubborn one, my sister. She doesn't take anything from you unless it's her idea, unless it's part of a great con. She won't take my breath, not even if her life depends on it.

"Breathe!" My voice is half plea, half shout.

She's never listened to me.

"Breathe." A whimper.

All I can hear is the accusation of my own gasps. She's leaving me behind again and there's nothing I can do. I look up, in the direction of heaven, see only the cracked ceiling with its web of hairline fractures. Come on, Daddy, God. Somebody.

I feel a flash of anger, that no one's listening, no one's doing anything, and a roar comes from somewhere deep inside me and I collapse against her. I don't have anything left.

Then, in the ragged pauses between breaths, I hear something I didn't expect to hear again. Not from her.

A heartbeat.

Her chest heaves, creaky as a rusty hinge, because, yeah, she's been at death's door.

235

I stare at her. "Meghan?"

She blinks, trying to put me back in focus, trying to make sense of things. "I guess that St. Christopher medal was good for something," she wheezes. She pulls it from underneath her shirt. She laughs at her little joke, a yip of a laugh, like a dog brought up short on a leash, the collar choking its neck. "It's a miracle, a fucking miracle."

"What happened?" I ask.

"I don't know," she murmurs. "I had the strangest dream. Bone was in it. A gun fired. Something hit me on the head."

I hear a creaking sound—Mama's pot rack, hanging by a link of chain. The main suspect in Meghan's head injury, the sauté pan, has slid over into the corner. I hadn't noticed it before. A stray bullet must have knocked it loose—and Meghan unconscious. I wad up a towel and put it under her head. "You'll live. But you might need stitches."

"Are the bad guys gone?" Teeny calls from the stairs.

I crawl over to the window. Lights flash in the alley across the street. A guy walks out with his hands raised. A cop pushes him against the car and handcuffs him. I can't see his face. "Looks like it. Is Si-si still snoozing?"

"Uh-huh." Teeny cradles one of the damaged dolls from the closet in her arms.

Si-si has slept through the whole thing.

"I'd forgotten about that old thing." Meghan glances at the doll, which has a missing eye and a bald patch from a bad haircut she'd given it when she was about Teeny's age.

"She's not a thing." Teeny strokes what remains of the doll's hair. "Her name is Annabelle and she needs a hug."

"How do you know that's what she needs?" Meghan murmurs, her breath still coming in shallow gasps.

"Because she told me." Teeny holds the doll in front of her, as if to confirm her version of the event.

Meghan nods so slightly, it's almost imperceptible.

Teeny sets the doll in her lap, making them both face Meghan. "Mom, what are you doing on the floor?"

"I'm having a religious experience." Meghan stares at the ceiling.

"More like a near-death experience." Now that the relief of her being alive has passed, my anger stirs. I turn to Teeny, jaw tight, voice sweet. "Teens, why don't you check on Si-si? I thought I heard her crying."

"Okay."

When I think she's out of earshot, I take a deep breath. "This has to stop. Now."

Meghan's still trancy. "It already has."

"No. It hasn't," I insist. "Otherwise those creeps wouldn't have come looking for you."

"That's in the past." She toys with the chain of the St. Christopher medal.

"Don't you get it? Your past followed you."

No response.

She owes me an explanation. She owes me more than that. "Did you steal from them?" I ask. "Did you owe them money?"

Still no reply.

"Don't you realize that what you do affects all of us? We could have died today. Every single one of us."

"But we didn't." Her voice comes from far away in her own personal nirvana. I want to shake her. "It was a sign, a—"

"I know. A miracle." I look at her face, at the pale freckled skin, the dear turned-up nose, the irrepressible smile now softened and beatific, a saint herself perhaps, having gone through trials and emerged, if not unscathed, at least alive. I remember a book of the saints Ginga had, the portraits painted with artistic precision and a touch of melodrama, the stories decidedly gruesome, full of rapes and dismemberments and burnings, of sacrifice, judgment, and mercy. It isn't hard to imagine Meghan's profile among them, the druggie trying to go clean, failing, trying again. A long-suffering Jesus forgiving her each time.

I want to forgive her. I want to believe. I do. But there's a part of me that can't. It's as if I'm holding on to the edge of that mine shaft again and if I let go, I'll fall. I can't rely on her to save me any more. I remember when we were kids we pricked our fingers and smeared our blood together and I almost fainted from the sight of it and she laughed, because I was scared and weak. "It's only blood, silly. There's lots more where that came from. It's not like you're going to run out." I'd pass out every time I had to get a shot or a blood test. I can't stand needles, a problem she's never had. She'd sit calmly and watch the point go in. She said it was only a little prick, that she didn't feel a thing. "It's making me better. See?" The flow of her blood from her body, or the flow of the immunization into it, fascinated her. Maybe it would have been better if it hadn't. Though in the end, it probably wouldn't have made a difference. She would have found another way to erase herself.

I feel like a fool for weeping and carrying on. "Tell me you weren't faking."

"Faking what?" Her eyes are pools of green I could drown in.

"Being dead. Getting me to say those things."

"I didn't hear anything but angels singing." She grins. There's no getting the truth from her.

Teeny taps me on the shoulder. "There's a man sleeping outside the front door. He won't wake up." She takes me by the hand and drags me over to the screen.

"Teens, the cops have the bad guys," I assure her. "You don't have to worry any more."

The screen hangs by a single hinge, as if it's been hit by a tornado. On the porch, there's a figure in a baggy brown coat. "What——?" I choke on the words, because I know who it is.

Bone. Bone crumpled into a heap, bleeding, bleeding. "Teens, go back in the house with your mama."

"Are you going to wake him up?" she asks. This isn't the first time she's seen someone unconscious and bloody. She doesn't even cringe. But she's concerned.

"I'll take care of it." I fight to keep my voice steady "Go." I crouch down beside Bone.

"Hey, girl," he wheezes.

"How did you——" I can't stop the tears from coming.

"I followed them here."

"Hold on, Bone. You just hold on." He's bleeding from a wound in his stomach, worse than Meghan, much worse.

An aid car screeches to a halt outside the gate. I wave. "Over here!" I see that Yo-ho's flying his war flag. It ripples and snaps in the breeze. Maybe he's got 911 in his arsenal. God bless him.

Bone blinks his eyes. "The little girl," he rasps. "She all right?"

"Teeny?" I lean closer, barely able to hear him.

He smiles, pain in his eyes. "What kind of a name is that? Yeah, Teeny."

"She's fine."

"She has the prettiest eyes," he sighs, slipping into unconsciousness. "My mother's eyes."

CHAPTER 14

L ike any Meghan story, this one's complicated. It goes something like this: she and her boyfriend-at-the-time owed a dealer money. They skipped on him, then skipped on each other. The boyfriend claimed she had the stuff. She said he did. Who knows what the truth is, though since she was living hand-to-mouth before she came home, she's either telling the truth or she blew it all. Must have been quite a bundle for them to chase her this far. She said something like two hundred thousand.

The answer to your prayers. The start of all your problems.

Then she heard that the boyfriend was living high in Mexico, in more ways than one. That's what she says, anyway, which almost absolves her of the worst offenses.

The pirates from California are awaiting arraignment on various charges. They'll be extradited back to their home state, where they're wanted for murder. I guess we should count ourselves lucky.

After Bone gets out of the hospital, he says he's checking himself into rehab. He means to get clean this time. He wants to be there for Teeny. I hope he can just be there for himself.

Joe and Ray helped us clean up the glass, repair the screen, caulk the holes. We bought a new TV—they were on sale at Best Buy. On the surface, things are back to normal, as normal as our lives will ever be.

Teeny's even watching Scooby-Doo. Some things never change.

I sit down next to her. I'm so tired I feel like I'm a hundred years old. I'm the only one home with the kids. Mama's driving Meghan to the treatment center, where she'll spend the next month.

"Where's Mom again?" Teeny sucks on a stand of her hair. We've been trying to break her of the habit, that and biting her nails. *People do worse things,* she told me.

Yes, they do.

I put a pillow behind my head. I could fall asleep right now and it's only 4 P.M. "She's taking a spa vacation."

Teeny raises her eyebrows at me, a look that seems strangely out of place on such a young face. "She's trying to kick again, isn't she?"

Drip-drip-drip goes the faucet. Tick-tick-tick goes the clock. Why did I think I could sugarcoat it? She knows how things work, even though you shouldn't have to when you're that age. "Well, yeah."

"Is she going to stay there this time?" Teeny knows Meghan's never finished a program before.

I know better than to lie to her a second time. "I hope so."

Teeny looks back at the screen, but her mind is on something else. "Are you going away too?"

"Nah. I'm not a spa person." I know that's not what she's talking about, but I'm dodging.

"No," she persists. "I mean for good." She winds the drawstring on her pj pants around her wrist, tight enough to cut off the circulation and make her skin change color, before she lets go and does it again.

She's making me nervous. "Hey, I know what we're missing." I change the subject.

She lets herself be distracted for a moment, curious. "What?"

"Popcorn!" I slip into the kitchen before she can say anything else and stick a bag in the microwave, hoping that by the time the zapping's done, she'll have forgotten about it. Because the truth is, I still don't know what I'm doing. With everything that's happened, I feel more tied here than ever. Maybe I will stay, depending upon what happens with the slides Daniel and David sent to their buddy in L.A. They said something about me getting listed in a fashion magazine, about setting up my own Web site. Maybe I will stay, because of my family. Because of Ray. One of the songs in *The Wizard of Oz* pops into my head: *Because, because, because, because, because—*

For always, Teeny says.

Nothing's for always. There are no guarantees. I know that better than anyone.

• • •

When calls come at eleven o'clock at night, you pretty much know it's not going to be good news. I walk into the kitchen as Mama hangs up the phone. She puts her head in her hands. "She's gone."

I don't have to ask who. The kitchen light bulb buzzes and flickers, on the verge of burning out. Bugs crash into window screens, then fall down stunned or dead, wondering why they couldn't reach the light. "When?"

She runs her hands through her hair, newly streaked with gray at the temples. "They're not sure. Some time tonight."

My sister, the escape artist. She's could probably break out of Alcatraz, if it were still a prison.

"You would have thought, after everything—" Mama's voice trails off.

"Yeah." You would. But Meghan survived again. She keeps thinking she can push the envelope, push it until she tears everything apart. The life she's built for herself is made of paper. The fibers break down. Dust to dust. But she still doesn't see that. She doesn't see.

Mama's almost talking to herself more than me. "She'll show up again."

I lean against the door frame, against the penciled markings with which we recorded our height when we were kids. Meghan's got a couple of inches on me. Give her an inch, she'll take a mile, my father used to say, a glint in his eye, approving her fearlessness. Little did he know the direction it would take. "What are we going to do when she does?"

Mama closes her eyes. "I don't know."

But we do. We understand what's required, what's always been required, though we haven't been able to bring ourselves to do it.

"Why can't she—" Mama's question hangs in the air, incomplete. It's a question we've asked ourselves many times.

Why can't she? Why can't she? Why can't she?

The words echo inside me. Meghan does this. Or we allow her to. She scoops us out, a human bulldozer, eating away at us, at herself, a blight to the landscape of our lives. And yet we remember what was supposed to happen, the times before the promises got broken, before people started to die and use and use themselves up. I keep thinking, someday things will change. Someday, Meghan will finally cut the shit and get her act together. But she never stops long enough to see the damage she's done. She's a storm that drops down one place, wrecks a house or two, then moves on.

A storm with a mother. A sister. Two children.

Mama bought Teeny one of those tornado-in-a-bottle things. It sits on the kitchen table, two pop bottles joined together with a red plastic segment, a simple science experiment. I wish I could cram Meghan inside it, contain the tempest, make her stop for a moment, make her listen, make her see us, see herself.

"Do you want me to find her?" I'll go if I have to. I'll try to fix everything again, because that's what I do.

Mama shakes her head. There's a hardness in her voice I haven't heard before, a set to her jaw. "Let her come to us this time."

. . .

Alex calls me at work the next day, says she needs me to stop by and see her at the Perkatory, ASAP. She won't say why. She sounds keyed up. I figure maybe she and Matt are getting serious. I swing by at 5:30, ready to hear the dirt. Inside, the devil's eyes gleam more brightly than usual, the fires of hell burn a fiercer shade of red.

Alex has someone take over the counter for her. Even though there are plenty of free tables, she motions me outside. We sit by a busted steam clock with an empty bottle of Thunderbird at its base, one of Bone's prime spots, before he was shot and decided to dry out.

Alex bites her lip, uncharacteristically at a loss for words.

"So, what's up?" I ask, wondering what it could be. God, I hope she's not pregnant.

She watches an Oldsmobile with a bad muffler rumble by. Nobody we know. There's not much traffic. Most of the activity takes place down the hill, in the land of McDonald's and Taco Time. Out with the old. In with the new. "She's back."

Meghan. The tripped-out sister who makes my heart trip over itself, not from love, but from the effort of trying to love her.

"I saw her by the Fillmore," she says.

"Did you talk to her?"

Alex shakes her head. "No. By the time I parked the car, she was gone. I guess she didn't feel like shooting the breeze."

"She was probably shooting something else." I kick at a loose chunk of cement in the sidewalk, more damage for Joe to fix. "We thought it would finally stick."

"Yeah." Alex nods. "After what happened."

"I guess it wasn't enough." The atmosphere is hot and still, making it hard to breathe. We might be in for a thunderstorm tonight.

A train whistle blows. I listen to its mournful wail. Meghan and I used to spend time at the tracks when we were kids, imagining the exotic places we'd go someday—New Delhi, Rome, Vienna, Timbuktu.

"Doesn't she realize she could have died?" Alex asks.

"But she didn't." I sigh. "That's the crucial point. She thinks that if she can cheat death, she can cheat anything."

"That's such bullshit." She snorts.

"It is what it is." I hear the crash of a dumpster lid, a drunken yell from a bar across the street, the ghost of a child, laughing, the way my sister and I rarely do any more.

Alex bites her lip. "What are you going to say to her if she shows up?"

"I don't know," I reply. The possibilities are endless, are pointless: Get straight. Clean up. Get a clue. Fuck off.

Is there anything that will convince Meghan to change? Maybe people don't. My father didn't. He was an alcoholic for years, then he died and left us. Maybe everyone goes through life being slightly different versions of themselves, but basically the same. Meghan, too, might always be addicted. In a wasteland within this wasteland that is our hometown. "I'd better go," I say finally. "My mom needs to know."

Alex gives me a hug. "You want me to come?"

I shake my head.

"Phone me later, okay?" she calls after me as I walk along the beat-up street, streaked with dust, the only sound my footsteps on the pavement, taking the path I need to take. Alone.

I'm on the porch, mending garments from the past, wondering about the people who wore them, what their problems were, why they gave these things away. Mama's inside doing dishes with such gentle hands you'd think she was baptizing them. I'm taking extra care too. Bugle beads and sequins catch the light of the setting sun. I like working here after the heat has gone from the day and the sky still holds a blush of color. The beads form flowers and birds—or they used to, before the threads broke. It's my job to set them right.

In my back pocket, I carry two pieces of paper. One is another acceptance letter from the art school in New York that came in today's mail, asking why I haven't responded. The other is the phone number of David's friend in L.A. Turns out he likes my work and wants to see more. I'll have to produce a lot of pieces in order to make much money, but it's a start.

I should be happy. Instead I feel very, very still inside, immobilized by indecision. I don't know what comes next, and I'm scared to find out. I haven't told anyone my news. Instead, I sit here sewing, letting my hands go through the motions, waiting. There's a charged atmosphere around me, partly generated by my own restlessness, partly coming from something else.

Ray called after I got back from talking to Alex. He asked me out for tonight. I told him I couldn't, and why. He fell silent for a moment. He wanted to be here for me—and I almost gave in and said yes, come, and hold me in your arms, and make it all go away.

But I didn't. I couldn't.

Minutes pass. An hour. It's dark now. Still no decision, still no Meghan. The kids went to bed a couple of hours ago. Mama spoke to Joe on the phone earlier in the evening. He insisted on coming over, but she said no, we had to handle this on our own. It's family business. No knights in shining armor allowed.

Mama has settled in the rocking chair. I hear the sound of it creaking through the open window, a determined rhythm that should steady us but doesn't. The light does a long, slow fade behind the hills, until it reaches the point I can't see what I'm doing and I stab myself in the finger with the needle. The short, sweet pain startles me, as if I've been in a dream. A dot of blood wells up on my fingertip, but it's not enough to make me feel faint. A car rattles along the washboard road and pauses outside the gate, headlights illuminating clouds of dust and bugs. I can't see who's inside. I wonder if they can see me, here in the shadows, and I feel a tremor of fear. It couldn't be the drug dudes. They're in custody. No one else is after us or Meghan, though she's probably left other angry people in her wake. The car huffs, as if it's asthmatic. Maybe Meghan is in there, deciding if she's going to get out. Maybe she's got a new winner of a boyfriend. I stand up, trying to see. The scissors clatter to the porch, blades open, cutting air. The spool of thread rolls down the steps, unraveling in a thin trail of white. Then the car slides away, a shark into deep water. Tail lights wink, a parting tease.

Meghan?

No.

Someone looking for another address.

I suppose it's time I went inside. The house releases a burst of pent-up heat. We threw open all the windows to cool it, but the air won't move. I take the seat opposite Mama, hunkering down on the couch. We glance at each other briefly, then fasten our eyes on our work, the task at hand. Her knitting needles tap like bones, marking the passing seconds. We don't speak. We wait.

I'd sit there and sew naked if I could, though it wouldn't do any good. The heat would still get me. It always does. I stitch under the light of the living room lamp. Stitch and stitch until the seams are straight, the holes are patched, the sequins shine, until my eyes close.

Sometime in the dead of night—when else would she come?—we wake to the rattle of the screen door. I'd locked it after I came in, because I didn't want Meghan to get inside unless we let her, because I'd kidded myself into thinking that we could make things happen on our terms.

I tiptoe into the hallway and stand in the shadows, shivering despite the lingering heat. Mama hovers in the doorway out of Meghan's line of vision, not trusting herself to come closer.

"Erin, it's me." The motion-activated porch light flicks on and weirdly illuminates Meghan's face.

I don't say anything.

"Don't be mad." She turns on the charm, her smile a flash of teeth, the dying sparkle in her eyes flecks of quartz.

"Don't tell me how to feel." I have every right to be mad. Mad as hell. Mad for the rest of my life.

"C'mon. Open the door." She knows how to get what she wants, knows how to get to me. I've always given in before. Why would tonight be different?

I glance at Mama. She shakes her head and presses her lips together, a vow of silence. Her eyes shine with tears.

I slide down the wall and press my hands between my legs to stop myself from undoing the latch. "You're not supposed to be here." I face the dark kitchen, the place where we'd eaten many bowls of cereal at many breakfasts when we were kids— Meghan had always gotten the prizes from the box first, first always first. The fridge ticks, keeping things cold. The table is bare except for a crumb or two that we forgot to wipe away.

Meghan takes another tack. "It wasn't the right place for me." Her mascara gently weeps.

I rest my head against the side of the hall table. Everything feels heavy. I can hardly move. "Nothing is ever the right place for you."

"What's that supposed to mean?" Her tongue runs the words together. They're barely comprehensible.

Before I have a chance to reply, a stair creaks behind us. Teeny.

"Go back to bed, sweetie," Mama whispers.

Teeny doesn't move. She's a little angel, the ghost of childhood past. "Don't open the door."

"Teens, don't be silly. It's me." Meghan pushes her face

against the screen, distorting her features and making herself appear momentarily monstrous, then pulls back, a grid of red marks printed on her face, a prisoner to the end, whether she knows it or not.

Teeny doesn't move. "I'm not going with you. I'm staying here till you get better."

Meghan touches the screen with her fingertips, long, jagged nails scratching the mesh like claws. "I *am* better. I know what I need. I know what *we* need."

Teeny sits down on the stairs and draws her knees to her chest. "No." She shakes her head. "You don't."

"I'm your mother." The words echo in the hall. We consider them in silence. They don't mean everything Meghan wants them to. They mean birth. They mean love, but the type of love that's diluted by the force of her own needs, by the siren song of her addiction.

Meghan's face is a mask beyond the screen. She must have been to one of the bars. She doesn't lay on the blush, the eye shadow and liner that thick otherwise. Or maybe she did that so someone would stop along the highway near the treatment center and give her a ride. She couldn't have walked the whole way. It would have taken days. Was it a lonely long-haul trucker? Or someone looking to prey on the vulnerable, someone she had to fight off. A couple of her nails are broken, and there's a scratch on her cheek. Hard to say. She could have fallen down. She has before.

Her lower lip trembles. She wipes a hand across her chin, perhaps realizing, in a searing moment of clarity, what a mess she is, suddenly conscious of how she appears to us. Her lipstick smears even more. Flakes of mascara dot her eyelids beneath the brows. Her blush is clown-bright. She wears a ragged, black spaghetti-strap dress, hem torn off at the upper thigh. Her hair's drawn up in a ponytail, a few strands straggling around her face. She looks like a ballerina who's fallen into a coal bin.

"Listen. Just listen——" She falters. She doesn't know what else to say.

Neither do we.

Mama takes Teeny's hand and they make their way slowly and purposefully upstairs. The only sound is the creaking of the steps as they move farther and farther away, into the deep reaches of the house, to the room that belonged to Meghan in another life.

"Mama!" Meghan yells. "Mama!"

Mama doesn't reply.

Meghan swipes tears away with the back of her hands. "How could you? How could you turn them against me?"

"It's easy to blame someone else, isn't it?" I glare at her. "For your information, I didn't do anything—other than be here when the kids needed me."

Meghan rubs her cheek hard, as if she's trying to peel off the skin. The itch is down deep, where she can't scratch it. "That's a cheap shot, even from you."

I shake my head. I don't feel anything any more. I can't be angry. I can't be sad. "Speak for yourself."

She takes a wheezy breath. "Let me talk to them," she says through gritted teeth.

I have to let her go, have to let her fall. I can't catch her any more. I'm not strong enough, so I say the hardest words I've ever had to say, words I have to mean this time. "You heard what Teeny said," I whisper. "Leave."

"What? How can you say that to me?" She pounds on the door. The metal frame shakes.

The door bows slightly but doesn't give. "I don't have a choice."

Mama watches from the landing. She'll come down if Meghan breaks through. We'll stand together for once. We have to.

"Stop fucking with me, Erin, or I swear——" Meghan balls up her fists and sticks out her chest. She wants to fight something. She punches the air.

"You can't come back until you get clean," Mama says.

Meghan shrieks, a sound so inhuman it makes me shudder, as she bangs on the door, kicking and flailing.

I push myself into a standing position, as tired as if I've walked a thousand miles, as if I'd gone nine rounds in the ring, and close and lock the door. I put my foot on the first step leading away from my sister, then the next and the next, because that's the way it has to be.

Upstairs, we all fall into Meghan's old bed. We don't bother to change our clothes. We lie prone, the way we are, and listen to my sister rage around the house for what seems like an hour, wondering if she's going to get in. If we'll have to fight her off. If we'll have to call the police, or if somebody has already.

But no sirens wail. She doesn't shatter the glass. She bounces off the screens, a giant moth, fluttering, buzzing, fuming, wanting to get at the light, wanting it so bad she'd burn for it, if she could only break through.

In the morning, when I open the door, I think I'll find her collapsed on the front porch, bruised and beaten. But there's only a tattered scrap of cloth from where her dress caught in the latch and tore, a piece of black, a remnant of the endless night.

CHAPTER 15

all is coming, brief as it is, before winter blasts down on
us. That's the way it is here. There's no transitional season. You have to shift gears and go at a moment's notice.
Teeny's starting kindergarten at Meghan's and my old school.
We bought her supplies—paper, crayons, a nubby pink eraser,
a Scooby Doo lunch box, new jeans and flowered tops and coat
and tennis shoes. She gives us a big gap-toothed grin, because
she's ready to make friends and learn something and be a normal kid. Maybe she'll play in the slag-heaps and try to fly and
rollerblade down the biggest hills she can find, a shadow of the
child Meghan used to be, riding with her unseen. She'll have her
first school picture taken and we'll put it alongside ours, the
ones with the colors that are starting to shift as the years pass
and the emulsion ages. Us, with our bobbed hair and missing
teeth, me with my chin ducked shyly, Meghan with hers thrust
out, grinning confidently, no hint of who we would become.
There are empty spaces left in the multiple-shot frame, for the

years of school she didn't finish, reminders of our loss. And there are empty spaces on the wall, for the years to come, that we might fill—the space that gives us faith that anything's possible, because it hasn't happened yet, good or bad. That Si-si and Teeny will explore this rocky world as Meghan and I did when we were younger, grandly, full of hope and brio, that the only saving they'll have to do will involve the minor scrapes of childhood present, not the broken pieces of childhood past.

As for us, we're getting by. The big news is that Bone's sober for the first time in years. He's returning to school in Missoula after a long absence, finishing his degree, says he's going to write and teach and get to know his little girl better. He takes the bus or bums a ride home every weekend to see her. Teeny adores him, thinks he's an angel God sent down to watch over her, and he wants to be, he wants to.

Joe comes over for dinner. He brings Mama vegetables and gorgeous tropical flowers he grows in his hothouse. He visits often enough to make them—and her—flourish.

Ray's still around. *You seem to be going nowhere fast,* I tease him. He just smiles at me from behind those mirrored lenses as he tosses Teeny in the air and sits down to meals with Joe and the rest of us. Mama goes on a cooking frenzy because she wants them to stick around.

I do too.

Me? I'm still working at Funkified and completing my first jewelry collection. A movie star bought one of my pieces, which means something, according to Daniel, because everybody wants to have the latest thing, everybody wants to be like her, at least for the moment. There was a picture of her wearing the necklace in a magazine. David has it framed at the store. He helped me construct a Web site to sell my designs. The orders are starting to trickle in, but it'll take time. Everything will take time.

I guess I'm not as ready to leave as I thought. I figure it isn't so much where I am geographically, as where I am within myself that's important—and the place I am now, while not perfect, is pretty damn good, all things considered. In the end, it's my choice, whatever I decide to do. And for now, I choose to stay.

As for Ginga's ring, I keep it in a velvet box, as if the drawer in my room is a safety deposit for the day my sister finally finds the right key.

We haven't heard from Meghan since the night we told her to go away. We don't know where she is or what she's doing. Maybe she's strung out in a squat. Maybe she's in treatment. Maybe she's dead. Maybe she's finally learning how to live. We tie ourselves in knots over it, human macramé projects of worry. But mostly, we try to keep going, to make things better, because that's all we know how to do, because, in the end, what else is there?

We'll be here trying to make roses bloom in the parched garden. We'll be here sweeping the dust from the front walk. We'll be here rocking on the porch and staring up at the mountains, watching for the first snow to fall. We'll be here, looking for her footsteps in the snow, leading to the house. Waiting for the knock at the door, the face to appear on the other side of the screen, tired, but clear-eyed and true. We'll be here when she's finally ready to come home.